HIGHBALLS IN THE HAMPTONS

Girlfriends of Gotham - Book Two

DELANCEY STEWART

ISBN: 978-1-956195-12-5

Highballs in the Hamptons

Girlfriends of Gotham
Book Two

Delancey Stewart

CONTENTS

1. Waxing and Other Dangerous Pursuits 1
2. Crutches and Crowns 17
3. Girls in Glass Stalls 27
4. Not a Fingerbowl in Sight 41
5. Green Monsters 53
6. Five Cents 59
7. Elevator Tango 73
8. Vodka Solves Everything 84
9. Adventure Lunch 92
10. Bathroom Ballyhoo 102
11. Once Upon a Hallway 113
12. Voicemail Tag 126
13. The Inebriated Hamster 132
14. Playing Homeless 145
15. Party Pants 156
16. Nantucket Reds 171
17. Buffalo Beckons 187
18. Team Tippy 196
19. Chasing Cabs 201
20. The Rabbit Rides Again 210
21. A Sushi Situation 221
22. Tippy Goes Downtown 229
23. Hunting for Heads 240
24. Page Six Can Suck It 249
25. Alive at Twenty-Five 253

Preview of Book 3 261

1. A Cougar on the Prowl 262
2. Along Came a Spider 270

Also by Delancey Stewart 275

Chapter One

WAXING AND OTHER DANGEROUS PURSUITS

Natalie

THE DENSE NIGHT air hung thick around our small group as we wandered down the sidewalk, arm in arm. Moving as one, we were an intimidating force in stilettos and platform boots—a group of four women in our early twenties—loud, tipsy, silly, and in love with one another and with life in New York City.

That evening we were in search of a place we'd been to several times before in ones and twos, but never all together. The bar may have had a formal name, but we just called it "Speakeasy." We found the place by the single blue light sticking out of the side of a building on 52nd Street near Ninth Avenue. You had to lift a phone receiver next to a dark, anonymous-looking door to get into the long and narrow space on the garden level of a building that had been there for over a hundred years, and maybe did operate as a speakeasy during the supposedly dry days of the Volstead Act. Prohibition-reminiscent bars had become fashionable in the Internet days of New York's late nineties. There were numerous hidden venues, intimate little bars, and even full-blown clubs, with no name posted outside. It was a test of your knowledge of insider cool to find one of these spots.

"Here it is!" Lulu called back. She'd run ahead at the sight of the blue light and was motioning and pointing as if she were part of a charades game. "I found it." She watched us approach from the top of the stairs. "Pepper, why are you walking funny?"

I did not want to tell her why I was walking funny. I really didn't want to be walking funny at all and thought I'd done a pretty good job of covering up my issue that night. Evidently, a few cocktails were enough to bring back the awkward gait that allowed me to move forward without piercing pain.

"Never mind," I said.

Now Candace and Maggie were both staring at me.

"It's nothing," I hissed. "It's embarrassing. I'll tell you later."

"Now you totally have to tell us." Candace was grinning her evil grin.

"Well, I'm not telling you anything on the sidewalk. Think we could maybe just go inside?"

"Good idea," Maggie smiled, patting my arm. "We'll get you a drink and then you can tell us all about it." Maggie was always the caring one, but the huge smile on her face told me that she was just as eager to hear about my issues as Candace was. It was going to be a long night.

Lulu was down the steps and lifting the receiver. "How many are we?" she called back to us.

"Four, Lu," Candace said. "Just like we were four a minute ago. Do they count differently in Brazil?" Candace didn't always have patience for Lulu—especially when Lulu was tipsy and silly.

The door swung inward, and we filed into the bar, momentarily quiet, hushed by the low yellow lighting and the soft jazz floating on the air. As we moved through the long space, eyes fell on us. Aside from one older gentleman in a black turtleneck, staring from the end of the bar, the other patrons were mostly couples, heads together, locked in various stages of intimacy. The bartender shook his head as we sauntered toward a set of low couches in the back, looking none too happy to be the host of a noisy group of silly girls. Once we seated ourselves, the atmosphere regained its momentum, and hushed conversations picked up again.

We procured drinks and settled in. The ability to hear one another in a bar was a novelty; one that was missed only by Lulu, who talked loudly enough for every table in the venue to hear.

"Tell us why you're walking funny, Natalieeeee." Lulu always drew out my name. There was something about it that charmed me, even as everyone around us now turned to see if my walking problem was perhaps written across my face.

"Keep it down," I said in a harsh whisper. "I'll tell you. I just don't really want to share with everyone in the bar." I took a sip of my martini and prepared myself for the inevitable laughter, but the girls were already guessing.

"Did you meet someone new?" Lulu asked, her eyes wide. "Someone ... large?"

"Or is something stuck in there?" Candace's green eyes flashed.

"Candace!" Maggie said, looking shocked. "Maybe she just tried something new," she said. "A different ... venue?"

"Will you guys keep it down?" I said, embarrassed by the couple leaning towards us from a nearby table, clearly eavesdropping. "None of the above, and you guys suck, by the way. It was a waxing accident."

Candace snorted and spit out a mouthful of her drink, grabbing a handful of cocktail napkins from the table and covering her mouth. "What?" she shrieked.

"You heard me. I had a little issue."

"How do you have a waxing accident?" Maggie said. She managed to look genuinely concerned.

Lulu just looked confused.

"I bought a do-it-yourself kit at the drugstore. It's still weird to me to go to one of those places and let some woman I don't know deal with my lady parts." I stared into my martini. I wondered if this admission would lead Candace to call me "Midwestern" again. I was from California, but she seemed to think I had some kind of sheltered naiveté about me, and used the term "Midwestern" like a slur. I glanced at her, but she was smiling, waiting for me to continue. "Maybe we could talk about this another time? Somewhere more private?"

Lulu was still staring at me, a question on her face. "That's so silly. You can't see your own parts. You have to have help to do that. Why didn't you call me?"

"Sure. That's a fun invitation: 'Lulu, please come help me wax my pubes.'"

"I would have helped." She looked mildly offended.

"What, you know about waxing because you're Brazilian?" Candace said, rolling her eyes.

"I know about waxing because I keep things neat down there," Lulu told her. "It has nothing to do with Brazil."

"Whatever," Candace said. "So tell us what went wrong."

"Fine," I said. "The kit had those strips. They're supposed to make it easy. You warm them up in your hands, and then slap them on, and rip them off after a minute or two. So I slapped one on and then my sister called, and I left it there for longer than I should have. When I went to rip it off, it was all cold and wouldn't rip right. It kind of peeled, and all this wax was stuck. I got up to get a washcloth to try to wash it off, and the wax kind of got into some ... areas ... where it didn't really belong. And it was very hard to get off, and it's still there, so things are sticking together, and it just hurts, okay?"

"Oh my God!" Lulu shrieked.

"That's pretty funny," Maggie said, her brown eyes wide as she patted my arm.

"Not to me," I told her. "Can we change the subject, please?"

"Yeah," Candace said. "Enough of Pepper's sticky pubes. What happened with your boy, Lu? What was his name?"

"Oh yeah," Maggie said. "You said you weren't seeing Ethan anymore."

"I'm not," Lulu said, her lower lip extending. She was gorgeous, even when she was pouting. Her long, dark hair hung straight down her back, and her skin glowed in the low light as she raised her dark eyes to us. "He broke up with me." For a second she looked genuinely sad. Then, in standard Lulu fashion, she seemed to get over it and veered into loud Lulu-land again. "I wasn't completely heartbroken. I mean," she put her hand on my arm, seeking my agreement, "the sex wasn't even good."

The couple at the table against the wall turned to openly stare, along with a few others nearby. Evidently, this was more interesting than my waxing mishap.

"He wanted to go down on me, so that was good, but I think he doesn't have the genes to make taco tongue. You know taco tongue?" she asked us all, making her tongue into a "u" shape and pushing it out between full glossy lips. "Not everyone can do it. And I think men who can't do it just aren't good at going down."

Despite our embarrassment at her volume, we couldn't help but nod in agreement. Lulu made her points with passion, and it was easy to be drawn to her side. Plus, if you didn't agree, you risked a volume escalation.

"You're right," Maggie said, her dark, wavy hair falling over one shoulder as she leaned in. At least Maggie knew how to whisper. "We did a genetics survey in my bio class in high school. We had to interview our family members about a bunch of stuff, and one of the things that is passed down genetically is taco tongue. I think we might've called it something more scientific."

"Like cunnilingus tongue?" Candace offered.

"Pretty sure that wasn't it." Maggie said. She took a long drink of her cosmo, then looked around her.

"We might need to watch our volume," she suggested.

Candace leaned forward and tried to whisper, her green eyes glinting. "So Lulu, you and Ethan are through, then?" Candace had taken unnatural pleasure in the downfall of Lulu's relationships since Lulu had dated Damon—one of Candace's exes—several months before.

"Definitely." She looked confident and secure. Then her face fell suddenly, her slim shoulders slumping forward. "You guys," she whined. "Why does this always happen?"

That was a valid question. But not one that any of us could answer definitively. Lulu brought a certain undefinable element to her dating life. She was just Lulu. She was tall, beautiful, opinionated, and inevitably loud. And there was something indistinct about her, an exotic element of unpredictability. Part of it was her occasional difficulty with American lingo, which could lead to some ridiculous conversations, but most of it was just Lulu. She was a force to be reckoned with. It would be the rare man who could handle that.

"Aww, Lu," Maggie chirped, leaning forward to hug Lulu.

We all joined in a group hug then, my knee knocking two of our drinks from an ottoman to the floor where they smashed unceremoniously, again attracting the attention of the rest of the crowd.

"Party foul!" Maggie cried loudly, then cringed when she realized that we were a spectacle. "Maybe we should go now," she said, her face imploring.

"Maybe we should," I agreed. I stood and approached the bartender. "I'm sorry about the glasses. Can I sweep it up or something?"

"No," he said, his jowls unnaturally red as they swung over his collar. "But I think you might want to move the party elsewhere."

Irritation fired in me, though I knew he had a point. "I think we will," I told him, turning back to the group. "Girls, let's go," I said.

"Yeah," Candace agreed, then added loudly, "I think they water the vodka here anyway."

The perturbed looks of the other patrons and the bartender almost made up for the mild disappointment I felt in knowing that I'd never be able to come back here.

Hangovers on Friday mornings had become almost routine for me, something I bemoaned as I stared into the keyboard on my desk at work the next day. I felt heavy and bleary. I was trying to remember what time I'd gotten to bed when a figure appeared in my doorway, ushering in a familiar sense of calm.

"Morning, CJ."

CJ's short, blond hair and full-wattage smile reminded me why I kept coming back to work, when my job had become a disaster in the past months. Even though I couldn't have him, I could be near him, and being close to the man of my dreams made taking constant abuse from my new boss almost worth it.

"Hey, Natalie." CJ slid into one of the chairs across from my desk and leaned forward, his dark eyes assessing me. "Rough night?"

"That obvious?"

"You just look tired, that's all." CJ grinned at me, and my heart clenched. "We still on for lunch?"

I lived for Friday lunches with CJ. Though I wanted more—much more—Friday lunches had become our routine and I looked forward to that one hour like nothing else. "Absolutely."

"Cool. What time should I pick you up?"

I grinned back at him. I couldn't help it. Besides being blessed with all-American good looks and a body to match, CJ projected an air of genuine goodness. It was as if he had a feel-good force field, and just being near him always made me feel like things were getting better, no matter how bad they might be. "Noon?"

"Where we headed today?" In the past, we'd taken our Friday lunches as far away as Brooklyn and Coney Island. Sometimes Friday lunches turned into Friday afternoons and neither of us bothered to come back to work. But now that I was under my boss's magnifying glass, I doubted that would fly. Plus, I was still having some walking issues, thanks to a certain amount of wax that I hadn't been able to scrub from my nether regions.

"Not too far away today. I've definitely got to come back and get some stuff done."

"Okay," CJ said, rising. "Maybe just a deli or Korean BBQ?"

"Sounds good." There were a million Korean BBQ places hidden along 37th Street, where my company's building rose to tower over the streets. Herald Square and the world's largest Macy's lay in its shadow, and the Empire State Building loomed over us just a couple blocks away.

"See ya then," CJ said, disappearing down the hallway.

When he'd gone, I turned to face the glass wall behind me. Sometimes I just stared out my window, marveling at how a girl from California ended up in a fancy office looking out at the Empire State Building every day. But it was usually when I was staring out my window that someone walked into my fancy office and caught me wasting time. And that person was usually Lanie Bill, the VP of Marketing. She'd been hired after me, so I'd gotten comfortable in my role as director before she'd arrived to show me all the ways I was failing at pretty much everything while proving herself completely incapable of remembering my name.

"Nellie." And it seemed today would be no different.

I turned, and the short wide form of Lanie Bill filled my door. She was not an attractive woman, though she carried herself as if she believed she was Miss America, and appeared comfortable anywhere she went. She lurched into my office and threw herself into the chair CJ had just left. Her lanky, brown hair was pulled back into a severe ponytail, and she wore no makeup on her pallid face. She leaned back into the leather seat, multiple chins pressing out over her chest as she relaxed into the seat.

"It's Natalie," I reminded her. She'd gotten my name right maybe twice since arriving almost four months earlier.

"Just testing you." She winked grotesquely. "So ... last night was craaaa-zy." Sometimes Lanie spoke to me as if we were girlfriends, telling me about her adventures in the city. Other times she was condescending and bossy. I had already decided that keeping me off balance was part of her management strategy, and I hated it. I tried to respond as little as possible. "I met up with some of my friends—bankers, all men, all ridiculously hot—and we went to Scores. Have you been?"

"No." Scores was an upscale strip club. I'd been there once, but wasn't about to have that discussion with my dislikable manager.

"Yeah, it's a little out of your league—you should probably stick to the college bars."

And there it was. Every conversation I'd had with Lanie seemed purposefully designed to make me feel small. It had stopped working once I'd gotten used to the routine. I just smiled back at her.

"One of the girls got me up to dance with her—after we'd been doing shots all night—and I swear she wanted to take me home. I don't really go that way, you know, but she was gorgeous, and she was so totally into me. It was almost tempting." Lanie was chuckling, her chins jiggling. "But, you know," she leaned forward, lowering her voice to a whisper. "I'm pretty sure Damon's getting ready to make his move on me. He's completely hot for me."

I swallowed hard. Damon Michaels was the office playboy. Dark hair, icy-blue eyes, and a panty-dropping smile all wrapped up in one sarcastic, Armani suit-wearing package. He'd briefly dated my friend Candace, and even I'd been lured into one ill-fated make-out session during one of my less proud moments. And while I didn't believe that Damon's standards were too very high, I was fairly certain that Lanie Bill was not on his sexual radar. I smiled and nodded, hoping that would pass for agreement and that she'd let it drop.

Having her in my office was not helping the headache that had been lurking behind my eyes all morning. "Lanie, is there something you wanted to talk to me about? About work?"

She sat up. An evil look flashed across her face but was quickly replaced with a more benign expression. "Yeah. Look, right now I think we're both overloaded. We've been orchestrating the new agency search and redeveloping the trade show schedule, plus handling all the PR and investor relations."

I hated it when Lanie reviewed all the functions of our two-person marketing department as if I didn't know what it was we did. I'd done it all by myself before she'd come in, but she'd never given me credit for anything except screwing up.

"Anyway, it's a heavy load for the two of us. And I think you'd benefit from having someone under you. He, he," Lanie chuckled and raised an eyebrow, then let it drop. "Let's get some recent college grad—I mean more recent than you—in here to do the crappy little shit. Write press releases, man the trade show booth. That stuff."

I liked the idea of having someone to manage. At best, I'd have someone to help out, and someone to share the burden of reporting to my evil boss. At worst, a direct report would look good on a resume.

"Okay," I said. "You want me to handle the search?"

She looked skeptical. "I hadn't really planned it that way, but sure. Think you can manage it?"

"Yes." I stared at her, willing her to stand up and leave. "I should be fine."

"Well, should be and will be are not the same thing. Let me know if you're over your head."

"It will be fine," I told her through gritted teeth.

Finally, she excused herself and I got started.

Hunger was just beginning to push past the nausea of my hangover when the phone rang.

"Natalie Pepper."

"Hi, Natalie. It's Allen Page, from Kenneth Lowton recruiting?"

"Hi," I said. Why was this guy calling me?

"Listen," he said. "Any chance you're looking for a new position? I've got a new Internet company looking for some marketing talent, and they're very interested in you."

"They are?" I was flattered, but confused. "How do they even know about me?"

"The party you threw for your pre-IPO at the New Year has been the talk of the town. Fantastic but tasteful—right on target, unlike some of those belly-dancer fiascos going on at other Internet shops."

"Oh." I had no idea what to say, but had definitely heard about the party he was referencing. Some of the techie nouveau riche had made some bad decisions for their recent party and it was scandalous, even by Internet standards.

CJ appeared in my doorway.

I smiled at him and gave him the "just a sec" finger.

"Listen, Allen? Can you maybe email me your information? I'll give you a call if it seems like the right time."

"So now is not the right time for you?"

"I don't think so."

"That's too bad," he said. "Keep in touch, Natalie."

I hung up, shocked and flattered that anyone knew who I was

or what I did. My ego was a couple sizes bigger than it had been an hour before as I smiled at CJ across the desk.

"You ready?" he asked.

"For lunch?" I winked.

"For whatever," he said, an earnest smile on his face. CJ and I had a complicated relationship. There was a mutually acknowledged attraction between us, and I'd shared the two very best kisses of my life with him. Unfortunately, it just wasn't part of my plan to get involved with someone at work—for a whole slew of reasons. So despite our incredible chemistry, we were doing our best to enjoy a friendship instead. But CJ made no secret of his desire for more.

"Let's start with lunch. I need to get out of here," I said, grabbing my bag and coat.

"I'll take whatever I can get." CJ didn't move as I approached the door of my office, and I had to squeeze between him and the doorframe. The proximity allowed me to get close enough to smell the minty leathery scent that surrounded him. My nerves always started firing when I got that close to him, and I pushed past him quickly, blushing. He stood still just a beat longer as I waited for him to get going, and I was fairly certain that he had leaned in to smell my hair before finally stepping from the doorway.

We wandered to a Korean barbecue that was on the second floor of a nearby building. I would never have ventured in on my own—the signs were in Korean and the place was clearly a favorite with those who knew what constituted good Korean. Luckily, CJ had done this before.

We were seated in a private booth next to the window overlooking the street below. A small grill was built into the table in front of us, and CJ grinned at me as I looked around with great interest.

"I'm glad you're not a vegetarian," he said.

"Nope. Totally carnivorous." I smiled, part of me embarrassed.

When I was with CJ, it seemed like even my most innocuous statements took on an unintended sexual tone. "Why, will this be a meat-heavy meal?" There it was again. I flushed.

CJ was grinning at me again, the full lips pulled wide to reveal the adorable dimples on either side of his jaw. He shook his head slightly, the dark eyes shining. Evidently, I wasn't the only one getting the innuendos that seemed to keep falling out of my mouth. "Yeah. Fairly meat heavy."

Our lunch arrived, and it turned out that we would be cooking it ourselves. The grill in the middle was lit for us and each of us had a long fork that we used to put strips of raw meat onto the grill and pull them off. We also had kimchi to compliment the meat. It was a unique experience, and I found CJ smiling at me at several points as I tended to my barbecuing.

"What?" I asked him at one point toward the end of the meal. "Am I that much a novice? Are you laughing at me?"

"No," he said, his face finally serious. "I just ... Natalie. This is hard for me. I want more."

He put it out there simply, honestly, and I admired him for that. If there was one trait of CJ's that never failed to impress me, it was his genuine nature. He didn't seem capable of subterfuge; never seemed to worry about what was cool. He was just himself. "I guess I still have trouble accepting your reasoning. It's so obvious to me that there's something between us. We're great friends. Why can't we be more?"

"CJ ... " We'd had this conversation. Lots of times. And every time I explained my reasoning, it sounded less and less reasonable. "I've told you that I don't want to get involved with anyone at work."

"Right. If things go badly, yadda yadda."

"Yeah, yadda yadda." I smiled at him, feeling sad suddenly. "But it's more than that. My dad just thinks I'm such a royal fuck-up. He always has—or at least he has since my mom died. It was like once she was gone, and he didn't have her to focus on anymore, he shifted his attention. To me. And to how I just couldn't seem to do anything right."

"You haven't told me that."

"I've told you parts of it."

"Go on."

"My mom was sick for a couple years. And Dad's life became about taking care of her. All our lives did. I moved to a college closer to home, my sister came home for a while to stay with them. Even though it was because she was sick, my mom pulled us all together. She was our center. And then she was suddenly gone, and we all kind of spun outward. Like we didn't have anything to hang onto anymore."

"I'm so sorry, Natalie." His eyes shone, and he reached across the table, covering my hand with his.

"The point is, I guess, I was kind of lost. Maybe I still am a little bit, but I'm working on that. But my dad ... he took all the energy he'd been putting into my mom's care, and suddenly put it on me. I was the only daughter still home since my sister had already gotten married and moved. And at the same moment that he decided to care so much, I was completely lost."

I looked at CJ's hand covering mine and closed my eyes for a minute, taking strength from the warmth of his soft skin. I wanted to melt into his arms.

"But I still don't see why that keeps us from being together."

I sighed. "Because. My dad has been disappointed over and over again. My mom died. My sister went back to her family up north. I changed majors twice. I quit two jobs. I ran up my credit cards, and he had to bail me out. I dated a guy he despised. And finally, now that I'm here—and he was totally against me moving to New York, by the way—he's finally proud of me. And I can't do anything to risk that. I think my dad is happy for the first time in four years, and it's actually because he thinks that he succeeded in raising me. I can't screw it up." I stared at CJ, wishing he could understand. "I think it would break him."

CJ stared at me for a moment, and I could tell he was trying to find the right words to say whatever was about to come out of those amazing lips. "Natalie. You have to know that your responsibility is to yourself. To live your life. To make Natalie happy. Your dad is responsible for himself. He's a grown-up. You don't have to protect him."

My heart clenched as he said it. He didn't understand. He wasn't in the same situation, and he just didn't know. "Maybe you're right," I said, hoping we could end this conversation. "But that's just how I feel about things."

CJ stared at me for a moment longer, and the pull of his deep dark eyes almost had me leaning over the table. The moment was interrupted by the arrival of the waiter with our check.

"Let me," CJ said, taking it.

"No," I said. "This isn't a date." I reached for the bill.

"Just let me pretend, then," CJ said, a sad smile on his face.

We walked back to the office in silence and CJ said goodbye to me at the front doors.

"You're not coming back up?"

"No." He shook his head. "I think I've had enough for today."

I went back to my desk feeling defeated, and spent the rest of the day in a depressed funk. I wanted CJ. I knew that in my heart, in my soul ... and in other parts that I wasn't about to acknowledge while sitting at my desk at work. But there were two things keeping me from running after him and throwing myself into his arms. For one thing, I didn't have a fantastic track record in the working world. My quick success in New York and in the Internet industry was too new for me to be able to assume that things would continue that way. I couldn't jeopardize my job. The bottom line was that I couldn't stay in the city without the income it provided, and I wasn't confident that I could easily land another—no matter what some misguided headhunter might think.

The second thing keeping me from CJ was fear. I'd had

boyfriends. But those relationships had just happened. They'd been the result of proximity, mostly. I'd never wanted anyone like I wanted CJ. I'd never had to consciously choose to be with someone. And I'd never had so much at stake. If it didn't work out ... I could barely stand thinking about the ragged wreck my heart would become. And it had only recently begun to be whole again since Mom had died. I just couldn't risk it.

Chapter Two

CRUTCHES AND CROWNS

Lulu

THE SUN WAS high when I left my apartment to run. I took deep breaths and pushed off, happy to feel light and free.

The only thing wrong with staying out late enough to need sunglasses on the way home was it killed my desire to run. Most days, I ended up running the path by the Hudson in the late afternoon. I preferred the very early morning—no tourists wandered into my way. But in life, sometimes you choose between sunrise and vodka. For now, I choose vodka.

I didn't talk to the other girls about running. To me, it was religion, and you don't talk about religion. I didn't go to church growing up, but I ran a lot. Away from some things, toward others. So I continued to run in New York. It was part of who I was. The steady beat of my feet against the earth connected me to whatever higher power I answered to and helped me stay just ahead of the things I feared.

The river on my right, I pushed forward, my body falling into stride, every cell focused on breath and movement. And after a mile or so, my clarity arrived, and I found what I came for. Freedom. I took a deep breath and closed my eyes for just a moment to enjoy the lightness.

But today it was just a moment too long.

Pain shattered serenity as I hit something solid, hard. As I fell to the ground, it registered that it was someone else's head that I'd hit. The pavement rose to meet me, and the next thing I knew, I was sitting on my ass, looking up into very concerned blue eyes.

"Are you okay?" A deep voice, full of worry.

A cloud circled my head. "I'm not sure."

He took my hand and pulled me to my feet, and the world spun again.

"Shit." I sat back down. My ankle throbbed. "Not all right, I think." I squinted and peered back up at the man squatting beside me again. "Did you hit me?"

"Not purposely, but yes, I did. I'm so sorry." He smiled and shook his head lightly. He did look sorry. "In my defense, you were running with your eyes closed. I'm not sure that's the safest way to go."

"The best way to do a thing is not always the safest."

He smiled again and nodded. He had golden-brown hair. The fog around me cleared a bit, and I realized I'd been knocked out by a very handsome runner. "I guess I'll have to try it sometime."

"I don't advise it. It can be quite dangerous, as it turns out."

"I'm a risk-taker." He grinned.

I tried to stand again, since my head was feeling clearer. But my ankle was not doing well. "I think I need to get my ankle checked. I'd better get a cab."

"I'll take you." The man pulled my arm over his shoulder and began slowly walking me toward the street.

"Take me where?" I tried to pull away.

"St. Vincent's is closest. And I know someone who works there." He patted my hand and pulled me forward.

"Connections. Good. Yes." I let him lead me to a cab, and settled into the back seat. He began to sit and I stared at him. "I'll meet you there." I didn't know him. I wasn't going to share a cab with him, even if he was handsome.

"Uh, okay. Sure." One big hand ran through his golden hair. He squinted up at the street. "You wanna just wait outside the emergency?"

"Okay," I said.

I watched him hail another cab as my car pulled away. He was very cute. Tall, broad-shouldered, nice features. But at the moment I was more concerned about my ankle. I pulled up my running pants to see blue and green already snaking up from my sock. "Fabulous," I whispered. No running for a while. And an immobile Lulu was not a happy Lu.

The cab delivered me to the hospital, where I realized I had no money at all.

"I'm so sorry," I explained to the driver. "I was running. I got hurt. I didn't plan to take a cab."

"This is New York, lady. You don't leave home without cash." The driver was not sympathetic.

"I did not plan things this way," I told him, anger and pain making me louder than I intended to be. I sat still, because it hurt to move and because he clearly wanted to be paid. Then I scooted over and opened the door, putting one foot on the curb, thinking about what to do.

"Well?" said the driver.

I was trying to come up with a solution when the man from the path jogged up and ducked his head in the door. "Here you go, thanks." He handed the driver twenty dollars and lifted me from the seat, pulling my arm over his shoulder.

"You didn't have to pay for my cab," I told him.

"You bring money out running?"

"No."

"So you were going to pay him with ... " he was smiling at me, and I tried not to be enchanted by the twinkle in his blue eyes.

"I was going to have him take me home and then bring me back."

"Where is home?"

"That seems like a very personal question."

"Just curious how long I would have been waiting. This just worked out easier, didn't it?" He smiled and there was no irony in his expression.

I relaxed a bit. "Thank you."

"That seems the more appropriate answer." He paused as the doors slid open for us.

I didn't like having to thank people for things. And I was more than capable of paying my own way. But it was kind of nice to be in the arms of this handsome man for the briefest of moments, even if the entire situation was ridiculous.

We limped through the doors to the emergency department and approached the desk.

"Morning, Libby," my companion said to the woman behind the desk. "I'm playing ambulance this morning. Can you get her paperwork pulled together while I go scrub? Stick her in the first room open and I'll see her myself."

"Okay, Dr. Barton."

I raised an eyebrow as my new friend deposited me gently into a wheelchair next to the desk.

"You have good luck," he told me, smiling. "I'll see you in just a minute."

I was not always lucky. Some parts of my life were horrible and something completely different from lucky—whatever the English word is that means the opposite of lucky. That. But that is exactly why I loved living in New York. Since I'd been living in the United States, he was right, I had been lucky. In college I'd won the green card lottery—something many people try for years to do. That meant that for the next ten years I was allowed to work here. I hadn't found any work that I wanted, but having the option was good. So maybe I did have good luck.

I watched the doctor's broad form disappear through the door behind the desk and whistled quietly to myself. This morning was not turning out quite as expected. I hadn't decided if it was a lucky accident or not. The pain in my ankle had me thinking no.

"Do you have your insurance card, dear?" Libby asked from behind the desk.

"I don't have health insurance," I told her. "I'll pay cash for whatever needs to be done."

She stared at me for a second, and then began punching things into the computer. She clipped some forms to a board and slid them to me.

I filled out the health forms just before a man in a white uniform came and took the handles at the back of the wheelchair. He steered me to the back, where the other runner—Dr. Barton—waited for me in an exam room.

"Okay, let's take a look at that ankle, Miss ..." He took the clipboard from me. "Miss Rossi. Lucia." He said my name slowly, as if he planned to remember it.

"Lulu," I told him. I was Lucia only to people whom I hoped never to have to speak to again.

"Mind if I remove your shoe and sock?" he asked, kneeling down in front of me.

"Most men buy me dinner or at least a drink first, but go ahead."

"I did pay for your cab," he reminded me.

My embarrassment must have shown.

"Sorry about that," he said. His face was sincere. "I'm Andrew, by the way. And if I didn't already make it clear, I'm really sorry for hurting you."

"I would say it was okay if I wasn't sitting in the emergency department at the hospital." I smiled. It was hard to be mad when he was so cute. "I'm sorry I ran into you, too."

"I didn't say I was sorry that I ran into you." He was staring up at me.

"Yes you did."

"No, I very specifically did not." He smiled.

The wheels turned in my mind as I went over our conversation. English was not my first language and sometimes I misunderstood things even though I'd been living in the United States a long time. He was sorry, but he was not sorry. It didn't make sense. English could be very frustrating.

Despite the pain, the situation was feeling more ridiculous by the moment.

Andrew's hands were warm and careful, but pain shot up my leg as he worked to remove my shoe. The pain and confusion were working together now to make me angry. I yanked my foot out of his grasp, sending a yelp of pain flying from my lips.

He looked up at me, confusion making his eyes wide.

"I don't understand. Are you sorry or not sorry? Because if you are not sorry, then maybe I'd like to see another doctor here." I knew that my face was reddening and I wanted more than anything to be able to stand at my full height and walk away. But I couldn't stand.

He smiled then, which felt even more infuriating.

"I said what I meant, but I will explain," he said, speaking slowly.

"I'm not an idiot," I told him. "I'm Brazilian."

"I didn't think you were an idiot," he said, taking my foot in his hands again. "I am very sincerely sorry that I hurt you. But I am very sincerely happy to have an excuse to spend just a little more time with such a beautiful and interesting girl." He stared up at me openly then, and my heart fluttered just a bit.

"You are flirting with me now?"

"You're not making it easy, Lulu."

The blue eyes danced and my frustration dissipated a bit. He was adorable.

"All right."

"You mean it's all right to flirt with you?"

"Yes. You may flirt with me." I felt silly. This was not the way I usually met men.

"Good. Do you think that maybe I can try to flirt a bit more over dinner some time?" He tilted his head to the side and grinned at me.

I couldn't resist him. "Okay. Yes."

He grinned. "What do you do when you're not running into people along the river, Lulu?"

"You ran into me." I knew he was teasing me, but pretending to be angry was becoming amusing. "And to answer your question, I don't have a job at this point."

"A student?"

"No." This topic sometimes became difficult, and I didn't like offering too many details to people I didn't know well. "I am just between jobs, that's all." That could be considered true, as long as you didn't consider the fact that I'd never had a job. But I wanted one. I just had no idea what I might be good at.

I was at the hospital with Andrew for another hour and he didn't leave my side. He x-rayed my ankle, and I was pleased to find that it was not broken. He gave me an air cast and a pair of crutches that I assured him I would not be using, and then put me back in a cab to my apartment. He pre-paid the driver after having me enter my number into his phone.

"I will call you tonight, Lulu Rossi, to see how you are doing, and to arrange that dinner." He gave me a card with his name and number on it.

I smiled as the cab pulled away. What a strange morning.

Sunday brunches were a usual outing for us, and I met the other girls at Cafeteria on Seventh Avenue. Normally I would walk, but today I took a cab. When I limped in, the girls' eyes got wide.

"Lu," Maggie said, "what on Earth happened?"

The large, ugly air cast did not fit into any of my heels, so I was wearing my running shoes again, the right one unlaced and bulging.

"I got hurt." I sat next to Candace and gave her a hard look. She often seemed smug when things did not go my way, and I didn't feel like putting up with it today. "Did you order my mimosa yet?"

"It's only eleven forty-five," Natalie said. "They brought us orange juice. You have fifteen minutes to regale us with the tale of the injury."

I felt disappointed. My injured ankle meant that I had spent the weekend in my apartment and not out running around, as I would have liked. I hadn't answered the phone, mostly because I was feeling down and didn't like people to know me that way. I watched television and felt sorry for myself. Today was my introduction to the world again, and I wanted champagne. I waved at a passing waiter. The rule that restaurants couldn't serve alcohol before noon on Sunday seemed prehistoric to me.

"It is only ten minutes until noon," I said. "I've injured my foot. The doctor suggested that mimosas would help." I gave him my best sad eyes.

"Did he now?" The waiter was young, cute. He smiled at me and then gazed around at the other girls. Candace was grinning, her short bob shining as always, and Natalie and Maggie were also putting on their best friendly flirting faces. "I'll see what I can do." He walked away.

"I fell down," I told the table.

"That's not very entertaining," Candace said. "Even Natalie's waxing incident was more interesting than that."

"We agreed never to speak of that again," Natalie said in a hushed voice.

"No," Candace said. "You agreed."

"How did you fall?" Maggie asked, her dark eyes shining. "What were you doing?"

"I went for a run," I said.

Candace laughed.

"That is funny because ... ?"

"Sorry, I can't picture you doing anything athletic." Candace often said "sorry," but rarely looked sorry.

"Well, I was. I run most days while you are at work. I just don't feel like I need to tell everyone about it."

Candace's eyes narrowed for a minute. She had a habit of telling us about her accomplishments, so I guessed that she would know this was aimed at her.

"Okay, so you were running, and what happened?" Natalie smiled as the waiter returned with mimosas for the table.

"Thank you," I said to him, raising my glass in a toast. "Now I can properly tell the story." I took a long sip and then smiled at the girls. "I met a nice man. A doctor."

"You hurt yourself on purpose to get his attention?" Maggie said.

"No. Don't be silly. He ran into me. It was just a coincidence. But he knocked me down, and I twisted my ankle when I fell. And he took me to the hospital where he works, and then called me later that night to make a date."

"So you're dating a doctor!" Natalie declared.

"Yes, I'm dating a doctor. Dr. Andrew Barton." I had been looking forward to telling them about him but I was embarrassed about the accident. "We are going out next weekend."

"Wow," Maggie said, smiling.

Candace raised an eyebrow and appeared to be thinking about something.

I ignored her and put his card on the table for them to

inspect. "He gave me his card. Plus, he treated me at the hospital, so I know he is who he says he is."

"Andrew Barton," Candace said. She said his name slowly, as if she were thinking about it. "May I see the card?" She held her hand across to Natalie, who handed the card to her. "Andrew Elliott Bancroft Barton." Her green eyes narrowed again. "Why does that name sound familiar?"

I reached for the card. "I have no idea."

"Dating a doctor is a whole new ball game," Candace said, her voice like a warning. "And one with four names sounds fairly pretentious."

"He was not pretentious at all." I felt defensive suddenly and didn't want to discuss the doctor any more. I pulled my menu in front of my face, trying to discourage Candace from pursuing this conversation.

"It's not like he's French, after all," Natalie said.

I lowered my menu to smile at her. She was trying to lighten the conversation, since Candace had recently fallen in love with a Frenchman named Gregoire. Of course, he wasn't pretentious at all.

"Gregoire isn't pretentious!" Candace's voice rose.

"I'm kidding," Natalie said, her voice soothing.

"Let poor Lu enjoy a first date at least," Maggie said.

"Yes please," I sniffed, folding my menu.

The conversation moved to other topics, and I nursed my mimosa and my foot, trying not to spend too much time thinking about the way Andrew Barton's eyes sparkled when he smiled at me, and trying even harder not to think about Candace's warning. Why would dating a doctor be any different than dating any other kind of man? I didn't know, and I was sure Candace was wrong.

Chapter Three

GIRLS IN GLASS STALLS

Natalie

THE WEEKEND WAS MOSTLY MISERABLE. Despite my ability to entertain an intermittent belief that something might eventually happen with CJ and me, I knew I was leading him on. I needed to tell him to give up. I needed to stop our Friday lunches. I needed to walk away.

But I couldn't.

In my darkest hours—and in my drunkest—I pictured the way his close-cropped, golden hair offset the dark eyes and ridiculously lush lashes. I thought about the way those full lips had felt pressed against mine, about the way he'd approached our two amazing kisses. He'd begun slowly, as if testing to make sure that I was a willing partner ... then he'd steadily increased his rhythm and pressure, expertly, moving slowly from a delicious teasing tempo to something far more carnal. It was impossible to forget the feeling of his hands on me, pushing me for more. There was something exhilarating—if frustrating—about knowing that something I wanted so much was completely within my reach.

But I knew that CJ wouldn't wait forever. I was constantly torn between my desire for the all-American man of my dreams and the desire to keep my job and my heart intact.

"Naomi." Lanie Bill stood in my office doorway, pulling me from my ruminations. "You ready for this?"

Lanie referred to the spate of interviews that today held for us. I'd put the notice out Friday, and a half week later, there were six people slated to discuss the marketing assistant position we offered. I'd interview them first, then pass them on to Lanie. If they weren't worthy, she'd said, there was no need to waste her valuable time.

"Remember, Nell, if the glove does not fit, do not acquit."

I cringed at her ridiculous and totally improper usage of Johnny Cochrane's OJ defense.

"Got it," I told her, shooting her the thumbs up. Lanie lived for cheesy hand signs and stupid clichés. It was part of why I had no respect for her as a marketing VP or as my boss.

"Incoming," she said loudly, backing away from my door.

A mousy girl in a short skirt and flat black shoes approached my door, the receptionist just ahead of her. "Chantale Deveraux," the receptionist said.

"Hi," the girl said.

"Come on in," I said. As she sat, Lanie appeared in the glass panel next to my now-closed door, her eyebrows high as she shook her head and mouthed the word "no." I consciously decided to give the girl a fair chance.

"Hi, Chantale," I said. "How's it going today?"

"Well," the girl said, placing her resume delicately in front of me. "This is not really the job I was hoping to be interviewing for."

The interview went downhill from there.

Other potential candidates told me stories of ex-boyfriends, bong accidents, and previous firings, giving me little hope of finding anyone that I might actually be able to work with. During the entire day of interviews, Lanie danced outside my door making faces and openly mocking the candidates. She seemed to pause only when Damon walked by, at which time she gaped at him, blushing furiously. Damon had that effect on women. All women. And it was clear that Lanie had a thing for him.

Finally, toward five o'clock, Jennifer, our receptionist, walked a candidate back who seemed outwardly capable. Her name was Justine. She'd worked as a public relations intern in college and had some previous event planning experience.

"I didn't graduate top of my class," she explained during our interview, leaning across my desk, "but I did pretty well. And UCLA is a tough school."

"I'm from California, too," I told her. "How did you end up in New York?"

"A twist of fate, I guess," she said. "I followed a boy. It didn't work out."

"Enough said." I smiled at her. I had a good feeling about this girl. "I'm going to walk you down the hall to Lanie's office. She's the VP." I hesitated before offering anything else, but I wanted this girl to work with us. She'd be an ally against Lanie, I thought. A force of normalcy in our otherwise insane marketing department. "Just take everything she says with a grain of salt."

"Um, okay," she said, smiling as she followed me down the hall.

"Lanie," I said, as we entered Lanie's office. "This is Justine."

Lanie spun around dramatically in her chair, a strange look on her face. "Have a seat, Jessie," she said. "Nattie, you can leave us. Oh, and if you see Damon, tell him I'll be ready in fifteen minutes." I gave a reassuring smile to Justine and walked out, hoping she'd weather the crazy storm. And then I set out to find Damon.

The man in question was leaned so far back in his office chair that I thought he might be seconds from toppling over. His feet were crossed on the edge of his desk and I could see him only in profile as I entered his office. He appeared to be sleeping, so I took just a second to appreciate the vision. I might not want anything to do with him, but I had to admit, he was ridiculously attractive.

"Like what you see, Pepper?" he asked, opening one eye and arching a perfect dark eyebrow. He pulled his feet down and turned in the chair to face me.

"Long day?" I asked.

"You could say that," he said, a thin smile pulling up one side of the sculpted lips. "What's up?"

"It's none of my business," I began.

"Oh, this should be good," he said, smiling fully now.

"I just wondered if there's anything going on between you and Lanie."

Both eyebrows shot up now and Damon suppressed something between a bark and a laugh. "What?"

"That pretty much answers my question."

"Listen Pepper, you're right—it's totally none of your business, but that is not the kind of rumor I'd want getting around. No, I'm not hot for Jabba the Hut."

"Ouch, that's pretty low."

"She's been hanging out in here, harassing me, making innuendos that make even me uncomfortable. And it takes a lot," he said.

"Well, she told me to tell you she'd be ready in fifteen minutes."

"Oh crap," he said, springing to his feet and pulling his suit jacket off a hanger behind his door. "I better go before she comes looking for me."

"The indomitable Damon? Running from a woman?"

"Yes, I'm running. The 'woman' part? Debatable. See you later,

Pepper." Damon passed me and practically sprinted toward the lobby.

At least that question was answered. I almost felt sorry for Lanie. But not quite.

In the end, Justine made the cut. A week later, she started as our new marketing assistant. She sat out in the cube farm, though she had a great view of the Empire State Building, and her cube was larger than most at other places I'd seen. The All Night Media offices were not exactly corporate in feel. We had a media lounge that included a Mortal Kombat machine and a full-sized Ping-Pong table. Half of the staff wandered around in jeans and T-shirts, while the other half wore suits. It was all part of the Internet culture, and Justine fit right in. She dressed in business attire, but seemed to have no problem getting along with some of the less socially-capable developers who made the technology work.

"How are things going?" I asked, when she'd been working for almost a week. "Did I overwhelm you with reading?" I'd given her a huge pile of reading material to help her get up to date on the Internet advertising world and some of the competition we faced as an advertising network.

"No, I think I'm getting it," she told me. "Everyone has been so nice."

Just then, Damon walked by, sauntering in typical Damon fashion. I watched her watch him and then caught him giving her the "I'll be back" eyebrow. I knew all too well where that could lead. It seemed no woman was immune to Damon's charms, and he saw every woman as a potential target.

"No," I said, my voice calm. "Just. No."

Justine raised an eyebrow.

"I'm not gonna tell you how to live," I told her. "But be here long enough to see how Damon operates before you commit. That's all I suggest."

"That's fair," she said. "But he is really hot, you have to admit." She tossed her long, dark hair over her shoulder and her light blue eyes flashed.

"He is. No argument."

"So," she leaned toward me, her eyes flashing. "You've tasted that?"

I stared at her for a second. I hadn't been with Damon in the carnal sense. But I'd veered pretty close, at a time when he was dating one of my best friends. And it was a closely guarded secret. "No," I said slowly. "But he dated a friend. It didn't end well."

"Ah," she said. She seemed to be thinking about that. I wasn't responsible for this girl's decisions, and she was only a few years younger than I was. But I was her manager, so I decided that I could at least mentor a bit in this department. "My recommendation? Steer clear of guys at work."

"Sure," she agreed.

"Okay," I said. "See you Monday."

She stood and pulled her bag from the floor. She was tall and slim, dressed well, and seemed fun. I could see her fitting in with my friends, but wasn't sure it would be a good idea to invite my new employee out. I didn't want to have to play manager while we partied.

"You have plans this weekend?" she asked as we walked toward the door together.

"Not really," I said, and then felt guilty. "But there's an Internet party tonight over at Limelight."

"Seriously?" she asked. Her face lit up.

"Yeah, I think my friends are heading over around eight."

"Do I need to be on the list?" she asked.

"I'll take care of it," I told her. I'd found that one benefit of my position as marketing director at a big Internet company was that it afforded certain privileges.

We parted ways and I called Audrey, the PR representative for RocketOwl, as I walked to the subway. "Hey Aud, it's Natalie. Can you add my new marketing assistant to the list for tonight? Her name's Justine Watters. Give her a plus one. Thanks!" I decided that I didn't mind her going to the party. I just didn't think she should go with me.

My phone rang as soon as I hung up. "Hello?"

"Pepper."

"Candace."

"I am so pumped for this party tonight. Gregoire's out of town and I'm on the prowl. Limelight is the perfect venue."

"You're not cheating on your perfect man?"

"That's not what being on the prowl means, loser. I'm just ready to have fun. I've been all coupley forever. I'm ready to dance and flirt and maybe disavow some chauvinistic banker of his misogynistic ways."

"Well, when you put it like that ... "

"Meet at Lu's at eight?"

"Sounds good."

I rode the subway home to my Upper West Side walk-up. I was relieved to find that Tori, my semi-parental roommate, was not home when I arrived. It gave me a chance to relax a bit on the couch before I got ready to go out. When Tori was home, I stayed mostly in my room, only because I felt like the apartment was more hers than mine for some reason. I guess it was because she'd been living there longer, and all the furniture in our sparse living room belonged to her. It was nice to stretch out. The tiny space that counted as my room held only a bed and my clothes, and made me feel like the walls were closing in on me.

When I heard her key in the lock, I was already dressed to go out, and we passed in the hallway.

"Headed out?" she asked, her pale face drawn and tired.

"Yup. Wanna come?" I asked, knowing the answer."No. Thanks, though. I'm beat. Have fun!"

"Okay, bye!"

I slid out the door and down to the street, relishing the constancy of the city's noise and movement and the fact that it always waited there, just outside my door.

We rallied at Lulu's place at eight o'clock, Maggie and Candace arriving with Catalina, a girl I could hardly stomach on the best of days. The feeling was mutual.

"Pepper," she said, her bored tone making me feel irritated.

"Catalina," I returned, before hugging Maggie and Candace. I had no idea how Maggie could put up with the always-superior Catalina. The girl had dated CJ briefly a few months ago, and I just couldn't put it behind me. Neither, it seemed, could she.

"How's CJ?" she asked. "You guys still doing that high school 'I want Jimmy, no, I want Timmy' thing?"

"What does that even mean?" I asked her.

"Oh, never mind. I don't care." Catalina wandered to the kitchen counter and poured herself a glass of wine. She was thin and waify and purposely cultivated an Audrey Hepburn look that was starting to strike me as pathetic.

I turned in the other direction, fuming.

"Ignore her," Maggie whispered. "She's still upset about CJ."

"So am I," I hissed.

"Let it go," Maggie said.

"When are you seeing the prominent doctor, Lu?" Candace asked loudly, stalking around the small studio apartment, poking at items on shelves and reading the backs of CD covers as she moved from place to place.

"Tomorrow," Lu said. She was still in an air cast and looked unhappy out of her signature four-inch heels.

"How long are you in that thing?" I asked.

"Three more weeks," Lu pouted.

We all settled around the small coffee table in front of Lu's futon.

"This is so nice," I moaned. "I want my own place so bad."

"Are you moving?" Lu asked innocently. She had a nice apartment thanks to her family. Candace was the same. I, on the other hand, rented what I could afford, which wasn't much.

"I wish."

"You should!"

"I'd love to. I just don't have the first, last, and broker's fee. Plus, the cheapest studio in a decent neighborhood would be what, fifteen hundred?"

"About." Candace sighed. She seemed bored whenever money was the topic at hand. Unless it was the money of investors whom she was trying to woo—but then she was discussing sums in the hundreds of thousands. My own paltry rent was hardly a blip on her radar.

"Well, maybe after the IPO," I said. All Night Media had an IPO coming in the months that followed. Since Lanie Bill had been brought on board, the plans were not part of my daily briefing.

"You have options, right?" Candace asked, her interest piqued now that we were veering toward business talk.

"Yeah," I told her. "A lot."

"So when you go public, you cash them and use the cash for a new place. Just be ready for a huge tax hit."

"This is so outside my realm," I said.

"Welcome to the Internet economy," Candace said. "I can help you."

"Thanks, Candy Cane."

She scowled at me. Candace hated being called Candy, but we all used the nickname now and then just to watch her reaction.

Eventually, we convinced a cab driver to take all five of us and rode up Sixth Avenue to 20th Street. We disembarked in front of an old church building. The dark stone exterior was foreboding, and little outside hinted at the bustling thrum of the club inside, except the pulsating light visible through the large, round, stained glass window facing Sixth. We approached the velvet rope and I checked us in with the doorman. We entered as a group, a dry ice-induced mist swirling around us as we came through the door.

The dance floor in front of us was dark but lit from beneath to make the fog hanging over it pulse and glow. A DJ occupied a stand at the far end of the open dance floor, with bars on three sides and a lounge area to the far right of the dance floor.

Candace shimmied off and into the mist, pulling Catalina along with her. Lulu, Maggie, and I headed for the bar, where I found Justine swaying next to a tall, dark-haired man I didn't know, a smile on her face and her light eyes bright.

"Hey," I said.

"Hi, Natalie." She smiled and nearly tripped walking toward me. Her dark hair was pulled into a high ponytail and her blunt-cut bangs hung straight across her forehead. She looked great.

"Been here a while?" I asked.

"Yeah," she smiled sheepishly. Despite the fact that she was tipsy and stumbled a bit, she was cute and I couldn't help but like her. At least until CJ appeared at her side, holding two drinks.

"Hey, Natalie," he said. Did he look strangely guilty?

"Hi," I responded.

He handed Justine a drink and then put an arm around me, standing between us. "I was hoping to see you here."

"Really?" I asked. It seemed like he had enough company.

"I hope to see you pretty much everywhere," he said softly in my ear, giving me the sheepish grin I couldn't resist.

"Just looking out for our new marketing recruit, then?" "She came alone, Natalie. I think she's pretty blitzed."

"So you're feeding her drinks?"

"This is her second seven and ginger, actually." He grinned. "She hasn't noticed."

Relief flooded me. This was typical CJ. Taking care of people, looking out for his friends. "That's really nice of you."

"Pepper," Lulu leaned in. "Come with me to the bathroom."

"Okay," I said, excusing myself with a bit of disappointment at leaving CJ's arm.

The bathrooms were quieter than the main club was, but not much. Lulu went into a stall and then shrieked loudly as soon as she'd flipped the lock.

"Lu? Are you okay?" I ran to the door.

"No! Get away from the door!"

"What?" I backed up and she burst out of the door again.

"Could you see me?"

"What?" I asked again. I was utterly confused. "Are you gonna pee or no?"

"Go in there!" she ordered.

"Okay," I said. I entered the stall and pulled the door shut.

"Lock it!" she said.

I did as ordered and began giggling madly when the oriental dragon pattern on the door disappeared and the entire panel became clear, revealing the restroom beyond the door, Lulu's shocked face directly in front of me.

"Did it happen?" she asked, her voice intense.

"You mean can I see everything outside the door?"

"Yes."

"Yes, I can."

"But I cannot see you."

"Good," I said. "Then I think I'll pee."

Lulu looked annoyed and then looked around her. "But I have to go!" she whined.

"You gave up a perfectly good stall," I told her.

"I thought everyone could see me."

I talked as I took care of business. "I'm surprised that would bother you. You've been known to continue conversations from the bathroom while you poop." Lulu wasn't what I'd consider shy.

She'd told us before that Americans were far too prudish in our attitudes about nudity and sex.

"That's at someone's apartment. It's different," she said. "Hurry up."

I finished, Lulu took her turn, and we returned to the bar.

CJ was nowhere in sight when we returned, and I tried to convince myself that I wasn't looking for him, though I couldn't keep my eyes from scanning the dance floor and peering into dark corners trying to find that golden head. I tried to keep up the conversation with my friends, but CJ's appearance and quick disappearance was bothering me more than I would have liked. Or maybe what had me bothered was the fact that Justine had disappeared too.

I sipped my cocktail and stared out into the club.

"What's your beef tonight?" Candace was at my elbow, squinting into the crowd to see what I was looking at.

"Nothing." I turned back to the bar.

"If you're mooning over your biz dev director, he's been propping up your drunk marketing assistant all night in the corner by the bathroom." Candace waved across the crowd, raising an eyebrow.

"Oh!" I sounded excited and immediately tried to cover. "I figured he left. Am I that transparent?"

"Like the bathroom stalls, my friend." She winked at me.

"Maybe I should go see if he needs a hand?"

"I'd expect nothing less."

I wandered in the direction of the bathrooms and found CJ sitting in a low booth, Justine at his side looking dazed.

"Hey," I said.

"Hey!" He looked happy to see me. "Wanna join us?"

I raised an eyebrow and CJ scooted over, allowing me into the booth. Justine offered me a weak smile and then her mouth drooped. She was hammered. "This has gotten ugly quick."

"Nah," CJ said. "She was over served."

"Right," I laughed. "It happens to the best of us." I turned to Justine, who was trying to keep her head propped up on one hand, but seemed to be having some problems with balance. "Hey, Justine. Should we get you home?"

"Nah," she slurred. "I'm fine."

"Right," I said. "Well just for conversation's sake then, where do you live?"

"Upper Swest," she slurred.

"Okay. We'll share a cab," I told her.

"Hang out a little bit longer?" CJ suggested, putting a warm hand on my arm.

My skin tingled and my stomach twisted with anticipation, and I leaned toward him. He was like a magnet to me, and I wanted to turn my mind off and just let my body react. "I'd love to," I said. "But I feel responsible for her. Especially since you've been the one watching over her all night. I should do something."

"I don't mind," CJ said, turning to look at his drunk charge. "Besides, I knew if I stayed close to her, you'd check in eventually."

"I would have checked in with you, too," I said.

"No you wouldn't. You make a point of avoiding me at these things."

He was right. I usually watched him and pretended I wasn't watching him. I made excuses not to get too close, despite wanting to throw myself into his arms. I gave him a weak smile. "I'm sorry."

"I don't want you to be sorry," he said. His hand was on my thigh now, and my mind was threatening to take a vacation as his fingers squeezed gently and caressed my skin. "I want you to be with me."

Justine swiveled her head around, and I pulled away from CJ before her drunk mind connected what she might have thought she heard, with my body language confirming it.

CJ's face fell, but the disappointment was quickly replaced with his neutral smile.

"I do want to be with you," I whispered. "But ... "

"I know." He turned to Justine and put an arm around her shoulders, shaking her gently. "Let's get you guys into a cab, huh?"

That was my cue. My heart sunk as I rose and helped CJ get Justine out to the curb, waving to the girls as we passed.

It was after two o'clock, and as Justine and I rode in the cab toward the Upper West Side I found myself wondering what exactly I expected from CJ. Half of me wanted him to demand more, to forcefully give me no choice in the matter. But that wouldn't be the CJ I'd come to respect so much. The other half wanted him to do exactly what he was doing. Wait for me. But even that selfish part of me realized that a guy like CJ wouldn't wait forever.

Chapter Four

NOT A FINGERBOWL IN SIGHT

Lulu

ANDREW CALLED Thursday to confirm that we would still see each other on Friday. I had spent part of the day at Bloomingdales looking for something to wear. I'd begun the search in my closet, but for some reason Candace's warning about pretentious doctors had me feeling uncertain about things that I normally wouldn't give a second thought.

When the phone rang, I was listening to Fat Boy Slim at a volume that generally irritated my neighbor—I'd seen him go out earlier—and trying on my new clothes.

"Hello?" I turned down the music.

"Lulu," Andrew's velvet voice rolled through the phone line. There was something that sounded like a smile in the tone of his voice. "Hi."

"Andrew."

"How's the ankle? Are you using your crutches?"

"The ankle is getting better. And I told you I wouldn't use those ugly things."

"It must be a lot better then. I'd predicted that you'd give in when you figured out how much it hurt not to use them."

"I'm sure you have been wrong before, Doctor."

Andrew laughed. "Hmmm. There's a first time for everything, right?"

"Ha ha." He was right, actually. It did hurt to wobble around on my ankle, but the ugly metal crutches were even worse. I'd chosen to just stay home most days instead of use them or endure the pain. "Did you call just to check in on my medical compliance?"

"Of course not. I wanted to see how you're doing, and find out if we're still on for tomorrow night."

"I'm looking forward to it."

"Great." His voice was happy, and it made me feel happy. Everything about him made me feel happy. I didn't know what I was supposed to take from Candace's warnings about Andrew, but he seemed perfectly genuine to me. "I've made two reservations. Do you want to keep it casual or go all out?"

"What would 'all out' be like?"

"A coat and tie for me. Lots of waiters, multiple forks, and probably a finger bowl."

I cringed. I'd done "all out" lots of times, and the thought of hovering waiters brought back bad memories. "And casual?"

"If we do that one, I'd like to keep it a surprise. But jeans would work fine. And you can eat with your hands."

"I don't eat with my hands. I can manage forks."

"I'm sure you can." I could swear he was winking, though I couldn't see his face.

"Casual sounds good."

"Done. I'll pick you up at seven-thirty. Where do you live?"

"Barrow and Grove. I'll wait downstairs at Grove and 7th so you don't have to locate the building." No one could ever find the tiny stretch of the West Village street where I lived unless they had spent years wandering the village.

"Are you in number nine? The big one on the corner?"

I was surprised. "Yes. You've been here?"

"I grew up in New York, Lulu. I know the village well. I went to NYU."

"Oh." I could think of nothing clever to say.

"I'll just ring up with the doorman when I'm there."

"Okay, good. Yes, that will be easier."

"I don't want you hobbling all over the place."

"Okay. See you then."

"Lulu?" His voice was higher, uncertain.

"Yes?"

"I'm really looking forward to seeing you again."

"Me too," I said.

When I hung up, I felt a lightness that I hadn't felt in a while.

I dated a lot. Or at least I flirted a lot and kissed a lot of men. I had more romantic interludes than maybe I should have. I'd sampled the local population. And I hadn't felt this excited about anyone in a long time. I smiled at the walls of my apartment and chose an outfit to match my optimism about Dr. Andrew Barton.

At exactly seven-thirty, the doorman buzzed, and I asked him to send Andrew upstairs. I was dressed, but still needed to brush my teeth and collect a few things. The doorbell rang shortly after, and I limped to the door to find a gorgeous Andrew standing in front of me, red roses in hand.

"For you," he said, a wide smile on his face. In the glow of the hallway lights, I noticed that his golden-brown hair curled slightly around his face, and a scatter of freckles fell across the bridge of his nose. The blue eyes sparkled, matching the smile on his full lips. There was an angularity to his features that was refined, chiseled.

"Thank you." I accepted the flowers and stepped back to make room for him to enter. "Red means passion, you know." I wanted to slap myself the second it was out. Why did my mouth insist on moving before my brain? Now he would think I was putting him on the spot.

"Does it now?"

"Not to suggest that you are passionate, I mean." Oh, that wasn't better. "Or maybe you are." I waved my hands awkwardly, shaking the flowers. "Never mind."

"Passion works," he said quietly.

I had no idea what to make of that and busied myself waving him in. "Come in for a moment."

"I did a little research yesterday after we talked. This building is from the late 1800s. It used to be a horseshoeing operation!"

I was surprised, and glad he'd changed the subject. "I love that," I told him. "I love the history of the buildings here. They've led so many lives. It makes me believe that it is possible for things to be reinvented, no matter how they began."

"A great way of putting it."

"I need to brush my teeth. Sit down," I said, planting the roses in a vase in the kitchen and then hobbling to the bathroom.

I returned to find Andrew looking at the one picture of my parents that I had. They were young in the photo, my father holding me in his arms and my mother holding my infant brother. I smiled and picked up my purse. "I'm ready when you are."

"This is your family?" he asked, replacing the photo.

"Yes." I opened the front door. "Where are we going?"

He looked at my short skirt and smiled, almost sadly. "I should have mentioned that we'll be sitting on the floor. Will you be comfortable?"

"We are sitting on the floor? What kind of restaurant forces you to sit on the floor?"

"Trust me?"

I looked down at my skirt. It would undoubtedly creep up if we were sitting on the floor. And what kind of place would make you sit on the floor? But I expected that I'd have a napkin in my lap, and I wasn't usually shy. Plus, I had already spent at least two hours choosing this outfit. Changing now was not something I wanted to consider. "I'll be fine." I'd managed to find some strappy sandals that could accommodate my brace, and the ankle was feeling well enough to brave two-inch heels.

"Those would not be my first choice in footwear—as your doctor," Andrew said as he put an arm around my waist and walked me to the elevator. "But you look amazing."

"Thank you," I said, feeling the lightness again. I looked into his handsome face as we rode the elevator down to the lobby and felt a stirring of nervousness in my stomach. I loved it. This feeling, this initial excitement about somebody or something new, it was addictive to me. Maybe that was why my relationships never seemed to last long.

Andrew hailed a cab and sat near me in the back, his arm still over my shoulder, his thumb lightly grazing the skin exposed by my sleeveless shirt. Chills ran through me. He looked good, he smelled good, and he was adorable.

We pulled up outside a restaurant in Soho called Casa La Femme.

"Have you been here?" Andrew asked, helping me from the cab.

"No."

"It's wonderful. I can't wait to show you."

We went inside, and after a brief chat with the hostess, we were led to a tented table which was surrounded by large pillows covered in fabric laced with gold thread. The pillows were overstuffed, and everything about the setting felt opulent. The dark table was low to the ground, and we were waved toward it by a woman who could have been a belly dancer for her thin revealing outfit, which consisted of sheer harem pants and a corseted bra top. Dark kohl surrounded her eyes. As we settled onto the pillows, she walked around the tent, pulling the sides shut. High notes of exotic music filled the air, and it seemed as though we'd entered another world.

I stared at Andrew with a silly grin on my face.

"Isn't it fantastic?" he said. He was grinning too, and I had a strange sensation that the two of us were alone in the world for a moment. The closed walls of the tent helped the illusion.

A woman stepped through the hanging panels with water glasses in hand. She smiled at us and then explained the menu and how to order. She arranged the pillows behind us and we reclined into them.

When our wine arrived, we were snuggled side by side into the soft pillows. We ordered our food and then resumed our positions, drinking wine and watching one another as we talked.

"You are very young," I said. "How is it that you are a doctor?"

He flashed the boyish grin that I was coming to adore. "I'm not that young," he said. "But I did start college a year early. I'm still finishing my residency at St. Vincent's."

"So you are not a doctor yet?"

"Technically you're a doctor when you graduate medical school. But the residency gives you the hands-on experience."

"I see."

We drank in silence for a moment, but it wasn't uncomfortable. I wanted to know more about this perfect man.

"So you grew up in New York City?"

"I did," he said, his smile wide.

"Do your parents still live here?"

"They do."

"Are you close with them?"

"I am," he said, putting his glass on the tabletop. "I see them often. I don't know what I'd do without them. It's easy to be overwhelmed by all the stuff that goes along with medical school. It's stressful. I think having them nearby has helped me stay grounded."

"They sound like good people," I said.

"The best."

I smiled. There was something about knowing that Andrew loved his family that made him seem even more perfect.

"What about you, Lulu? Are you close to your family?" Andrew took my hand as he asked the question, and a wonderful warmth moved through me at his touch, even though the question generated a chill in my bones.

"Not really." Andrew's eyebrows raised and concern spread across his face. "I mean, my uncle—he is like a father to me. It's his apartment, where I live. He bought it when he worked in New York and let me move into it when I finished school." I moved closer to him, dropping my hand to his thigh as the feeling of electricity in the air seemed to grow around us.

"That's nice," Andrew said. He looked down at my hand and then back up at me. His tongue darted out to wet his lower lip, and butterflies jumped inside my belly. "But your parents ... ?"

I didn't want to avoid the question completely, but I wasn't ready to talk about all of that with him yet. And his mouth was just inches away from mine, distracting me. I put my wine glass on the table and then slowly moved to trace my finger over the lip Andrew had just touched with his tongue. His eyes widened and then the lids dropped partway, and the look in the sparkling blue eyes darkened with lust. I leaned forward and took his lip between my teeth gently, and was rewarded when Andrew sucked in a surprised breath.

My body was tingling as I darted my tongue out to taste his mouth. He let out a low growl and then his arms were around me, pulling me toward him on the soft pillows, his mouth hard on mine. Just as I opened my mouth to meet his tongue, the waitress announced that our food was ready and we moved slowly apart, our eyes fixed on one another.

. . .

I gave Andrew a smile as I moved back to my spot and listened to the waitress as she showed us how to eat with the bread, making it into a scoop. She smiled and wished us "Sahtain" before refilling our water and wine and then backing out, leaving us alone again.

"Wow," Andrew said.

I couldn't tell if he was talking about the food or our kiss, but the deep breaths he took seemed to indicate that he needed a moment to steady himself. He grinned at me and then picked up a piece of bread and served himself.

I sat, uncomfortable, while Andrew began.

"Lulu," he said. "You're not eating."

"This is strange to me. I am not used to eating with my hands. It is never done in Brazil. It's very rude."

"But we aren't in Brazil. This is Egyptian, and in Egypt it is completely proper to use your hands. Your right hand, at least."

"Why only the right?"

"They use the left for ... other things."

"Such as?"

"Personal duties."

"Like?"

"You're going to make me talk about this while we eat?" He was smiling again, the blue eyes liquid and warm.

"No, I think I see where you are going with that."

"Can you eat? I'm feeling very rude." He took a big bite.

"Okay," I said, and served myself from the main dish.

The food was wonderful, and the company was better. When the food was gone and we'd had rich coffee, we shared a hookah with apple tobacco in it, reclining in the pillows. Andrew kissed me again at the end of each course, and his lips were becoming one of my favorite things. I began to dread the end of our date.

Finally, we had to leave the separate world that existed inside our little tent, though I would have liked to keep it for the whole night. Andrew helped me to my feet and we made our way outside into the cool spring night.

"That was incredible," I told him.

His arm went around me naturally and he pulled me to his side as we moved slowly up the sidewalk. I'd had enough wine that my ankle didn't bother me, and I was able to walk almost normally. I leaned into him, resting my head on his shoulder for a moment.

We stopped walking and he turned me to face him. He kissed me again, and my stomach quivered and then felt as if it dropped out of me completely. I was melting in his arms and wanted to continue kissing him forever.

"I don't want to take you home, Lulu."

"What if you came with me?" I smiled at him.

He looked uncertain for a brief moment, then said, "Okay." The happy smile overtook his face again. Just then, flashing lights lit the dark sidewalk as a photographer dodged out from behind a parked car. "Another kiss, Mr. Barton!" he called.

"What the hell?" I shielded my eyes from the sudden flash.

Andrew turned us in the other direction and guided me up the sidewalk, away from the man holding the big camera.

"I'm so sorry," he said.

"What the hell was that?"

"Paparazzi," he said. "They follow my family sometimes when the gossip is slow."

"What? Why? What does that even mean? Will we be in the paper?"

"Only local stuff," he said, looking sheepish. "It's not a big deal. I'm sorry, Lu. Does it bother you?"

"Why do the paparazzi care about what you do, Andrew?"

"It's kind of a long story," he said, his voice low. "Let's get a cab and I'll try to explain."

As the cab crawled north, Andrew began several times to explain why he had paparazzi stalking him, but then stopped. I let him stutter and look embarrassed for a few minutes before becoming completely frustrated.

"How complicated can it be?" I asked. "Are you famous?"

"Not really."

"Are you a criminal?"

Andrew laughed and shook his head.

"The American press cares about celebrities, criminals, and billionaires from what I can tell. Which one are you?"

"The last, I guess."

I laughed. But Andrew wasn't laughing. "Oh." So he was rich enough that the press cared what he did at night. "So you are very wealthy, then?"

Andrew narrowed his eyes as he nodded.

"Why didn't you tell me that?"

"Seriously?" He shook his head. "It's a tough way to begin a conversation, and a really bad way to start a relationship. 'Hi there, I'm rich, how are you?'"

I laughed, and he turned his head to watch me. "It is so ridiculous that this should matter to anyone," I said. "Why a newspaper photographer would be interested in taking pictures of you just because you have money ... it doesn't make much sense to me." I watched him for a moment, and realized that he wouldn't meet my eye.

"They don't care so much about me personally," he said quietly. "It's more like they're in the habit of tracking my family. My great-grandfather did well in oil investing, and he was always happy to have his picture in the paper. I guess they've just gotten used to covering my family."

It didn't make sense to me, but the American public was very interested in wealth, from what I could tell. "Do you think it matters to me?" I asked.

"Does it?"

"No," I said.

His shoulders loosened and he appeared to relax a bit.

"Does it matter to most women?"

"What do you think?"

I thought about that. I guessed that it would. Especially in a place like New York City where it seemed like you spent money just to walk down the street. Everything was expensive. For many girls, I could see that finding a rich boyfriend might be a good solution. Lucky for him, I wasn't one of those girls.

We dropped the topic of money as soon as we got to my apartment building, but it took another hour, lots of kissing and a vodka tonic for Andrew to relax again. In the end, he stayed all night. We lay kissing, talking and drinking until almost four in the morning. As we both got sleepy, he pulled me into his arms and tucked the blanket around us. I was surprised at how comfortable I felt with him, and also at the fact that we hadn't done anything more serious than kiss. It was serious kissing, but still, just kissing. I wanted more, and I tried to push things forward, but he gently kept things from progressing.

Eventually I slept in the warm circle of his arms, waking to find him still next to me, bright light streaming through the windows. And despite the sweetness of the situation, I was confused. I couldn't remember the last time I'd spent the night with a man whom I didn't actually have sex with. When someone came to my bed, it was an expectation. If not his, then mine.

"Good morning," I whispered, rolling over to face him.

"Morning, beautiful," he said.

I smiled at him, tracing a finger down the high cheekbone, across the line of his jaw, and over the full lips. Maybe Andrew was a morning sex man, I thought. He lay quietly watching me. The light blue of his eyes grew darker as I continued tracing his neck and chest, memorizing him with my fingertips. As I traced lower, toward the waistband of his boxers, he let out a low growl and the look on his face became more focused and practically carnal.

"Lulu," he whispered. "It's our first date. I don't want to move too fast."

"It can be our second date," I whispered back. "It's a whole new day."

He smiled at me, the desire never leaving his eyes as he stopped my hand. "No," he said. "Stopping you now feels like the hardest thing I've ever done, but I want to take it slow. I really like you. I feel like there could be something here."

I stared at him for a moment. "Okay," I said, relaxing slightly. I realized that I had begun trying to initiate things that morning because I believed I should—that sex would be the expected next step. It was both a disappointment and a relief to find that he wanted to wait. The only thing that bothered me was that I wasn't sure why. Did he not find me attractive? Or did he not trust me now that he'd told me he had money? I settled back into his arms, my hand wrapping around his neck as I considered the possibilities. We lay like that, staring into each other's faces, for what felt like hours, and I pushed the sense of confusion that was creeping up on me down as firmly as I could.

Chapter Five

GREEN MONSTERS

Natalie

I MET Candace and Maggie to lounge in the sun on Sunday after Lulu called to cancel our regular brunch. She didn't give a reason, but she'd been less mobile since hurting her ankle. She also didn't share anything about her date Friday night, despite each of us calling her to ask.

"It didn't work out," Candace ventured as we tilted our faces toward the sun, lying on a blanket in Sheep's Meadow with the Sunday paper scattered around us.

"We don't know that," Maggie said.

"Otherwise she would call to tell us," Candace said.

I didn't know much about Lulu's dating habits. Maggie and Candace had known Lulu in college, so they were more familiar with the way she handled men. All I'd seen were men falling over themselves to get near the tall, tan girl with the long, dark hair, her wowing them with her slight Brazilian accent, and then deciding whether or not to take them home for sex. Lulu seemed to approach the entire world of men and sex much more casually than I ever could. Sort of like a salad bar.

"She would call to tell us how in love she is, and how they'll undoubtedly be getting married soon." Candace yawned.

"Really?" I asked. "That doesn't sound like Lu."

"She's different when she really likes someone," Maggie said. "She's kind of an all or nothing girl. She either uses men or falls completely in love with them."

"Huh." I supposed I'd only seen the side of Lu that used men for fun and recreation. I had always thought that dating was kind of a hobby for her. "It seems like she could have just about anyone she wanted. I've never seen a guy not fall for Lu."

"No," Candace said quickly. "You've never seen a guy who didn't want to sleep with her."

I raised an eyebrow. I understood that there was a difference, but I didn't picture Lulu struggling with men. I knew that the last guy she'd been with, Ethan, had broken up with her, but she hadn't seemed wildly in love with him.

"Think she was completely in love with Ethan?"

"Probably." Candace looked bored.

"She didn't seem too upset when it ended," I said.

"She's actually pretty private," Maggie said, rolling over and propping herself on her elbows. Her dark hair fell around her shoulders and I was struck by the thought that she should consider being a hair model. "She doesn't share the big stuff unless you pry it out of her."

"I wouldn't have thought that. I sort of thought it was just all out there with Lu," I said.

"Some stuff is. She doesn't have much of a filter," Maggie said. "But the stuff that is important to her ... not so much." Maggie crossed her arms and laid her head on them. "What an amazing day."

"Hmmm," Candace smiled. "Gregoire comes back tomorrow," she said. Her voice turned to honey whenever she talked about her boyfriend, and I had to turn my head to make sure it was still Candace speaking.

"That's great." I meant it. Gregoire was incredible. Besides being ridiculously handsome and falling into the category of jet-setting businessman, he mellowed out my friend Candace. She was sometimes more hard, sharp edges than anything else, but when Gregoire was around, she softened and was more understanding and forgiving. It made me think that they were made for each other—the kind of couple that is better together than apart.

We relaxed in the park for a couple hours more, eventually heading in different directions as we said goodbye and went home to prepare for the week ahead. I drew the day out as long as I could. I was not eager to return to the office and the growing sense that I needed to make a decision about CJ. I wanted to do the right thing, but I feared that the right thing would be letting him go, and I didn't know if I was strong enough to do that.

"Nicole," Lanie Bill bustled into my office, holding several flapping sheets of paper in front of her. "Did you want to take a look at this before I pass it on to Jessica?"

"What is it?" I'd gotten past bothering to correct Lanie about my name. I felt only a little bit better to know that I was not her only name-slaughtering victim. Justine rarely heard her actual name leave Bill's lips, either.

"The trade show schedule. I've booked us into quite a few now that we've got a dedicated marketing assistant to make 'em happen. And with the IPO and everything, we're sponsoring a few, too."

"Sure," I said, reaching for the schedule. "Wow." I looked it over. "She'll be traveling every other week!"

"She's young, she'll enjoy it."

"You're probably right," I said. A tiny well of jealousy began bubbling away in my gut. I'd never traveled much. And Justine, who was two years younger than me, was going to be seeing many of the major cities in the country. On the company's dime. "I'll pass this on to her," I said. "Hey Lanie," the VP had almost reached my door. "Do you have this in Excel so I can just email it to her? And so that we have something other than a paper record?"

"You know my philosophy, Nina."

I said the words with her; I'd heard them so many times. "Put it on paper and make it real." It made no sense at all, but Lanie hated using the computer. She didn't seem to realize that she could print anything she wanted to, thus "making it real." I still had no idea how she'd landed a job at an Internet company. I shook my head at her back as she left my office, and pulled up a new spreadsheet so that I could enter all of her handwritten trade show plans.

After lunchtime, I found Justine at her desk. My heart jumped into my throat as I rounded the corner and found a familiar blond head leaning across the partition on the other side of her. CJ's low laugh rolled through the air, which suddenly seemed thick and oppressive. He looked up to see me standing there, and straightened, smiling. "Hey, Natalie."

Justine turned and smiled, too, remnants of whatever joke they'd shared still lingering in her grin. I swallowed hard as jealousy erupted in me for the second time that day.

"Hey guys," I said, my voice coming out stiff. "Justine, you have a minute? I just wanted to go over the trade show schedule with you. Lanie's already registered for most of these, so we need to get you some plane tickets for the first couple pretty soon."

She sat straighter and clapped her hands in front of her, her ponytail bouncing. "I'm so excited!"

"Mind if I take a quick look at the first couple?" CJ asked. "There's one in San Fran that I think I'm gonna need to go to."

"Sure." I spread the newly-printed spreadsheet out in front of Justine, and CJ and I both stood behind her, bending over it.

"You're gonna be busy," CJ said, his voice low.

"I can't wait," Justine said. She looked up at him then, and caught his eye. As a look passed between them, I felt the small bubbling well that had popped up earlier begin to churn madly. I felt sick. Was there something going on?

"Um, so," I began, having no idea what I was going to say, but feeling childishly triumphant that I'd wrenched both sets of eyes away from one another and back to me. "So maybe if CJ is going to the San Francisco show, we don't really need you there." I pulled this from thin air, realizing as CJ opened his mouth that it made no sense.

"I'm not going to be able to man the booth the whole time, though, Natalie. I've got meetings," CJ said, seeming to think about this. "Plus, this is a pretty big sponsorship. It might make sense to have a few people there to make sure it goes smoothly."

He was right. "Right, sure," I mumbled. Then inspiration struck. "Maybe I'll come along, too. I can help you make sure that the sponsorship and booth setup go smoothly, Justine. And then you'll be all set for the next one." The San Francisco show was only two weeks away.

"That'd be so fun!" Justine said, seeming to mean it. She was always enthusiastic and upbeat. It was part of the reason I'd hired her, but at that moment it was just irritating.

CJ was looking at me over her head, a strange expression on his face, as if he was trying to understand something.

"CJ?" I said, knowing I'd already made up my mind and hoping he didn't have any good reasons why that wouldn't work.

He smiled, not the big CJ grin, just a small smile that felt like it was just for me. His blue eyes darkened for a moment. "That'd be great," he said. For that second, I felt like we were alone in a room, like the office buzz wasn't all around us, and like Justine wasn't practically vibrating with excitement just in front of us. "Great," he repeated louder, breaking us out of the illusion.

"I'll check into flights for that first event, then," I told them both, "and see what we can get."

I waited a minute longer to watch CJ turn and head down the corridor to his office before I turned to head to my own.

"Natalie?" Justine said as I moved away from her desk.

"Yeah?" I walked two steps back.

"This is totally none of my business," she began. "But is there anything, uh, going on there?" She pointed a finger toward the hallway CJ had just disappeared down and then waved it at me.

"What, us? CJ?" I felt the flush beginning in my neck and put a hand to my throat, as if I could cover it. "Nope. Just friends," I said.

"Huh." A thoughtful dreamy look came over her face, and warning signals flared within me.

"Bad idea to date people you work with, Justine. Terrible idea."

"Right," she agreed.

I went back to my office and worked on finding a flight full enough that I could get two seats together and one far, far away.

Chapter Six

FIVE CENTS

Lulu

I SAW Andrew almost every day the week following our date. He came over when he was done with his shifts, sometimes in the middle of the night. We'd gotten into the habit of just lounging in my bed together, snuggling and sleeping. But even after seeing him for five straight days, we still hadn't had sex. For me, this was a record.

The phone rang next to my bed, waking me Thursday morning just after four. I reached for it. "Hello?"

"Hi gorgeous. Can I come over?"

"Mmm." I stretched and yawned into the phone. My voice was thick but I was wide awake, knowing Andrew would be there soon. "I should say no. These late night visits are very inappropriate. What must my doorman think?"

"Do you care?" His voice was low. I could tell he was tired.

"Not at all."

"See you in a few."

I hung up and stood slowly to go to the front door. I picked up the handset to call the doorman. "Tom?"

"Yes, Miss Rossi?"

"Andrew is coming over, just send him up please."

"Sure thing."

I didn't care what the doorman thought. He'd seen plenty of men in and out of my apartment in the six months I'd been back. I doubted that he was in contact with my uncle,. and even if he was, I doubted that my uncle would care very much, though he might try to have some kind of fatherly talk with me if he knew. I opened the front door an inch and crawled back into my warm bed, pulling the comforter around me.

Soon, I heard the front door open and a bag drop to the floor. The door shut quietly and I could hear the shuffle of Andrew moving toward me around the corner that separated my living space from the bedroom area.

"Hello," he said, his voice low.

"Hi." I pulled the comforter back next to me.

I heard clothes being removed and then a comforting weight depressed the mattress and shifted toward me.

"Hi," he said in a sleepy voice as his arms went around my waist, rolling to pull me on top of him. "How are you?"

"Good," I said, letting my head fall to his shoulder, nuzzling the skin of his neck. "You sound tired."

"I am." His warm hands were running slowly up and down the length of my back, stopping to cup my butt when they were at the end of their journey before heading back up. "But it's easy to forget once I'm with you."

His bare chest was broad and warm, and there was something comforting about Andrew that I'd come to depend on. He came to me almost every night, rarely pushing for more than a few kisses. I felt like he valued our companionship more than anything else, and while it was hard to control myself when I felt his erection pressing against my stomach as we lay in my bed, I tried to honor that.

"I'm glad you came," I told him, finding his lips with my own.

His arms tightened around me as he responded to my kiss, and his tongue teased its way between my lips and began doing things that made my stomach tighten and my muscles clench deep inside. I pressed myself against him, rocking slowly back and forth, and Andrew moaned low into my mouth.

"God, Lu," he growled. "You're so incredibly hot." The hands were firmly on my butt now, pressing me into him. He pulled me closer, rocking against me.

"I thought you were tired," I purred.

"Not anymore," he said.

My blood rushed in my ears as my pulse accelerated. I believed this would be it, and even though I had been trying to play cool, the thought that maybe he didn't want me had crept into my head once or twice. And though it was easy to pretend that wouldn't be a big deal, it would be. It might break me. I hadn't been this interested in a man in ... maybe ever. And that was just after five days.

Andrew's mouth became more insistent on mine, his tongue plundering my mouth and his hands pulling at the thin T-shirt I wore. I slid off him to pull it off over my head and his hands moved up the sides of my body as his head fell back to the pillow. I heard him sigh deeply just as his hands cupped my breasts, and then ... nothing.

I leaned forward, teasing his lips with mine, but his hands just pulled me close as he let out a low moan and then began breathing deeply. He was tired after all.

I rolled off him and let out a frustrated huff. What was going on? No one had ever fallen asleep while I was seducing him. I sat up abruptly, anger and confusion bubbling in my stomach and racing through my veins. This was unacceptable.

With one finger, I poked Andrew in the bicep, hard. "Hey!"

He shifted, but didn't wake up, moving his hand up as if to swat at a fly.

"Hey!" I said louder, shoving him with my hand.

"What?" he said, his voice groggy. He rolled toward me and reached for me, "sorry, babe. So tired ... " And he was asleep again.

I left him there and got up to limp around the apartment, my mind spinning. Was I just a friend? I didn't believe that at all—you didn't kiss friends the way Andrew had been kissing me. And I'd felt his interest pressing into my stomach. So he wasn't gay, and he did want me. But for some reason, he didn't want to actually have sex with me. Was Andrew a virgin? I stopped pacing and thought about that. Not possible. He was twenty-eight. And he kissed like a man with a lot of experience. Was he afraid to get too close because of the money thing?

I spun on my heel and watched him sleep for a few minutes, no answers coming. This was a new experience for me. And though I might be flattered by his desire for my company and conversation, I was beginning to doubt myself in other ways. And I didn't like it.

Andrew left just after ten in the morning Friday, and we still had not had sex. I couldn't help but feel insecure despite his tender kisses and constant phone calls. I was used to men wanting me. I wasn't very used to men wanting things beyond wanting me. Maybe I was an object to some men, and in some ways, that suited me. I controlled my image. I could play the role in bed. I didn't have to divulge much truth—since that was not what most men were after.

As I limped around my small apartment Friday, forcing myself to think of other things, the door buzzer rang.

"Hello?"

"Miss Rossi? There are some flowers here for you. Shall I send them up, or would you like to collect them later?"

"Thanks, Tom. Send them up." I never did understand exactly when Tom slept. He seemed always to be on duty.

The doorbell rang, and I pulled the heavy door inward to reveal a large bouquet of Gerber Daisies held in the arms of a young deliveryman.

"Oh! Thank you," I said, reaching for the bright yellow vase.

"Have a nice day," the man said, turning.

"Wait!" I called, grabbing my bag from the chair by the door and finding a tip for him.

He thanked me and I let the door close as I turned to admire the flowers. They were my favorite. Not exotic or fragrant. Just pretty and colorful and simple. Andrew and I had talked about flowers at some point this week during our late night marathon chats, and I realized now that he might have asked certain questions with a purpose in mind.

I smiled as I dialed his pager number and hung up. When the phone rang a few minutes later, I couldn't help gushing. "Thank you so much, they're amazing."

"So are you, Lu. You deserve something beautiful to look at—besides the mirror."

I giggled. "Are you sure you won't be too tired to meet us tonight?" The girls and I were going dancing at one of our favorite bars, and Andrew and Gregoire had both promised to meet us out later.

"I think I can manage," he said. "I'll be there around eleven."

"You know where it is?"

"Gemini, right?"

"Yes."

"I'll be there, Lulu."

"Okay. Bye."

"Goodbye, sweetheart."

I hung up and sat in front of the flowers to let my mind run away with me for a few minutes. Then I called Candace.

"Kanie, HellCat." Candace worked at a company called Hell-Cat, and she'd begun answering the phone this way a while ago. I had told her several times that I thought it was rude, but that only seemed to make her enjoy continuing to do it.

"What time are we meeting up tonight?" She knew it was me. We were years past identifying ourselves on the phone.

"Your place at nine. And I'm bringing someone."

"You mean Gregoire."

"No, his real estate agent."

"Why?" I asked.

"Because she's awesome," Candace returned.

"Why my place?" I said, looking around at the clutter.

"Because you don't work and therefore have the most time to procure alcohol for the pre-party and to clean up your apartment."

"That's fair," I said, conceding the point.

"Plus, it's on the lower east. You're closest."

"True." That made much more sense to me. I saw no purpose in navigating the city in a direction different from our destination.

"See you then. Gregoire's coming out at eleven."

"Andrew, too."

"OH." Suddenly I had Candace's full attention. I hadn't realized that she'd been typing as we talked until I heard the keyboard sounds stop. "Really?"

"What do you mean, 'really?'"

"I'm just surprised."

"What, that he wants to meet my friends?"

"No, that you're still seeing him!"

"Why?" That wasn't very nice, but to be fair, I hadn't mentioned him to anyone but Maggie since we'd first gone out. If I was truthful, it was because we hadn't had sex yet and I wasn't sure if he was going to stick around. If he wasn't interested in me that way I didn't want to give Candace anything she could use to embarrass me.

"Just hadn't heard anything, that's all."

"Well, he's coming," I sniffed.

"Can't wait to meet him."

"See you later."

"Bye."

Candace was hard to read, but I knew that down deep we were like sisters. She had her pride and her foibles, but at heart I knew she loved me. She'd looked out for me in a big-sisterly way in college, helping me avoid or recover from the pitfalls of living in a foreign country and speaking my non-native language, and even though there was some competition between us, I loved her, too. I couldn't help feeling like I was seeking her approval, even though I hated to admit it to myself.

Candace was on my doorstep at exactly nine o'clock, as promised, looking poised and put together with her signature bob and short skirt. I had always thought Candace was very sexy. She had a small blond girl with her, whom she introduced as Tamara.

"Where are you from, Tamara?" I asked as I poured from our usual extra-large bottle of Pinot grigio. There was nothing about this girl that made me think she was from the city, but something in the tilt of her chin told me she was fierce and determined.

"I grew up in Indiana," she said, smiling as she reached for a wine glass. "'With those Indiana boys on those Indiana nights,'" she added, winking a bright blue eye as she held her glass in a toast.

"What?" I asked. She was cute, but maybe she was crazy. I flashed a look at Candace.

"It's a song lyric, Lu," Candace said, reaching between us to take a glass.

"Oh." I shrugged as Tamara and Candace sang about someone named Mary Jane.

"Tom Petty?" Tamara said, raising her eyebrow. She was at least a foot shorter than I was, but she projected confidence, and the three-inch heels on her boots were impressive. I hadn't figured this girl out yet, but decided to like her.

"She's from Brazil," Candace said, as if that explained everything.

"Whatever." I knew of Tom Petty, but I didn't know the song.

Tamara smiled. "That's so cool!"

I smiled. Being from a foreign country always seemed impressive to Americans. I hadn't figured out why yet. I knew plenty of assholes in Brazil. Being from there didn't automatically qualify you as a good person.

Candace and Tamara moved to the couch as the buzzer rang again, and I waited by the door to let Natalie and Maggie in. Catalina, Maggie's roommate, was with them, and I could see that Natalie was not pleased. They didn't get along, despite Maggie's constant efforts to mend whatever hurt existed between them. It all came down to jealousy, I thought. Catalina had gone out with the man Natalie liked from work. I honestly didn't see the big issue, since Natalie refused to date him. But I was trying to be neutral.

Natalie hugged me and immediately poured herself a glass of wine and went to sit across from Candace. I could hear her introducing herself to Tamara.

"I'm so excited to meet your man," Maggie said to me, a huge smile on her face.

"Is he handsome?" Catalina asked.

I poured wine for them and answered. "I think he's adorable. But that's just my five cents. I'm biased."

They looked at each other and began giggling.

"Honey," Maggie said, leaning in and putting a hand on my arm. "You only get two cents."

"What?" What the hell was she talking about?

"The expression, it's 'that's my two cents.' Not five cents."

Irritation made my skin tingle. "Whatever," I told her. "Maybe I get more because I'm Brazilian." American expressions made no sense at all.

We all sat down and Catalina shared my error with the other girls, which I didn't especially appreciate, but I just smiled as they laughed at my expense.

Tamara and Natalie seemed to be getting along. Their heads were close together on the couch as they talked about being newcomers to the city and real estate.

I drank and watched the clock. I was excited to see Andrew out for a change, and nervous to introduce him to the girls. After an hour, we made our way across town to the Gemini Lounge.

I'd forced my ankle into knee-high boots, believing the zipper would provide enough support to forgo the air brace for one night, but as we walked to the door of the bar, I knew I'd been wrong. I was limping painfully. I would not be dancing tonight.

Inside, there was a bar directly ahead with a big lounge area just to the left. Up one stair behind the bar was a dance floor. It was small, but had a DJ booth through a window and flashing strobe lights. On the other side of that, down one stair, was a big room with two pool tables and low couches. This had become our favorite place to come this summer. You could dance or just hang out, and there were lots of places to sit. It was the perfect bar.

I wanted a drink, but my ankle was throbbing and there was a low table open to the left. I sat at the table and hoped someone would just bring me a martini.

I was surprised when Tamara wandered over with two glasses in her hand. "I hear you like 'em dirty!" she said, over the music.

"You already know me so well!"

Maggie and Candace set their drinks on the table, grabbed

Natalie, and went immediately to the dance floor, where something by Bon Jovi was making people shout along. Catalina stood at the bar, already having been approached by a dark-haired guy wearing a rugby shirt and khaki pants.

"So your boyfriend is coming out tonight?" Tamara said, pulling my attention back to the table.

"Yes, well ... " I thought for a second. Maybe I could talk to her about Andrew. Who knew if I would ever even see her again? "I'm not sure if he's my boyfriend. I mean, actually, he's definitely not. So I don't know what he is." To my surprise, I felt tears begin to threaten as my face got hot and my eyes burned.

"What do you mean?" Tamara asked, leaning in.

"He spends the night. Almost every night. He comes to my apartment instead of going to his, even when he gets off shifts in the middle of the night. And we kiss ... a lot. And he has brought me flowers once and had them delivered once already this week."

"Flowers twice in a week. I'd say you're dating for sure, and he's definitely into you."

Hearing her say that made me feel better. "Yes, but, I don't think he wants to sleep with me."

"What?" She sat up straight and put her drink down. "Lulu, I just met you and I kind of want to sleep with you. And I hardly ever sleep with girls!"

I couldn't tell if she was joking or not, so I just waited for her to continue. She winked a light blue eye and reached across the table to put a hand on mine.

"If he comes to your house instead of going home, he definitely wants to sleep with you. Especially if he's really tired and he still comes over."

"But he doesn't even try. The one time I was sure it was going to happen, he fell asleep first."

"Oh, that's not good."

"He's a doctor. I think he works too hard."

"A doctor, huh? Nicely done." She raised her glass.

"But it's been a week of seeing each other almost every day, and no sex."

"No sex?" Candace called out loudly as she sat down.

I frowned. I hadn't seen her approaching and had not planned to share my dilemma with her.

"No sex for who?" She looked at me over the rim of her glass. "Oh, for you? What, with the doctor?"

I just looked at her. Even though I hadn't wanted to tell her about it, Candace's frank insights were usually on target where other people's relationships were concerned.

"Why not?" Her voice was softer.

"I don't know," I admitted. "I've tried. I wonder if he just doesn't see me that way."

"He comes over in the middle of the night," Tamara said. "He sees you that way. Unless you just have a really comfortable bed."

"It is a very nice bed ... " I said.

"Lu," Candace said, setting her drink down. "I meant to talk to you about this."

"What?" Now I was really confused. She had been "meaning" to talk to me about this? Why was Candace thinking about me having sex—or not having sex—with Andrew?

"I figured out why his name was so familiar. His family ... "

"I know."

Candace raised an eyebrow. "Do you really know? I mean, the Bartons are like Upper East Side royalty, Lu."

"He and I have discussed it. I don't care about the money."

"Money?" Tamara leaned in.

"But his family doesn't just have money, Lu. They have more money than God. It's an issue."

"It is not an issue for me." I hated that we kept coming back to this.

"How much money are we talking about?" Tamara asked.

I raised an eyebrow at her and she leaned back, sipping her drink.

"So the sex thing might be about his family. They're old school. He's probably just waiting an appropriate amount of time. He's a gentleman. He follows rules that other people don't even know exist." She looked pleased with herself and picked her drink up again, fishing around in it with her long fingers until she got the cherry to the rim, which she immediately popped into her mouth with a grin.

"I hadn't thought of that," I admitted.

"And maybe he's trying to be sure that you're not a gold-digger."

"A gold what? Like a miner?"

"No. After his cash," Candace said.

"I'm sure that's not it. He's just a gentleman," Tamara said. "And by the way, there's a very handsome man holding a rose and coming this way right now. Would this be the good doctor?"

I turned to see Andrew striding towards us, a huge smile on his face. I stood to say hello and his smile faded as he looked down at my boots.

"Where's your cast?" he said when he had arrived at our table.

"It's ugly. I wanted to look nice," I told him.

"Lu ... " His voice was low and frustrated.

I smiled brightly at him. "I'm so happy to see you."

"I'm happy to see you, too. You look amazing," he said. He held out the rose, and seemed content to let discussion of the cast drop. Then he pulled me into his arms and pressed his lips against mine, his tongue immediately parting my lips and finding my own.

I responded enthusiastically and was lost for a few minutes until I heard Candace's voice behind me.

"Bern chicka berneer ... " she was making her porno soundtrack music.

I laughed and pulled away from Andrew. "Guys," I said. "This is Andrew."

He smiled and shook hands with my friends.

"We've heard a lot about you," Candace said, her green eyes gleaming.

Her knowing stare had Andrew shooting a questioning look at me, but I played innocent. No doubt he thought I'd told them all about how much money he had. This would not help my cause.

"Nice to meet you," he said. "Can I get you ladies a drink?"

Andrew went to the bar with our order and the girls both smiled widely at me.

"Um, he's totally your boyfriend," Tamara said.

"Really?" I asked. I was not usually this insecure. But I had usually had sex by now.

"No doubt," she said, fondling my single rose.

"No doubt," Candace repeated. When Andrew returned, Candace accepted her drink and then said, "I think Tamara and I need to go dance for a bit." She pulled Tamara to the dance floor.

I smiled at Andrew over the lip of my drink. "Thank you for coming," I said. "And for the rose."

He put his hands on my knees, leaning toward me on the low stools. "Thank you for going running last week, and for being clumsy and falling down so I could help you."

"I am not clumsy! And I didn't fall. You knocked me down!"

"And for hitting your head so that you can't remember properly what happened." His eyes glinted as he grinned.

"Maybe you hit your head, too," I said.

"And thank you for letting me see you every day this week," he said, looking serious. "Would you be willing to come with me for dinner Sunday?" he asked.

"Dr. Barton, I'll have dinner with you any time you like," I told him honestly. "We don't even have to eat." Maybe that was too much. I couldn't help it. I liked this boy. I wanted more time with him. I wanted to have sex with him.

"Um, so. This dinner would be with my parents," he said.

I sat up straight. Parents. Candace's comments about his

family rang in my head. "Really? Sunday?" I had no idea what to say. I didn't want to meet his parents. At least not yet.

"Lu," Andrew leaned closer to me and took my drink, setting it on the table. Then he took both my hands and pulled until I was scooted so close that our knees and foreheads were touching. "Lu, look. I think this is serious between us. Or it could be. And my family is really important to me. I have dinner with them almost every Sunday. I want you to meet my mom and dad, and get to know my little sister. And I want them to meet the amazing girl that I'm totally falling for."

My heart raced with the end of his speech, and a buzzing began in my head. Did he say "falling?" I threw myself at him and lost track of time, but when I had finished attacking him, I was sitting in his lap, my arms tightly around him.

"So that's a yes, then? For dinner?" he asked.

"Yes to dinner," I said, and then kissed him some more.

Chapter Seven

ELEVATOR TANGO

Natalie

WHEN WE GOT to the Gemini Lounge, I went with Candace and Tamara to dance almost as soon as we arrived. From our spot on the dance floor, I could see Lu sitting at a low table, and I watched as her boyfriend arrived and the other girls went to meet him. I didn't mind dancing alone for a while—there was plenty of company on the dance floor—and I wasn't in the mood to watch the love fest. I was happy that Lu had found someone, though it honestly didn't seem to be a challenge for her. But even watching from my spot on the floor, I could see that she was different around this guy. Less secure, less poised ... less Lulu. She must really like him.

I closed my eyes and danced to Hippy Chick without thinking too hard about anything. As the song ended, I glanced back over to the table to see that Gregoire had arrived. Since Catalina wasn't sitting, I made my way over to say hello and spied her at the bar, looking bored as ever while a sad-looking guy in a rugby shirt fawned over her.

"Hey," I said, touching Gregoire's shoulder as I slid onto an empty stool next to him.

"Natalie!" he smiled, pulling me in to kiss me on each cheek.

"Did you just get in?"

"I have been here for two days, actually, but have been very busy. Did you meet Tamara? She is showing me some apartments in the city."

"I did."

"You should ask her about your situation."

"Maybe I will," I told him. "I'm not sure I'm in the market yet. I'm going to get a drink. Can I get you anything?"

"No, no," he said, standing. "Don't be silly. What would you like?"

Gregoire was always a gentleman. Candace was beaming on his other side.

"An apartment, huh? He really is moving here?" I said as he moved toward the bar.

"He won't give up his place in Dijon," she said. "But yes, we'll share a place here."

"You're leaving your place?" I was surprised. Candace lived rent free in her parents' place on the Upper East. Her patio alone was bigger than my entire apartment.

"Time to grow up," she said, winking as her dark bob caught the light, shining as always.

"Huh." I wasn't sure why, but the metamorphosis that I was seeing before my eyes bothered me. Candace was "growing up," Lulu was busy falling in love ... and I sat there wishing I weren't so confused. I was fine when I was busy, but when love was in the air —as it was that night—I felt a jarring sensation of absence. And my thoughts always turned to CJ.

"No hot blond co-workers around tonight to lead on?" Catalina slid onto the stool next to me and gave me a catty grin.

"Leave it, Catalina. I'm really not in the mood." Catalina's time with CJ had ended when he'd left her at a party to kiss me. Not that our kiss had left us any more together than we were before it happened, but Catalina wasn't the type to accept second place. "Isn't it about time you either fucked him or cut him loose? CJ doesn't deserve to be treated that way."

"You have no idea what you're talking about," I told her. Sadly, she did. And she was right.

Maggie must have seen me smoldering, because she came to kneel between our stools. "Did you meet Andrew?" she asked me. Catalina rolled her eyes at me over Maggie's head. It took everything I had not to stick my tongue out at her.

"Not yet."

"He's so nice," she said. "And check out his friend. John, I think his name is."

Another man had arrived while Catalina and I were "chatting." He was good-looking in a dark, Irish kind of way, but his best feature by far was a shock of perfectly waved dark brown hair. It was thick and luxurious. It reminded me of television newscasters, but in a good way. Tamara seemed to notice him, too. She was leaning toward him, even though his back was to her as they sat. Was she smelling him?

"Tamara!" I called across the dark table.

She jolted upright and then smiled a sheepish grin at me and gestured at the back of the handsome man next to her while mouthing, "SO HOT."

I grinned and nodded.

We made small talk around the table, which was a feat considering that the music seemed to increase in volume every ten minutes.

"So you run marketing for an Internet company, Natalie?" Andrew was asking me.

"I used to run it," I said. "Now I report to a VP." I took a long swig of my vodka tonic. The thought of my boss made me want to down the entire glass.

"Sounds really interesting, though," he said. "Do you get to travel a lot?"

I might've sighed loudly in discontent because suddenly Maggie was looking concerned and even Lu was facing me.

"What's wrong, Pepper?" Lulu asked.

"Nothing. No, everything's good. I'm actually going to San Francisco next week," I tried to sound bright and upbeat, but knowing that the only reason I was going was because I couldn't stomach the thought of CJ and Justine traveling alone together made me feel small.

"That's awesome," Candace said. "What for?"

"Trade show," I told her.

"Is anyone else going?"

"Um. Yeah. My marketing assistant Justine—you met her at Limelight last week."

"Oh, yes," said Lulu. "She drinks a lot, I think."

"Pot, kettle?" Tamara piped up.

Lulu looked confused, but everyone else laughed. Tamara's joke seemed to have earned her John's attention. He leaned into her to whisper something in her ear, and she lit up as she answered him too softly for me to hear.

"So you and Justine in San Francisco. That should be fun," Maggie said.

"And, uh ... CJ." I stared at the ice cubes in my glass, but could feel Catalina's eyes on me over Maggie's head.

"Oooh," Candace purred. "The perfect chance to seal the deal. Hotel sex is always kinky."

"There will be no sex!" I said, not realizing the volume of my voice. People around us gazed over. John laughed loudly, his face breaking into a gorgeous grin with dimples on either side of perfect teeth. I thought Tamara might fall off her stool. "I mean," I said, my voice lower, "it's just work."

"Right," Gregoire said, winking at me.

Everyone knew about my desire for CJ and about the convoluted history we had together. They were rooting for us to get together. It seemed like I was the only one who understood my rationale for staying away from dating people I worked with. And even I was starting to find that rationale confusing. I thought there were two things in the way of me and CJ—work and fear. But maybe there was only one. And it probably wasn't work.

"Dance!" Candace cried loudly, jumping up when Kid Rock's "Cowboy" came on. Everyone except Tamara and Lulu rose and followed Candace to the floor to get their cowboy on. Tamara was laughing into John's shoulder as we walked away. Why was it so easy for everyone else? I wished that I'd sat closer to John. Maybe I'd be the one laughing into his handsome shoulder just beneath that amazing hair. Maybe a distraction from CJ was what I needed.

The following week at work was complicated. First, there was the small issue of explaining to Lanie that I needed to go on the San Francisco trip.

"Why, Nester?"

"Nester? Really? Is that even a name?"

"What? No, seriously. I'm not sure we need three people out there. Isn't CJ going, too? He can show Justine the ropes." Lanie crossed her arms and leaned back in her chair. She'd wheeled the huge leather chair into the office one day, telling everyone that it was special-ordered because she had back problems. I'd glimpsed the invoice taped to the back and was shocked at the price. When I'd talked to David, the CEO, he'd confirmed that the company had purchased it for her. CJ and I called it the "million-dollar chair."

"CJ will be in meetings most of the time, and Justine's never coordinated all the aspects of a sponsorship of this size. It'd be good to have two of us there, so one person can man the booth if anything goes wrong." I'd thought this out ahead of time. "Even just setting up our booth is a feat. She's set up a booth before, but not this one. It's quirky."

"Aren't we all ... " Lanie spun around a few times in her chair, appearing to actually think about this. "Fine, but do it on the cheap. Share a room with Justine." A maniacal look came over her face then and she leaned across her desk on her forearms. "Or with CJ ... "

"What?" I could feel the blush creeping up my cheeks. Did Lanie know about CJ and me?

"I'd totally hit that," she said.

The mere thought of it almost had me gagging.

"Um. Right. So I'll book some tickets?"

"Sure, have a ball. Fly economy, Nancy."

"It's Natalie."

"I know."

I walked out of Lanie's office fairly certain that she was legitimately insane, but glad she wasn't going to fight me on the trip. And it seemed like her crack about CJ was meant to be a joke. I didn't think she had any real idea about our relationship—whatever it might be.

After that was settled, I had to coordinate with CJ to book tickets and hotel rooms. I took a deep breath and walked into his office, only to find Justine comfortably settled into a chair next to him behind his desk, looking intently at his monitor with him. Their heads were too close together for my comfort.

"Hey guys," I said, feeling awkward.

CJ had the grace to jump a bit in his seat, while Justine merely smiled at me. I couldn't tell if she was just generally sweet or if she had some deliberate intentions toward CJ. She'd already told me that she found him attractive.

"Hey, Natalie," CJ said. "Are we on for lunch this Friday? I need an adventure."

I was surprised he mentioned it in front of Justine. I stood a bit straighter, feeling as if I'd won some kind of small victory, then immediately berated myself for feeling that way. Stupid ...

"Sure," I agreed. "We can talk about our plans for San Francisco. I just got Lanie's approval for all three of us to go."

"Cool," Justine said, clapping her hands.

I deflated as I realized that I'd basically just invited her to my Friday CJ lunch. "Or we can talk about the details now," I suggested.

CJ was staring at me, a thoughtful expression on his face. He seemed to decide something. "Friday is better," he said. "We're kind of in the middle of reviewing our partner profiles."

"Okay," I said, coaxing a false brightness into my tone. "Lunch Friday, then." A wrenching ache began to spread through me. "Um, any preference for hotels in San Fran? I'm gonna book flights and stuff now."

"Oh, I can do that myself," CJ said.

"No, it's not a problem. I want to make sure we get on the same flights and get seats together. It'll make everything easier."

"That makes sense. Thanks," CJ said. He stood and pulled out his wallet, handing me a card. Here are my frequent flyer numbers. Justine, do you have numbers to give Natalie?"

"I'm not exactly a frequent flyer," she said, her dark bangs falling into her eyes. She blew them away, and I wanted to hit her for being so ridiculously cute.

"I'll help you sign up," CJ told her. "And we can add your numbers when we check in. Let us know what airline, okay Natalie?"

"Sure," I said, feeling more bleak and desolate than I had since arriving in the city. Was this happening? It seemed Justine and CJ were becoming cozy right before my eyes. Maybe going to San Francisco would be too little, too late. The worst of it was that I honestly liked Justine. If she didn't have a hang-up about dating guys at work then maybe it'd be fairer to CJ to just let it happen and not get in the way. "I'll send you the details by email." I turned to walk away.

"Natalie?" CJ was still standing, a strange expression on his face.

"Yeah?"

He looked at me for a minute like he wasn't sure what to say, his dark eyes wide, and an apologetic look on his face. "Thanks."

"Sure," I said, ripping myself from the scene in front of me.

I called the corporate travel agent from my desk, cursing myself for my stupid rules.

Once the hotel accommodations and flights were set, I felt a strange desolation settle over me. The walls of my office felt oppressive and all I wanted was to run. I forced the feeling down and set to work getting things arranged for the show the following week. Justine walked into my office just as I'd finished the list of items to ship and carry along.

"Hey, Natalie," she said. She was pert and fresh looking, her clear skin always rosy beneath her dark hair and eyes.

"Hey, Justine. Perfect timing. Let's go through some of the setup stuff for next week."

"Oh, great!" she said, sitting across from me and putting a pen and pad on my desk.

"There's a ton of stuff we need to ship out quick," I told her. "It should have already gone, but Lanie didn't get this sponsorship settled until just now."

"Okay, I can call the shippers. What stuff?"

I went over the list with her, and Justine promised that she could manage to get it all taken care of. There were a few printing items we'd have to get turned around quickly, so I took care of setting that part up. When I was finished, I was exhausted. It was only noon, but I couldn't take any more of the office or of Justine's perky and completely sweet attitude. It would almost be better if I didn't like her so much, I thought. Then at least I could hate her for getting along so well with CJ.

I decided that my day was over. I still had lunch Friday to get through with CJ and Justine. But for today, I'd had enough. I called the one person I was sure wouldn't be at work.

"Hello?" Lulu answered.

"Hi Lu, It's Pepper." Even I'd begun referring to myself by my last name.

"Hi!"

"What are you doing?"

"Nothing," she said.

"I need to get out of here. Can we hang out?"

"Yes! Oh ... fun! Come over!"

"Thanks. I'm on my way." I picked up my bag, leaving the office as quickly as I could without running. When the elevators opened to let me in, CJ was standing inside. He stepped out and held the door for me.

"Hey," he said.

"Hey," I repeated as I stepped into the elevator. I looked into his face for a second as the doors began to slide shut, and was surprised when he stuck a hand between them just before they met.

"Hang on," he said, pushing them back open and stepping in.

"You almost lost a hand there," I said, forcing a smile.

"Yeah, well." The doors closed, sealing us in. Alone. "Listen, about lunch Friday. I felt really weird about the way that all came out."

"It's fine," I lied. "We'll need to talk about how the week will go anyway."

"No," he said, rubbing a hand across his short, dark blond hair. He looked upset. "Look, it's just. I wanted to go to lunch with you. Like we always do. I wanted to have an adventure ... but then I realized ... "

"What?"

"That maybe I'm just an idiot." He was looking at me with a searching expression on his face.

I realized that he was asking me a question, even if he didn't phrase it that way.

"Maybe I'm just wasting all this time waiting for something that's never going to happen." He looked so sad. The dark eyes were liquid as he stared at me.

"No, CJ," I didn't know what to say. I couldn't promise him anything, but I had to say something to make the hurt in his eyes go away.

Just then, the doors opened to the lobby and a few people from our office and from the other floors piled in around us. I pushed to the front and held the door open. CJ stayed inside.

"It might ... I just ... " I stared into those dark eyes and wanted nothing more than to step into the circle of his arms and tell him that we could be together. All I wanted was to be together. What the hell was wrong with me?

"Up or out, lady," a guy in the back said in a harsh voice.

"Sorry, I ... " I pulled my hand away from the door and it immediately slid closed, sealing CJ inside and abruptly ending our conversation.

I stood in front of the doors for a minute staring at the cold steel. I could feel the pressure of gut wrenching sobs building in my chest, and I did not want to have a nervous breakdown right here in the lobby of my building. I took a deep breath just as a gray-haired woman arrived to stand next to me. She stared at the elevator panel in front of us and then fixed me with a steely look. "It won't come if you don't push the button," she told me, jabbing the "up" button with a long finger. "Idiot," she whispered as she turned away from me.

That was it. Tears broke loose and began running down my face as my breathing began to come in gasps.

The woman turned to stare as I pushed my way out of the lobby and onto 37th Street. I flagged the first available cab I saw and crawled in, barely able to tell the driver Lulu's address through the tears. I didn't even remember paying the cabbie or talking to Lu's doorman. The next thing I knew, I was standing in her arms as she hugged me while I cried on her doorstep.

Chapter Eight

VODKA SOLVES EVERYTHING

Lulu

Natalie arrived at my door a complete wreck. Her dark blue eyes were smeared with makeup and her hair was tangled and messy. She was wailing and crying, and I had no idea what to do besides hug her. We stood there, in my doorway, with my ankle throbbing as I held her tightly to me, hoping she'd stop crying soon so we could at least go inside.

Finally, she pulled back a bit and I closed the door.

"What in the world is going on?" I asked.

"It's the same stupid crap," she sobbed. "With CJ."

"I thought there was nothing going on there because you refuse to admit that you are in love with him." I hobbled to the couch and sat, putting my foot up. Then I thought better of it and stood again, limping to the kitchen. "We need drinks."

"Lu, it's one o'clock on a Thursday."

"I don't see your point." I poured two vodka tonics and handed her one. "Here."

"Okay," she sniffed, taking the glass and sitting down.

Once I was back in my spot on the couch, I waited for her to begin explaining why she was a messy wreck of a girl.

"I think CJ is getting tired of waiting for me to decide to date him."

"There are many things wrong with what you just said." Why did she not see any of this?

She stared at me, looking miserable.

"Okay, look. Maybe I am missing something. You tell me. You like CJ, right?"

She nodded, wiping her face with one hand.

"And he has told you that he likes you, right?"

She nodded again.

"But you won't be with him because you have invented a rule against dating someone you work with."

"Well yes. But no, I mean, it isn't that simple."

So far, she was not making a strong case. "Explain then."

"If I date someone I work with, and it ends badly, then we will have to see each other at work every single day, and it will be weird and horrible and uncomfortable. And then it could affect my performance at work, and I might lose my job. And I can't afford to live here with no job, and I'd have to go home, and my dad would end up being right."

"About what?"

"About me essentially being a total fuckup."

"I doubt he thinks that you are a fuckup."

"That's just it. Right now, he doesn't. For the first time ever, he thinks I'm doing well, he's actually proud of me."

"So if you date CJ and it ends badly, then you'll do poorly at work, lose your job and make your father not proud." This was insane.

"Right."

"There are so many uncertainties there, Pepper. You don't know that it would end at all, let alone end badly. You don't know that it would affect your performance, and even if it did, you don't know that you'd lose your job. Or that your father would find out or even care as much as you believe."

"Right."

"And so you are still torturing yourself because ... ?"

"I don't know." She sniffled and took a long drink. "But I think CJ likes someone else at work now, anyway, so maybe it's just too late."

"I doubt he would give up so quickly. Who?"

"Justine."

"The drunk girl?" I shook my head. Justine was cute, but she was not nearly as interesting as Natalie. CJ was not an idiot.

"She's not 'the drunk girl.' She was drunk that one time at Limelight. We're the ones swilling vodka in the middle of the day."

I raised an eyebrow and shook my head lightly. Natalie made everything complicated. "CJ likes you. All you have to do is decide that it will be okay and tell him."

"Which would be so wonderful," she said, "but what if something happened? And it doesn't matter anyway. He practically told me that he's done waiting."

"Natalie, stop. This doesn't make any sense. You cannot live your life worrying about what might happen. You have to take what is in front of you now. Or it will go away."

She sniffed again, looking sad. "I think it already has."

"Well it will if you do nothing." I stared at her. She refused to meet my eye and did not respond. I pushed. "So you are going to tell CJ that you can see him, right?"

"What? No!"

"Why not?"

"Because ... " She just stared at me. "I ... maybe ... "

"Just be brave, Pepper."

A slow smile spread across her face. "Maybe you're right. Maybe I should."

"Want to use my phone?"

"No, I can't tell him on the phone. I'll tell him at work."

I was happy when Natalie's crisis seemed to be over, at least for the moment. She poured us more drinks and then asked about Andrew.

"I'm meeting his parents on Sunday night."

"Oh my God, that's huge!"

"Yes. I think it is." For him, especially.

"So you guys are official. Boyfriend, girlfriend?"

"I think so ... but Pepper, we still haven't had sex."

"Seriously?"

Her shocked expression did nothing to make me feel better. "Right, so this is not normal, is it?"

"Depends on the guy, I guess."

"Candace says she thinks he's very old fashioned because of his family."

"Whom you're about to meet. Where's the dinner?"

"At their townhouse."

"Wow." Natalie seemed to be thinking about something. "What will you wear?"

"I have no idea. I think I have to wear this stupid brace or Andrew will refuse to take me," I said. My ankle was better, but the brace would be part of my wardrobe for at least another two weeks.

"Are you seeing him again before Sunday?"

"Probably. He practically lives here." I pointed at the chair where Andrew had begun piling his clothes. "I even sent out some of his laundry."

"Wow. It's so weirdly serious and yet very G-rated, huh?"

"I know. It's terrible. I'm going to make him have sex with me this weekend before we go."

"How romantic." Natalie arched an eyebrow and smiled.

"It will be." As I said the words, the plan formed in my mind. I was tired of this uncertainty. I would push the issue. If he didn't want me, I would find out and then I could move on. Though even the thought of his rejection made my stomach hurt. "I plan to seduce him."

"I wish you luck. Tell me how it goes. I plan to drink myself silly until it's time to get on a plane with CJ and his new girlfriend, Justine."

"No. You will be brave and tell him that you want him."

"Maybe."

Natalie and I eventually decided to move our drinking to a sidewalk table at the Cornelia Street Cafe and called the other girls to join. Maggie said she was too tired to go out, but Tamara came with Candace, and the four of us spent the evening watching people wander by as we drank wine and ate, enjoying the long dusky evening.

As darkness settled over the street, Natalie excused herself to prepare for work the next day. Tamara was making noise about having apartments to show, until a certain handsome man with amazing hair walked by on the sidewalk just beyond our table.

"Oh my," Candace whispered dramatically. "It's *him*. Tamara, it's 'The Hair'! Can you breathe?"

We had been referring to John as "The Hair" since we had met him at Gemini. And though nothing had happened between Tamara and him since that night, it was clear that she hoped something would.

"Quiet," Tamara said. She ran her hands over her hair and pinched her cheeks. "John!" she called out, as if she'd only just noticed him.

John stopped walking and turned just next to our table. He looked over the three of us and his eyes came to rest on Tamara. "Hey," he said. "Good to see you."

"Yeah," Tamara said. And then she seemed unable to imagine another word to utter.

"What are you up to tonight?" I asked, kicking Tamara under the table with my good foot.

"Just kind of strolling, honestly. I had a few drinks with friends after work. What are your plans?" he asked. "Seeing Andrew?"

"I think he's working until late," I told him. "Tamara was just saying something about getting coffee, but Candace and I both need to leave."

"Yeah." Candace produced a dramatic yawn and threw some cash on the table. "I'd better scoot."

I looked hard at Tamara.

"Um," she said. Then she smiled, her blue eyes shining, she turned to The Hair. "Would you want to have coffee with me?"

John looked up and down the sidewalk, and then reached to loosen his tie. "Yeah, actually," he said.

I stood and put some money on the table.

"I'll tell Andrew hello for you," I told him as he settled into the chair Candace had left.

"Thanks," he said.

Candace and I made our way out of the patio, and I turned to see Tamara smiling happily at John. I couldn't fix whatever was going on with Natalie and CJ, but at least I could help with this. I went home feeling like I had done something good.

Andrew called when he finished work that night, and we went to his apartment for a change. He had a nice one bedroom in Murray Hill just below 36th Street, and I wondered why we didn't spend more time there. It was much bigger than my place.

"But your place is much closer to work," he told me when I asked.

"I'm nervous about meeting your family," I told him, sitting on the couch next to him. I'd had enough vodka and wine that I should have been climbing into his lap the second I arrived, but the idea of meeting his family had me feeling very uncomfortable.

"They'll adore you," he said, slipping an arm around my shoulders and kissing me lightly beneath the ear, his breath hot on my neck. "After all, I do."

I looked into his deep blue eyes. "What?"

"I do," he said, his mouth returning to my earlobe.

I began to melt in his arms. "You do?"

"Yes, Lulu." He laughed and then pulled me onto his lap. "I adore you, and so will they."

"But you haven't ... we haven't ... "

"Sex?" he asked. He was still laughing, which made me feel like he was making fun of me. I stiffened.

"Yes."

"I didn't want to rush it. I care about you." He nuzzled my throat again and his tongue flicked against my skin, sending chills through me. "Do you know how hard it's been to wait?"

"Really?" I felt nervous with Andrew suddenly. That was not something I was used to. I leaned into him, turning to straddle his body with my legs. I looked down at him and put my hands along either side of his face. Leaning in slowly, I began kissing him. I put everything I had into it. This was my best "sleep with me tonight" kiss. I stopped and looked him in the eye. "Then why?"

His low voice sent tingles through me. "I just don't want to rush anything with you. I haven't felt this way about anyone in such a long time. I didn't want to ruin it all by making you think that I was in it just so I could mark 'sex with a hot Brazilian girl' off my list."

"You have such a list?"

"No, but that would be on it for sure."

I relaxed and felt my shoulders release a bit. "And that is all?"

"That's all. Do you feel better?" His hands slid up my back and down again, resting on my hips. He pulled me closer to him and his hands found their way under my shirt. I shivered at the feeling of his hands against my skin.

"Yes," I said, my voice a whisper.

Still kissing me, he scooted forward, and holding me tightly, he stood. I wrapped my legs around his waist.

"Should we move this to the bedroom?" he asked, a sexy grin on his face.

"Absolutely," I said, bending to kiss his neck. I loved the way the stubble of his jawline felt against my lips.

He laid me gently on his bed and stood looking at me for a minute, his wavy hair perfectly messy and a faraway look on his face. "You're gorgeous, Lu, you know that?"

"So are you," I said. Normally I would have added some kind of crass encouragement—played the role of vixen that I usually assumed. But with Andrew, I felt vulnerable and exposed. This was different. It was possible that I felt something for him beyond sexual attraction. The air between us seemed to dance and sizzle with anticipation. Finally, he began unbuttoning his shirt. I sat up and took over the job. Within minutes, we were both undressed, and when Andrew pulled back the duvet on his bed and rolled me into it, I knew that I was about to get everything that I wanted.

Chapter Nine

ADVENTURE LUNCH

Natalie

After a few hours of last minute pre-trip scrambling in the office Friday, CJ, Justine, and I piled into the elevator to head out to lunch. I'd tried to catch CJ alone a few times, though my resolve was crumbling now that the influence of Lulu's straightforward logic and several vodka tonics were just a memory.

We'd talked about lunch as an organizational meeting, but now that almost everything was done, spending time with CJ and Justine together just felt like unnecessary torture. I guessed it was good practice for the week ahead. I'd had some trouble with the elevator at work since my last talk with CJ—every time the doors slid shut, I felt a soul-thumping "clunk" of finality. CJ hadn't mentioned our last conversation since it had happened. But mentioning it would have meant that we'd actually spoken since then. And we hadn't.

"Where should we go?" Justine said, bouncing like a puppy. "What kind of adventure did you have in mind, CJ?"

I watched CJ look at her, surprised to see exhaustion etched into the lines around his eyes where amusement normally lived. "I'm not up for adventure," he said. "Let's just nail down the details and call it a day."

Justine's face fell a bit.

"I'm not sure we have time for an adventure," I jumped in. "Justine, we've had long lunches sometimes in the past when there's been nothing else going on at work."

"Oh," she said, some of the enthusiasm missing from her bright voice. "Okay, so where to?"

"Wanna go to Punch?" I asked, mostly to CJ. He steadfastly refused to look at me, despite my stare.

"Not today," he sighed. We'd been there before—it was a second-floor eatery just south of the Flatiron building, with a clever menu full of alliteration. The English geek in me loved it, and the last time we'd been there CJ had laughed along as I'd read the entire menu to him.

"There's that cafe at the bottom of Macy's ..."

CJ shook his head. We were out of the building now, wandering aimlessly toward Sixth Avenue.

"Deli?" Justine asked, pointing at a corner bodega.

"We need to be able to sit and talk, right?" I was talking directly to CJ now, daring him to acknowledge my presence.

He just walked, staring straight ahead.

I'd never seen CJ be anything but kind and friendly. It was such a shock seeing him act this way that I started to worry about him. Did I do this to him? Had I broken CJ? Or maybe there was something else going on. Maybe something had happened, and he was upset and because of everything between us, he didn't feel like he could talk to me about it.

Justine was looking uncertain, pointing out places as we passed them, and finally giving up. We were three co-workers, just strolling together under a strange cloud of weirdness.

Finally, I couldn't take it anymore. CJ's silence was killing me, and if he was upset about something other than me, I was probably not going to be his first choice for confidante at this point. I bowed out.

"Okay, end of the line for me," I told them. "I'm starving and exhausted. I'm gonna grab a sandwich and take it uptown ... get some rest. I'll see you guys in the town car on Monday morning, okay?"

I didn't wait for an answer, turning and walking back the way we'd come. As much as I hated leaving CJ and Justine alone, I hated CJ's silence even more. I did exactly as I'd promised, grabbing my stuff, getting a sandwich, and heading home. There was no way I could talk to CJ with Justine there, and it seemed like he wasn't going to give me the chance anyway.

I'd gotten to work Friday morning with the confidence of a firm decision having been made. I was going to tell CJ that I'd been an idiot. I was going to tell him that I was ready to take a chance on us—on him. But the day had been busy, and I hadn't been able to catch him alone. And now we had Justine with us, and he wouldn't even look at me. I began rethinking my decision to try to move forward. Maybe it was just too late. It seemed like CJ had already given up on me, and when I really thought about it—about how long I'd already made him wait—I wasn't surprised. I had the whole week in San Francisco to find out for sure.

I sat on the couch in my apartment, staring at the television, watching people I didn't know go through some serious issues on *Days of our Lives*. I'd watched the show in high school but hadn't so much as glanced at it since then. Strangely, I found that I could still follow a few of the story lines. I felt like my life might make a good plot. Everyone watching would be rolling their eyes, telling me to just go after the guy, only to realize that it was already too late.

I ate my sandwich and brooded, and when my cell phone rang in my bag it woke me from a stupor. I'd been staring at the television and hadn't even noticed when a new show had come on.

I scrambled to pull the phone from my purse on the floor where I'd dropped it.

"Hello?"

"Hey, it's Tamara."

"Hi, Tam." I was a little surprised to hear from her; out of our group of friends, I spent the least amount of time with Tam. But I was glad she called. There was a spark of energy and fun in her that made me want to get to know her better.

"Hey, are you still looking for an apartment?"

"Well, kind of. I can't pull the trigger on anything for a while because I need a few thousand bucks to handle the broker fee and first and last." My current situation wasn't bad, but my roommate sometimes felt like either a stranger or a displeased parent. I wanted to live on my own.

"Might not matter," Tamara said. "I know of a sublet, and they need someone, like, now."

"I'm about to head out of town for a week, Tamara."

"When? Now?"

"No, Monday morning."

"Well, if you want this apartment, it'd have to happen this weekend anyway. Let's go look at it."

"So fast?" I was shocked. Could I make a decision like that in one day?

"That's how things work here. You wanna go look or no?"

"Yeah, I guess so ... " It was almost the end of the month, though I hated the idea of leaving Tory in the lurch. "What's the rent?"

"It's amazing. It's twelve."

Twelve hundred dollars was double what I paid Tory. But to have my own place? "Wow."

"I know, right?" Somehow, I didn't think Tamara understood

that my "wow" was not the "wow" she thought it was. "Meet me outside my office? 56th and Seventh."

"Okay," I said, my brain still whirling. "I'll be there in twenty."

"Cool." Tamara hung up.

Twenty minutes later I stood beneath a towering office building, waiting for Tamara to appear. When she came out of the building, she looked far more corporate than I could have imagined, in a tailored skirt suit and shiny black pumps.

"You look amazing!" I told her.

"It's the uniform." She winked.

Tamara worked at a high-end real estate firm selling properties that I would most likely never see the inside of. I had no idea how she'd landed that job, but got the sense that she was probably good at it.

We grabbed a cab and headed downtown. "You excited?" she asked.

"Yeah, kind of," I said. "Things are just insane right now ... I'm not sure it's the right time to move."

"Well, it probably never will be if you look at it like that."

We rode in silence for a minute.

"Look, Pepper." She turned to face me. "Apartments—good apartments at least—are like hot guys. When they're available, you have to take a chance and go for it. They won't last long and if you hesitate, then someone else will be snuggled up on your window seat tomorrow."

"This place has a window seat?"

"Well, no. It has a radiator in front of the window. But you could put a pillow on it and call it a window seat." She smiled. "Some New York real estate takes a certain amount of creativity."

"So do some New York men, I guess."

"Exactly."

Tamara knew less about the CJ situation than my other friends did, so I didn't think that her metaphor was actually a quip about him. But it hit home nonetheless.

We pulled up outside a nondescript brown building on West 15th Street near Eighth Avenue.

"This is it," Tamara said, paying the driver. We walked up three steps and she unlocked the front door and the inner door. "No doorman," she said lightly.

The ground floor was dark and somewhat foreboding. I didn't get a great feeling from the row of rusty mailboxes on the wall and the aging checkered linoleum.

"It's on the second," she said, guiding me up the narrow stairs.

The door she opened was at the front of the building, and walking through that door was like entering another world. The apartment was wide and long; a studio with a clear bedroom at one end, living room in the center, and kitchen near the front door where we'd entered. The bathroom door was behind the front door when we'd closed it. There were windows all along the front and side of the apartment, and it was filled with light. There was a space between this building and the next that you couldn't see from the street, and though the neighboring building also had windows, they were offset so that you couldn't look directly across into someone else's apartment. The airy open feeling was amazing.

"Wow," I said, imagining myself living here. "Tamara, you don't normally do low-end sublets, do you?"

"No," she said. "And a lot of sublets aren't even legal. This is one of the other agent's places. He wants to keep it, but he's bought a co-op in another building."

"I see," I said. "Will he make any profit on the rent?" It had to be extra income for him, renting this place out.

"Not much at twelve hundred," she said. "But he has a crush on me and I told him that you'd be an exemplary renter."

"Wow," I said again. I wandered the length of the hardwood floor, peeking my head out onto the fire escape and then into the long closet as I walked back to the kitchen. The bathroom had a full-sized tub, and there was even a window in there. "I really can't say no," I told her.

"I know."

"When do I have to decide?"

"Nowish."

"Shit."

"Yeah." She smiled, a gleam in her eye. "I knew it'd be perfect for you."

"When would I have to pay?"

"I think he'll be flexible, but first and last towards the beginning of this month."

"I hate to dump Tory so fast. I need to give her at least a month's rent extra, I think." I did some mental math to see if I could even afford to do that.

"You gave her first and last when you moved in, right?"

"Yes," I said, seeing Tamara's point. "So if I pay her for this coming month, she's actually got it covered for two months."

"Right, and then you just need to come up with double for this place. Can you?"

I thought about my meager savings. "I think so." I could replenish it after the IPO.

"So you're in?" She looked as excited as I felt. "I can't wait to hang out here!"

"I'm in," I told her. "I'm so excited!"

We went back to her office with my head spinning. I met the agent who was leasing the place and signed the lease agreement. "Thanks," I told him.

"Anything for a friend of Tam's," he said, practically drooling on Tamara across the table. She flashed him an angelic smile.

"Let's celebrate!" Tamara said as we left the small conference room where I'd signed the paperwork.

"Don't I need to go get him my paystubs and stuff?" I asked.

"It can wait. He won't do anything until I tell him to," she smiled.

"He's pretty much your lap dog, huh?"

"Yeah," she said, waving it off like it wasn't a big deal.

"Not interested?" I asked.

"Oh, it's not that," she said as we got in the elevator. "I just don't shit where I eat."

It wasn't elegant, but there it was. "Thank you," I said.

She looked momentarily confused, and then clarity hit. "Oh, yeah. CJ."

"Yeah, CJ."

We found a bar around the corner and pulled up stools at the dark wooden expanse. The rounded lip in front of us was shiny and worn from years and years of people bellying up to this exact spot. I wondered briefly what other conversations had taken place right here. The bar appeared to be an ancient establishment. The sense of nostalgia that hit me and then quickly passed was one of the things I loved most about the city.

"So," Tamara said, as we sipped tall beers. "I think you have a couple of options in the CJ department."

"Okay," I said slowly.

"Though I completely understand your ideals—not to date people you work with—because I share that rule myself, I'm also not in love with anyone I work with." She sipped her beer and waited while that sunk in. "If I were in love with anyone at work, I'd have the same two options you do."

"Which are?"

"Simple. Get a new job. Or write off your rule and see what happens."

"Simple."

"It actually is, if you think about it, Natalie. What is there to get wound up over?"

I sipped my beer and thought about that as the glare of

sunlight lit the windows of the dark bar. There was something illicit about sitting in a darkened bar before four o'clock on a workday. "I can't leave my company before the IPO ... as much as I'd like to get away from Lanie Bill."

"Okay, so it's option two then."

"Just say 'fuck it'?"

"Right."

"I wish it were that easy."

"It is." She smiled at me, and her blue eyes danced.

"No, it isn't. There's one more part to it."

"Which is?"

"My dad."

"Your dad isn't here. He's a grown-up and he can take care of himself. He would be happy to know that you're doing things that make you happy." She nodded, pleased with her little speech.

"He's never been happy when I've done things that made me happy in the past."

"He's a grown-up, Pepper. And so are you."

"I know. I'm just enjoying the novelty of him actually being proud of me for a change. He was always so disapproving of everything I did when I lived at home."

"Is that why you moved to New York?"

"I kind of ran away. I'd moved back home, graduated from college, and started a job I hated. Dad was critical of my decisions no matter what I did. He said I shouldn't have moved home, he didn't like my major, he said my job was dead-end. So I looked for a different job and switched, and then he was unhappy that I didn't give the first job a chance. I'd been dating a guy for a while —whom he hated, of course—and when that ended ... I just couldn't take anymore. And then once I'd gotten the job here, he was so proud of me—it seemed like maybe doing well out here was the best way to make him happy."

"So—don't take this the wrong way, but ... the cord's already cut, right? You're three thousand miles away. What difference would it make if you dated CJ and everything went to hell?"

I put my head in my hands. "I don't know. I just feel like such a failure to my family no matter what I do ... It probably doesn't matter now anyway. Your two options assume that CJ actually wants to be with me."

"I thought that much was clear."

"It was. But I think he's moved on. There's another girl at the office. They've been spending a lot of time together. Every time I go to look for him, he's with her. I don't know if I'm just being paranoid ... but it seems like the more frustrated he is with me, the closer he moves to her."

Tamara appeared to think about that. "I wouldn't worry about her. He wanted you first. If he's looking somewhere else, it's only because he thinks you're unavailable." She lifted her glass. "To your new apartment. And to you deciding to give love a chance."

I raised my glass and met hers with it, not at all sure that I was brave enough to give love a chance.

Chapter Ten

BATHROOM BALLYHOO

Lulu

SUNDAY ARRIVED on the end of a weekend spent in Andrew's arms. But when he left to attend to some paperwork at the hospital early Sunday morning, I felt desperate over the dinner situation that night. He promised to pick me up on his way uptown. That gave me ten hours to worry before meeting what Candace called Upper East Side royalty.

I passed the time by trying on every outfit in my closet, looking for the one that said, "respectable single woman." It turned out that I did not have many ensembles that said that. When Andrew arrived at six, I was a high-strung bundle of nerves in slim-fit black pants and a lightly sequined black blazer over a pink tank top. I wore my sandals, and no brace.

"Um ..." Andrew said when I appeared in the lobby after Tom had buzzed to let me know that Andrew had arrived.

"'Um' is not good."

He smiled and crossed the marble floor to hug me. "You look great. I was just surprised by the bedazzled jacket."

"Bedazzled?"

"The sparkles."

"They're sequins. This jacket was very expensive. It's Michael Kors." I was already nervous, now I was becoming angry.

"It's nice. You look great." He was repeating himself. He was nervous too. That couldn't be a good sign. "Let's go, Lu. My parents will be expecting us. No brace, huh?"

I smiled and he let it go.

Andrew wore khaki pants and a button-down dress shirt with brown leather shoes. The shirt was fitted and emphasized the "v" from his waist to shoulders. His blue eyes sparkled and his light brown hair looked perfectly mussed. I stepped in close to him, running my hands down the smooth soft shirt, feeling the firm muscles beneath as I breathed in the familiar vanilla scent of him. His arms went around me and his hot breath was against my neck. I closed my eyes, glad we were out of Tom's line of sight as Andrew's lips found my earlobe. I gasped and felt the muscles inside me clench. If he continued, we would have to go upstairs before we could go anywhere else.

"You had better stop," I said, not really meaning it.

"I wish I didn't have to." His voice was like gravel.

I kissed him quickly and then pulled away. "To your parents' place?" I hoped maybe he would just say no.

"To my parents' place. Thanks for coming, Lulu." He took my hand.

I had expected a cab ride, but Andrew had a car waiting at the curb, a dark Lincoln. As we walked toward it, the driver got out and moved around to open the door.

"Thanks, Sheldon," Andrew said to the tall slim man who held the door. "This is Lulu."

"A pleasure," the man said.

"Hi." So it wasn't a hired car. Andrew knew the driver.

We rode uptown in silence, which was awkward. Andrew held my hand and glanced at me occasionally, which didn't help my nerves at all. I scooted around on the seat, trying to get comfortable, but my stomach was rolling and my upper lip had begun to sweat. I had never been quite so nervous.

When we got out of the car, I pulled him down the sidewalk, leaving Sheldon looking confused as he stood at the foot of a stoop in front of the townhouse.

"Look," I said, my voice a hiss. "I'm really nervous about this, I don't know why exactly. I'm usually fine with people."

"You'll be fine. You don't need to be nervous." He took both my hands in his and pulled me close. "You are fun and beautiful. And do you know how amazingly sexy you are?"

"Yes," I said. "That doesn't help at all. Your parents don't care about those things. I feel kind of sick." I swallowed hard and prepared to walk toward the stoop, but he pulled me back with one hand.

"Lulu," his eyes were deep and liquid as he looked down at me. "I am absolutely, totally falling for you." He leaned down and kissed me then, softly and sweetly, replacing my nerves with anticipation. He pulled back and traced my lips with his thumb. "You're gonna do great. Ready?"

Something about the way he said those last words set off a small alarm in my head. What if I didn't 'do great'?

"Yes," I lied, and followed him to the door, holding his hand.

Walking up the steps into Andrew's family's townhouse was terrifying. Sheldon turned out to be their driver *and* butler, and he ushered us inside to a formal sitting room where Andrew's parents waited.

"Darling!" A paper-thin woman with white-blonde hair fluffed into a bob rose from an ottoman and floated across the room to

Andrew. Her skin was powdered and rouged, and she had an ethereal quality that reminded me of renaissance paintings of angels. And vampires. She wore a fitted sheath dress that left skeletal arms and legs exposed. As she embraced Andrew, I actually shivered. She kissed both his cheeks and then took a step back, keeping a hand on his arm.

"Mom, this is Lulu, the girl I told you about."

The sunken skeleton eyes regarded me, tracing a line up and then down my body before finding my face.

"Hello." I stood there awkwardly for a moment, unsure whether I was supposed to kiss her or shake her hand. I extended a hand.

Ignoring my hand completely, she said, "Well, hello, Lulu. I'm so glad you could come. I'm Elizabeth, but I hope you'll call me Tippy, as all my friends do."

I smiled, pulling my hand back. Andrew's arm tightened around my waist, reassuring me. *Who would voluntarily want to be called "Tippy"?*

As the papery woman spoke, a tall broad man stepped behind her. He was built like a bear and towered over all of us by at least a head. I thought he might be able to carry all three of us around if he felt like it. "Lulu," he said, smiling in a way that put me at ease. "It's wonderful to meet you."

I didn't raise a hand after Andrew's mother had ignored my efforts, but Mr. Barton reached out and pulled me into a rough hug, so I returned it awkwardly. "Thank you," I said, my voice muffled in the plaid of his shoulder.

When he had released me, Mr. Barton stepped back and put an arm around his wife, who wore an expression of mere tolerance. "Shall we have some drinks, Son?"

"It wouldn't be a Barton family dinner without them," Andrew said. He led me to a loveseat upholstered in pink damask and kissed my cheek as I sat. "Martini?" he asked.

"Yes, please," I said, my stomach still lurching and rolling.

Andrew turned to follow his father to a bar at the far side of the room and Tippy settled herself across from me. Her knees poked out of the bottom of her skirt and I wondered if it was painful to be so thin.

"It's always nice to meet one of Andrew's friends," she told me. She wore a smile as thin as her waist, and I had a sense of foreboding. The way she'd emphasized the word "friend" told me everything I needed to know. This woman didn't like me. At all. There was a folded newspaper next to her, and she laid a hand on it, seemingly waiting for Andrew.

Andrew handed me my drink and sat next to me on the loveseat. His mother actually made a huffing noise when he put a hand on my knee, her eyes narrowing.

Mr. Barton appeared oblivious, taking a chair next to her and glowing at all of us with a short glass of scotch in his hand. He handed his wife a flute of champagne.

"To the doctor in the family," he toasted, raising his glass. "And to his beautiful girlfriend, Lulu."

I smiled, and Andrew squeezed my knee.

Tippy picked up the paper and opened it, holding a photograph up for us to see.

"I've been meaning to talk to you about this, Andrew, darling."

The picture was of us. Andrew's hand was on my butt, and my head was leaned in toward his neck, our mouths open. It was the one that the photographer had snapped outside Casa La Femme.

"Not to be indelicate, but dear, you need to keep your hands off other people's derrieres in public."

"Mom," Andrew began.

"No, I don't want to discuss it. I've been getting calls about it all day. Quite embarrassing. You know the rumors fly anytime you're pictured with a woman. You might try to be more selective about your outings. Or your companions," she said, eyeing me.

I flinched and Andrew's hand tightened on my knee.

She put the paper away and the evening dragged on, Andrew

and his father trying to lighten the awkwardness. Tippy, for her part, worked like an agent of evil, tsking under her breath and making comments that seemed neutral but could also be taken as sarcastic.

"Your jacket is lovely, dear," she said at one point.

I smiled. "Thank you."

"I believe I saw something like that in the window at Union Square as I passed that teenager store Cherry likes so much," she told us all, smiling as she looked around. "What is that place called, dear?"

She was asking me. I knew the answer, but I also knew that supplying it to her would make it sound like I had, indeed, bought my expensive Michael Kors jacket at some discount chain. And I did not shop at those places. I might not be royalty, but I knew something about fashion. "I don't know," I lied.

"Oh sure you do," Tippy laughed.

"I'm afraid I don't." I turned to stare at Andrew. He was just smiling and nodding.

"Oh well, it doesn't matter, does it?" She smoothed her own sleeve as she talked, and I imagined she was showing me the quality of her own garment in contrast to my cheap jacket.

"I bought this after Fashion Week last year." I couldn't help myself. "It was part of the line Michael Kors showed." I sat up straighter. My stomach gurgled loudly.

"Hmm." Tippy shrugged and then asked Andrew about his work.

We moved to the dining room a little bit later, and I tried to eat despite feeling increasingly unwell. I didn't know if it was nerves or if I was genuinely sick, but I desperately wanted to leave the table. Unfortunately, the meal dragged on, and as it neared its end, Tippy's attack picked up strength.

"So you are a foreigner, Lulu?"

"I am from Brazil," I answered. "I don't think of myself as a foreigner. I have a green card. I have lived here for so long now it feels more home than Brazil does."

"Ah, but you're not really American," she said, as if she were pointing out that I was covered in horse manure.

I had no idea how to respond, so I just smiled. My stomach twisted. The alcohol was not helping.

"For instance, you cannot become president," she pointed out.

"Mom, I don't think Lu is interested in running the country," Andrew said.

I laughed, uncomfortable under her sudden attention and because of what seemed to be happening in my stomach.

"No, perhaps not. She isn't working at all, I understand."

It wasn't a question, so I sipped my water. I did not want to defend myself. I didn't think I should have to.

"Are you un-hireable for some reason?" she asked, making her voice sweet.

"Not that I am aware of," I told her.

"Mom, Lulu is perfectly hirable," Andrew said. "She doesn't have to work and is looking for an interesting opportunity." We had discussed this before.

"Well, that's certainly nice. You don't have to work? Not many young women can say that much." She sipped her always-full glass of champagne. "Tell me, Lulu. At what age did you come out?"

What? I looked at Andrew, surprised. "No, Mrs. ... uh, Tippy. I'm not homosexual."

Andrew spit his coffee out.

"Andrew," his mother scolded.

He wiped his mouth with a napkin, laughing.

I felt my face reddening as I realized that I really needed to visit the restroom.

He put an arm around me. "Coming out also means being debuted to society. You know, debutantes? They have a coming out ball."

"They should call it something else. That is very confusing," I said, beginning to feel desperate.

Tippy sat back in her chair, an amused expression on her face.

"I was not a debutante," I told them, my words rushed. "My family ... we didn't do that. In Brazil, it is called the *Festa de Quinze Anos.* Your family makes you a party when you are fifteen. But I did not. Excuse me," I said, standing. "Where is the restroom?"

"Just around the corner," Andrew said. "I'll show you."

The bathroom was just feet away from the dinner table, down a short hallway. I cringed as I locked the door and rushed to the toilet. Whatever had been going on in my stomach was violent and noisy, and it was no less so on the way out. The sound seemed to echo off the close flowered walls, and I had no doubt that it was completely audible through the thin pocket door. With every spasm of relief, I became more embarrassed. I could do nothing to control the noises that were erupting, and I just hoped that Andrew and his family had returned to their conversation. But I probably would have heard them if they had. When the horror seemed to have ended, which was at least ten minutes later, I stood shakily and tried to pull myself back together.

My face was red and sweaty, and my mascara was running. I sponged at myself with a washcloth, but there was nothing to be done.

Humiliated, I returned to the table.

Andrew gave me a strange look, and Tippy sat back in her chair with what looked like some kind of triumph on her face.

"I'm sorry," I said. "I don't feel well."

"It's fine," Andrew said, though his voice was stiff. He didn't put his hand back on my knee once I sat down.

"I'm sure your family misses you," Mr. Barton said, breaking the silence that had descended upon us.

"No," I said. I should have just smiled.

"Why not?" Tippy asked, leaning forward.

"Ah ... " I stuttered. "It is complicated." Between my humiliation and my general discomfort, my family was something I did not want to discuss.

Andrew was watching me. I had avoided this topic when it had come up.

"Family can be complicated," Mr. Barton agreed.

"I'm interested," Tippy said, urging me on. "If this girl wants to be with Andrew, we should learn as much as we can about her," she told her husband. "Go on, Lulu."

"I ... well, my parents were killed when I was very young," I began.

Andrew turned to stare at me, his eyes shining with sympathy. His hand found my knee and squeezed gently.

"Sorry I'm so late!" A teenaged girl bounced into the dining room, her blonde hair in a ponytail and her face shining. "Andrew!" She ran to his chair and Andrew stood to give her a big hug.

"Cherry," he said, laughing. "Meet Lulu."

"I'm so happy to meet you," she said as I stood. She wrapped her arms around me, so I hugged her back, smiling over her head at Andrew. He still looked less than comfortable.

Cherry sat next to her mother and grabbed a roll from the center of the table. She began pulling it to pieces and eating as she smiled across the table at Andrew and me. "I'm so hungry," she said.

"You are also not a barbarian," Tippy said in a clipped tone, taking the roll from her daughter's hands. "I'll have Sheldon get you a salad."

Sheldon appeared, as if by magic, and bent forward slightly. "A salad, ma'am, of course." It was creepy.

"What have you been up to, sis?" Andrew asked his sister.

"I was at Sarah's. They got a new PlayStation. It's so much fun."

"Sarah is Cherry's best friend from like ... preschool. She lives next door," Andrew told me.

"That's so nice," I said. "To have your friends so close."

"It's awesome," Cherry agreed.

"How old are you?" I asked her.

"Thirteen," she said, beaming.

"My parents needed a good long break after me," Andrew said. "I was so perfect they felt there was no need to try again." He winked.

"Or maybe it's because they can't stand to touch each other," Cherry said.

Tippy stiffened, and Mr. Barton put his drink on the table loudly. "Now, Cherr..."

"Kidding!" She laughed. "Just kidding."

Uncomfortable looks were exchanged around the table, but Cherry continued to chatter about her friend Sarah and the games they'd played. The rest of the evening was lighter, thanks to Cherry's arrival. Tippy stopped poking at me, offering me snake-like smiles instead, as Andrew and Cherry bantered with their father.

Cherry hugged me tightly at the door as we left and whispered in my ear, "Don't worry about my mom. She's harmless."

I smiled at her, but I wasn't sure she was right.

Andrew walked me to the curb after I'd said stiff goodbyes to his parents. I was humiliated and still not feeling well.

"I'm so sorry," I told him. "I was so sick all of a sudden."

"Yeah, we heard," he said, then looked embarrassed. "I mean, I'm sorry you were sick. Do you feel better now?" I looked at him, surprised at the initial disapproval in his voice. "Andrew, I couldn't help it," I whispered. "Are you mad that I was sick?"

"No, no. I know that you couldn't help it. It was just such terrible timing. My mother ... she's very particular about ... " he glanced around us, looking grim.

"About everything, as far as I can tell!" I was becoming angry. "You could have shown me to a bathroom a bit further away. I'm certain the house has several of them!" I dropped my hand from his arm. He could not be angry with me for being sick.

"Well, I thought you just needed to freshen up. I didn't know you were going to be dropping bombs in there!"

I had no idea what to say. I just stared at him.

After a painful moment of silence, he softened a bit. "I'm sorry, Lu. I'm sorry you were sick, and that I wasn't more sympathetic. I just had very high hopes for tonight. I just really wanted my family to like you."

"I know that," I whispered. "I did too. But if they don't like me because I was sick, then I am not sure I care very much." My chest felt heavy. How could he blame me for the way the night had gone? His mother was insufferable.

"I'm sorry Lulu. I'm sorry that my mother was hard on you, and that you were sick." He pulled me close and kissed my neck just under my ear.

"I am sorry things didn't go better," I said. His hot breath was starting to melt my anger as his hands rubbed my back. "Your sister and father seem wonderful."

"My mother will grow on you," he said, stepping back and keeping his hands on my shoulders. "I promise. She just takes getting used to."

I didn't believe him at all, but the hope shining in his eyes made me nod along, agreeing to give her another chance.

"Listen, I have an early shift. Sheldon will take you home, okay?" He put two fingers under my chin and tilted my face to look into his. He looked at me for a minute, and then placed a soft kiss on my lips. "Goodbye."

I watched him walk back up the stoop to his parents' house as Sheldon pulled open the car door for me. I slid into the back seat, and rode home, hoping that we could put this night behind us. I was eager to see Andrew again without his mother looking on.

Chapter Eleven

ONCE UPON A HALLWAY

Natalie

"I'M SO EXCITED!" Justine had been bouncing since I'd met her in the dark town car outside my apartment. We'd picked up CJ last and Justine sat between us on the back seat as we fought traffic approaching JFK. "I've only been on an airplane once before!"

CJ smiled at her and I tried to push down my irritation. Though he'd said hello as he'd gotten in, he hadn't said much else and I was feeling uncomfortable. I hoped the whole week wouldn't go this way.

After check in, he excused himself to go find something to eat, and returned to the gate only when our flight was boarding. As we got on, I heard him talking with Justine behind me on the jet way. "You guys should sit together. You can go over last minute details. I'm sure Natalie has a lot of stuff to tell you."

"Okay," Justine said.

I turned to see them swapping boarding passes.

"I'm sitting with you, Natalie," she squealed.

I looked at CJ, and he met my eye briefly. His face was grim. He shrugged, then looked away. My heart felt like a rock, descending slowly through my chest and into my stomach. I wondered if he'd ever speak to me again. I took a deep breath, pushing down the tears that were threatening.

We boarded the flight and I let Justine take the window seat. Her enthusiasm lifted my mood slightly as I watched CJ take an aisle seat five rows behind us. I stuffed my purse under the seat and sunk down, offering Justine a weak smile.

The flight was long, and Justine's excitement didn't wane. She was thrilled about the movie, the lunch, and tiny bottles of wine. She loved the view of San Francisco Bay as we landed, and even seemed to believe that the San Francisco airport was somehow worthy of excitement. When we finally reached the hotel, I felt like I was going to slap her.

I remembered what Lanie had told me, but as I checked in, I quietly asked, "I don't suppose you'd have another room available, would you? We'd planned to share, but I think I might like some privacy."

"Certainly, miss," the clerk told me. "I do have another room on the same floor."

"Great," I said, sliding my company credit card across the counter.

As we rode in the elevator when CJ had finished checking in, I told Justine, "Great news. They accidentally booked us into separate rooms, so I guess we'll both have our own!"

She looked disappointed. "Oh. Okay."

"We'll both have more space. It'll be good," I assured her.

The bright smile returned as her dark bangs hung across her eyes. "Sure, okay!"

We went our separate ways after making plans to reconvene for dinner in the lobby in a half hour. I went to my room, knowing that I had a half hour to figure out how to get CJ to speak to me again, at least.

When I arrived back downstairs, CJ and Justine were waiting, talking with their heads close. Of course, my arrival prompted CJ to clam up completely. I might have actually rolled my eyes at him. This was getting ridiculous.

We opted to eat in the hotel restaurant instead of venturing out. Justine and I needed to go to the conference floor to check our boxes in and set up the booth. The show would start early in the morning.

As the food arrived, I began my campaign to make CJ talk. "How's your food look, CJ?"

"Pretty good," he said, not looking at me.

"What'd you get again?"

"The salmon." Still not looking at me.

"It does look good," I said, feeling like an idiot, but determined to keep him talking.

"It does," Justine agreed.

"Do you have meetings tomorrow?" I asked him. "What time?"

"I do," he said. "Not until noon."

Silence settled over the table as we ate. That wouldn't do. "Can I taste that?" I asked CJ.

"Um. Okay," he said, holding his plate toward me.

"Thanks," I said.

"Sure."

I was beginning to feel a little bit insane, enunciating my words with extra emphasis and speaking more loudly than I normally would.

"Is anyone getting dessert? CJ? Dessert? You like chocolate."

"No, I'm good."

"I thought you liked dessert."

"Not tonight."

"Not feeling it?"

CJ raised an eyebrow and looked at me as if I had three heads. "Not really, no."

As we finished the meal and paid, Justine headed to the bathroom.

"Natalie, what the hell?" CJ hissed across the table, finally looking at me.

"What? What the hell yourself!" I hissed back. "You won't even talk to me!"

"You noticed that, huh?" He said. "And yet you still keep picking at me?"

"I hate it, CJ. You can't give me the silent treatment."

"It's easier than the alternative," he said, his dark eyes brooding as he looked into mine. "Don't you know how impossible it is for me to be around you right now?"

"But nothing's even happened," I said, realizing this wasn't true.

"Right. And you've made it clear that nothing can. I'm trying to accept that. Just let me," he said.

"But CJ," I started, "we need to talk ... to ... " I began to try to tell him everything that had been on my mind. About the conversation with Tamara, about my willingness to take a chance. But Justine reappeared, ending my stuttering. "Can we talk later?"

CJ didn't answer, just watched Justine approach the table where he still sat.

"Ready?" Justine said. "I'm so excited!"

"Sure," I said, feeling my heart sink. "Let's go check in for the show."

CJ didn't respond, as Justine and I walked away from the table.

Thanks to the time change, 8:00 a.m. felt ridiculously late. I'd been up since six, stalking around my room, trying to figure out how to fix everything with CJ. I didn't expect to see him until after the show floor closed that afternoon, but needed to get some time with him.

"Good morning," I said to Justine as I entered our booth. She was already behind the low table, arranging media kits on its surface. "You ready?"

"Yup!" she smiled.

"You're going to be so tired of talking by this afternoon, you'll be shocked." I'd worked a few trade shows in my day, and the endless loop of repetitive info-dumping got old pretty fast. But it was fun meeting a lot of people in our industry, and there were always familiar faces around.

We took our positions in the booth, which was just a metal frame with All Night Media banners hung from it. The entire convention floor was brightly lit, and split into rows by lines of booths. You needed a map to get from one place to another, and every Internet company that had anything to do with media or advertising was there. Some booths were as big as my apartment, with multiple television monitors and girls in tight dresses demoing technology. Others, like ours, relied on the marketing reps to hand out media kits and pens. Despite our small booth, the All Night Media banners hung in the hotel lobby and at the doors to the convention floor, thanks to our sponsorship.

After an hour of repeating herself endlessly, Justine walked to the back of the booth and picked up a bottle of water. I had a break in traffic and joined her.

"Some of these people just want the free pens!" she said, looking totally offended.

"Oh, yeah. There are always swag hounds at these things. Some people just wander around collecting crap."

"That's what CJ said this morning," she nodded.

She had seen CJ this morning? Alarms began ringing in my head. "Oh, did CJ stop by the booth?"

Something passed through her eyes. Was it guilt? "No ... we had breakfast together."

"Oh." What the hell did that mean? In my mind's eye, I saw her sitting next to CJ in his bed, both of them wrapped in hotel robes and enjoying room service. I felt sick.

We stood side by side, something awkward in the air between us. While we swigged water, a man wandered into the front of the booth and picked through the pens and sticky pads arranged on the counter.

"They don't even care what we do!" Justine turned to me, laughing as the man wandered away with a handful of pens.

"Nope."

"But that's so wrong! I don't want to waste pens on them!"

I pulled myself together and put images of intimate breakfasts out of my mind. "That guy might use the pen where someone who is interested in what we do will see it. Or leave it on the counter at the grocery store or doctor's office. Think of people like him as messengers for us."

"Hmmm." She still didn't look happy. "Oh, here comes CJ!"

CJ was walking down the aisle ahead of our booth, looking around him and smiling at people as he passed. His golden hair glowed under the lights and the cut of his suit made him look trim and lean. I couldn't help but stare. CJ was the most handsome guy I'd ever met. As he flashed his amazing smile at someone nearby, I realized how much I wanted him to smile at me again. My heart raced and my skin tingled. God, I wanted that guy. But was it already too late?

"Hey," CJ said to the booth in general as he walked in and picked up a pen.

"Hi," Justine and I both said. I glanced over to see that she was also staring at CJ with a dreamy expression on her face.

"You look great," Justine said.

"Thanks." CJ looked embarrassed, straightening his royal blue tie and swallowing hard.

"So did you figure out what to do about the client?"

"Oh, the um ... distracted one?"

What the hell were they talking about?

"Yeah," Justine said, stepping closer to him. "Did you do what I said?"

"I tried!" CJ laughed.

They were having some inside conversation while I was standing right here. I watched, shock pouring through me, as CJ put a hand on Justine's arm as they laughed together. I was standing outside a bubble that they were in together. They'd had breakfast together ... and now they were sharing this intimate conversation as if I wasn't even here! It really was too late. I tried not to stare as they joked together, Justine standing much closer to the man I loved than I was comfortable with. And there was nothing I could do.

I stood in the corner of the booth and tried to decide what to do. I ran my hands over my skirt, smoothing invisible wrinkles. I tried to pull myself together. I'd been the one to put all the distance between us, after all. I had no right to be surprised that CJ had moved on.

When I looked up, CJ was standing directly in front of me. I jumped slightly. "Oh!"

"Sorry, Natalie," he grinned. "Didn't mean to scare you." The smile faded, and he leaned closer.

I could smell his skin—it was a soapy scent mixed with what I could only describe as masculinity. It made me think of leather and trees, cowboys and big sturdy rocks. I wanted to lean in closer and wrap my arms around him, push my nose into his neck. Instead, I stepped back. I was hurt and confused. And I had no right to be either. I glanced at Justine out of the corner of my eye. She was chatting with someone at the far corner of the booth.

"Hey," CJ said, his voice low. "I'm sorry about dinner yesterday."

"It's okay," I said.

"No, it's not. I was overreacting."

"Okay," I said.

"I miss you. This is just really hard for me," he said.

"I understand." I looked down, and then chanced a look into those dark eyes. My heart lurched. "It seems like maybe you're doing okay, though."

CJ raised an eyebrow and his dark eyes scanned my face, a question in them.

"I mean, you can't be too terribly lonely. With all your breakfasts, and client meetings, and ... " I made myself stop. "Sorry."

"What are you talking about, Natalie?" CJ put a hand on my arm, concern in his big eyes.

"Nothing."

"Okay, well ... I wondered if maybe you and Justine would want to come out with me later. I'm meeting some clients."

I hadn't noticed Justine standing close again, having finished her conversation at the corner of the booth. She bounced excitedly. "Sure."

"I'll pick you guys up here when the show floor closes," CJ said.

I tried not to show my disappointment. It seemed Justine would be our perpetual third wheel. Or maybe I was the third wheel at this point. Darkness narrowed my vision as I had the thought. "Sounds good," I said. As much as I wanted to be close to CJ, I dreaded the thought of spending an evening with him and Justine if they really were involved. I wasn't sure I'd survive seeing real proof of my suspicions.

When five finally arrived, I was exhausted. It should not be underestimated how constant talking can wear a person down, especially when the talking is essentially repeating the same information on endless loop and must be delivered while wearing a smile and standing in shiny pumps. I was feeling deflated when a certain hunky director of business development appeared at the end of the aisle before me. It was as if he walked in a spotlight toward me. He seemed to glow. And then Justine stepped in front of me.

"CJ!" She cooed, bouncing on her toes.

"Hey, Natalie. Justine." His smile was wide and friendly, and if I didn't know better, I'd think nothing had changed between us. "You guys ready?"

"Yep, let me just shut this down." I tried to keep my voice light as I turned off the monitor and lights in the booth.

"I'm meeting clients at this place a couple blocks away that makes good margaritas."

"Yay!" Justine clapped and bounced on her heels. Did she never get tired?

"Perfect," I said. I pulled my bag over my shoulder and we walked toward the double doors at the end of the room. I hoped it wasn't far. My feet were aching. "Do you know I haven't been out of this room all day?"

"Seriously?" he said.

"Is it nice out?"

"Not really," he said. "Kinda cold and windy."

"Typical San Francisco, I guess."

"Have you spent much time up here?" Justine asked me.

"Nope, I'm a Southern California girl, but my sister lives just a bit south of here in Gilroy."

"And your dad is still down South?" CJ asked.

"Yeah."

We walked in silence for a block or two, and I waffled wildly between my belief that Justine and CJ were involved in a secret tryst and the idea that maybe everything was exactly as it had been. No matter what was going on between them, I was sure that I could still feel the familiar buzz between me and CJ—the pull of attraction.

CJ opened the door of a Mexican restaurant, and we walked

into the dim interior. We made our way toward the bar, and a voice called out above the din, "CJ!"

There was a group of dot-com types gathered around a table near the bar motioning to us.

"That's them. Looks like they started without us," CJ said.

The group at the table pulled up chairs for us and immediately put shots of tequila in front of our places. CJ motioned to a chair at his side and I sat, Justine on the other side of me. I smiled, feeling like I'd won a victory. I glanced at Justine, but she didn't appear to be upset about being separated from CJ.

"Sam, Cooper," CJ said. "This is Natalie Pepper. She's the marketing director at All Night, and this is Justine, also in the marketing department."

"Hey," I said to the two guys next to CJ. There were some girls at the other side of the table who were leaning into each other, whispering. After a few minutes, one of them turned to me and stuck out a hand. "Hi, I'm Emily."

Emily and the other girls worked at the company hosting the trade show, so I'd actually spoken to a couple of them on the phone as I'd set up details. We made small talk as CJ chatted with the guys.

"Those aren't just for decoration, you know," Sam said, pointing at the shots.

CJ looked at Justine and me and raised an eyebrow.

"If you're game, so am I," I told him.

"I'm in!" Justine squealed.

We picked up our shots and threw them back in unison. Sam put a beer in front of each of us and I sipped mine gratefully.

"You'll have to do at least two more of those if you want to catch up," Cooper said, pouring another shot for each of us.

"How is it that you have an entire bottle of tequila?" CJ asked.

"I talked the bartender out of it for a hefty tip," Cooper smiled. He had dark hair that came to his chin on either side of his face. Something about him reminded me of the surfers I knew in San Diego. "Drink up," he told us. Maybe he was more frat boy than surfer. Or a blend of the two.

I did my second shot and sipped the beer. I began to wonder if maybe getting dinner would have been a better plan. CJ and Justine were laughing and enjoying themselves, so I did my best to smile and nod, even though I wasn't too interested in the show recap that Emily and the other girls were doing. Every now and then, CJ turned and smiled at me. There was something in his dark eyes, something more than just indifference, and between that and the tequila, I began to feel warm and giddy. I drank quietly, refilling my glass from the pitcher on the table and eating tortilla chips, wondering if what I thought I'd witnessed between him and Justine was all in my mind. Hope began to bloom in me again.

After a couple hours, the alcohol in my system had worked its magic and I was feeling more confident. I wanted to talk to CJ. I wanted to tell him that I was ready. I wasn't going to let fear rule my decisions any more. But as the night dragged on, I realized I wasn't going to get a chance to talk to him alone unless I forced it.

"Hey," I whispered to him, leaning closer than I needed to just to get a whiff of that CJ scent.

"Hey," he returned, turning the wide smile on me. "What's up?"

"I really want to talk to you tonight," I told him.

He raised an eyebrow.

"I mean, if you're talking to me again."

"I'm talking to you," he said. "I just ... "

"No!" I whispered. "Don't say anything else. I need a few minutes with you. I need ... " A hand landed on my shoulder as I whispered. I turned to find myself looking at a very drunk Justine. Her hand stayed on my shoulder as the rest of her body leaned forward, and a lopsided smile spread over her face.

"I think I'm all drinked up," she giggled, her words jumbling together.

"Yeah," I agreed. "I think you are." I sighed, giving CJ a disappointed smile as I turned to help push Justine back into her chair. She began trying to lay her head down on her arms on the tabletop. Tequila, it seemed, was not her friend. "Oh no you don't," I told her. "If you fall asleep here, I'll never get you home."

I nudged CJ and pointed at Justine. His eyebrows shot up.

"I'd better get her back," I said as I pulled her to standing. I looped her purse over her shoulder. She smiled at me, giving me such a sweet puppy dog look that I almost felt guilty for the murderous thoughts I'd been having as a result of her managing to keep me from talking to CJ again.

"I'll help you," CJ said.

Justine jumped, as if she'd been asleep. "Oh, hey," she slurred. She jabbed a finger into CJ's chest and then took hold of his tie, pulling him nearer to her. "You're so cute," she said.

I stood between them awkwardly holding her up as she tried to flirt with CJ. "Um, Let's get back to the hotel, okay?" I asked, feeling less than steady myself.

CJ apologized to his clients and then arranged with the waiter to pay for the remainder of their evening.

I raised my eyebrow at him as he left his card with the guy.

"I'll get it in the morning. How much damage could they do?"

I shook my head.

CJ and I guided Justine back to the hotel and up to her room.

She stumbled across the threshold and lay down on the bed fully dressed.

"Justine," I said. "Do you want to put on pajamas?"

"Mmmhmm," she said.

"I probably shouldn't be here when you get her ready for bed," CJ said, and excused himself.

I watched the door shut behind him and realized that I'd just missed another opportunity. Or rather, Justine had stolen another chance from me.

My heart sank as I helped Justine get her pajamas on and

climb into her bed. It was hard to be angry with her when she was so likeable, but I was still fuzzy on what exactly was going on between her and CJ.

As I finished hanging Justine's suit, I pictured CJ getting into the elevator and heading to his room. I set her alarm and turned off the lights. I'd gotten closer to talking to CJ tonight than I'd been able to since leaving New York, and I still hadn't told him anything. I glanced back at Justine to make sure she was all right and then went back into the hallway.

Chapter Twelve

VOICEMAIL TAG

Lulu

Since meeting Andrew, I had rarely gone more than four hours without talking to him—either in person or on the phone. The few times it had been longer than that, I knew he was thinking of me because he sent flowers. But I had heard nothing since getting into the car at his parents' townhouse.

As two days dragged by, I left voicemails for him at regular intervals. The first one was casual: "Hey, Andrew. Just missing you. Wanted to find out if you were coming over tonight." He did not come over that night. The next one, quite early the next morning: "Hey baby, it's me. It's so strange not hearing from you. I worry that maybe you are not all right. Please call me." No call came. Four hours later I left this: "It's Lu. Andrew, this silence is impossible. What is going on? I miss you. Call me."

At one point, the phone rang while I was in the shower, and I leapt across the apartment, naked and dripping, to answer it.

"Hello?"

"Hey, mamma!" It was Maggie. "There's a party tonight, you coming out?"

I did not feel like wandering out to any wild Internet parties. They were inevitably crazy and ridiculous, with free shots and men wearing button-down shirts and khaki pants as if they were some kind of techie uniform. My friends, whom I loved very much, all fell into some kind of pre-scripted industry talk—at least while sober—and I usually ended up bringing home some art director one-night stand. I wasn't up for it while my heart felt so fragile over Andrew's silence.

"I don't think so," I said.

"Oh, honey, what's wrong?"

"Nothing." I knew I wasn't convincing.

"I can hear it in your voice. What's going on, Lu?"

"Fine. Everything is shit. Andrew is not speaking to me because I farted at his dinner table." I spit it out like a child in having a tantrum. I had not even thought of it in those terms before, but there it was. Andrew had been silent since dinner. He had said that he was not angry at me for being sick, but what else could it be?

Maggie sputtered with laughter and then quickly stopped. "What? I'm sorry, you did what?"

"You heard me. I was very sick."

"Oh, God. Okay. Well, he can't be mad about that."

"I think he can."

"Well then he's an idiot. You couldn't help that."

"It embarrassed him in front of his parents. That and the fact that I'm an unemployable foreigner."

"You have a green card. You can get a job whenever you want."

"Whatever. His mother hates me, and now so does he. And he just told me he was falling for me and we finally had sex." Tears were rolling down my face, and I wiped them away, angry.

"Oh, honey. It's all been so fast, hasn't it? I'm sorry."

"It's fine."

"No, it's obviously not. What can I do?"

"Nothing. I'm sorry. You should go have free drinks and dance. I just can't do it tonight."

"Of course not, I understand. I would come down, but I have to go. It's a work thing for me."

So many of my friends' jobs required them to go drinking on a regular basis. Maybe an Internet job was what I needed.

"I understand. Have fun, Maggie."

"I'll call you tomorrow."

"Okay." I hung up and let myself cry for just a moment before pulling my heart back together. I'd been through much worse. This did not warrant tears. If he was going to be angry that I was sick at dinner, then I didn't need him or his horrible mother. As soon as I had this thought, my heart lurched and a tiny voice inside said, "But his hair is so nice, he smells so warm and comforting, and he said he cared for me ... " I ignored it and decided that leaving my apartment would be the best solution for now.

I would take this rejection one minute at a time. I was stronger than that little voice inside.

As I walked, my phone rang. Part of me wanted to ignore it. The past few days had been overwhelming with extremes of emotion. I could have used a day to just find my center again. But I had difficulty ignoring a ringing phone. And I was certain it would be Andrew, finally calling with an explanation.

"Hello?"

"Hey, it's Tamara. How did dinner with the 'rents go?"

"It was awful. His parents are horrible. Especially his mother."

"How bad can she be?"

"She's really terrifying. She hates me."

"Not everyone is gonna love you. That's her problem."

"And mine if Andrew thinks that her opinion is important." I pouted, even though there was no one to see. My ankle was beginning to throb as I walked. I found myself outside the Corner Bistro, so I hobbled in and took a table. "I also got incredibly sick right after dinner and had to relieve myself in a bathroom that was practically in the dining room. Andrew and his parents heard everything. And there was a lot to hear. And smell. It was ... "

"I'm getting a clear image, thanks. It just got louder. Where are you?"

"Corner Bistro."

"Ohhh, I want a burger."

"I'm not going to deliver a burger to your office."

"No, I'm coming down." She hung up.

So much for solitude. I ordered a soda and a burger and put my foot on the chair across from me to wait for Tamara. I looked around while I waited, and noticed a man sitting at the bar watching me. He smiled when I noticed him, and inclined his head.

Was he flirting with me? I looked like shit. I was wearing a one-shouldered T-shirt with a tank top and tight black jeans. I had running shoes on because I'd been too lazy to try to find cute shoes that wouldn't hurt. My hair was in a messy bun and I hadn't even looked in a mirror to see if my makeup from last night was still on. I guessed that it wasn't.

I ignored him and was pleased when my food arrived. Tamara showed up fifteen minutes later.

"I love your suit," I told her. She looked incredible in a crisp white shirt and tailored light gray pants suit.

"Thanks," she smiled, sitting. She gazed around and said loudly, "Who's the creeper?"

"No idea. He's been staring since I got here."

"Well, you do look beautiful, as always."

"I look like shit," I told her.

"Whatever. That Brazilian exotic thing kind of wafts off you, even when you're not trying."

"It does?" My friends all seemed to believe that I exuded some kind of otherness, just because I was born in another country. I didn't believe it. Well, maybe I believed it a little bit. It did seem to attract men, whatever it was. But I was very much uninterested at that moment.

"You know it does." She ordered her food and then smiled a wide smile. I was glad not to have to tell her more about Andrew.

"What's going on with you?"

"I have news," she said, her smile wide. "The Hair."

"Tell me." I was happy to have something else to think about besides Tippy and Andrew's silence.

"I finally went on a real date with him."

"You did?" Tamara seemed to keep her secrets better than the other girls managed to. Had it been Candace, I would have known about every detail before, during, and after.

"Yes. And he kissed me."

"And how was it?"

"I think it will get better."

"What does that mean? It was bad? He's a bad kisser. I'm so sorry."

"No, I think he was nervous." She smiled at the waiter as her food arrived, and quickly put two French fries into her mouth. "I was totally craving this."

"The Hair doesn't seem like a nervous man. He seems very confident."

"Well, don't underestimate my effect on men," she said, smiling. There were dried chives on her teeth from the fries.

"Of course not."

"Anyway, I think we're going out again this week."

I sipped my drink and watched her. I didn't feel like I could encourage the dating of a bad kisser. It could only lead to more disappointment.

"The kiss was the first goal. This time, I want to see where he lives. I know he has a place in Irving Square. That's a big deal in real estate terms. I can't wait to see it."

"Well, good luck."

"Don't sound too excited for me." She sounded annoyed.

"I'm not."

We ate in silence for a minute, and I began to realize that Tamara was actually angry.

"Sorry?" I wasn't, but it seemed like that was what she wanted to hear.

"No you aren't. You go on for hours about your doctor, but give me just a teeny bit of happiness, and you try to ruin it."

"I did not try to ruin it. I just think you should be careful."

"Because he's not a good kisser?"

"That's what you said."

Tamara sighed loudly and sat back in her seat. "Forget it."

I was happy to let the topic drop. John was good-looking, and he did have good hair. He also seemed to be successful, judging by what Andrew had told me, so I could definitely see the attraction there. But a bad kisser was a bad kisser. I waved at the waitress and ordered a beer.

We moved on to other topics and ended our lunch at about five o'clock, both of us drunk.

Chapter Thirteen

THE INEBRIATED HAMSTER

Natalie

I CAME out of Justine's room angry at myself for missing another opportunity to talk to CJ. But when I looked up, my mood shifted suddenly. CJ was leaning against the wall just down the hall from Justine's door, his hands in his pockets. He wore the smile that had won me over in the first place—warm, sexy, and completely disarming. He watched me walk toward him, and I knew that something had changed.

I was also a little bit drunk, and the slight bump in the carpet of the hallway did nothing to help my sexy saunter. Instead of gliding down the hallway toward the man of my dreams, I dove headfirst to his feet, skinning my knee in the process. So sexy.

"Are you okay?" CJ was laughing as he knelt down on the carpet next to me.

I lay on my stomach, supporting myself with my elbows, one leg pulled under me and the other stretched out. It was like a drunken yoga pose. Maybe it would be called the inebriated hamster. I was halfway between crying from the pain of the skin torn off my knee and laughing at the hilarity of the situation. And instead of doing either, I just hiccupped. Which was worse than either option.

"Seriously, Natalie, you're bleeding."

I looked into those concerned dark brown eyes, and CJ reached for me, gathering me into his arms like a child. I found myself practically in his lap as he settled with his back to the wall, my arms around his neck. His arms were around my waist and he put strong hands on either side of me, lifting me to sit on his thighs, my legs stretched before me.

My knee stung, but the deeper intensity came from the zing in the air between us. CJ was smiling at me, but it wasn't his full-wattage grin anymore. The sides of his mouth still curled, revealing the incredible dimples, but the look on his face was more aroused than amused. He stared into my eyes. Then his gaze shifted to my lips.

My drunken giggles died away, and I forgot that we were sitting in a ridiculous position in the middle of a hotel hallway. The atmosphere around us felt thick, imbued with the tension and desire that had been building between CJ and me for months. This was the closest we'd been in a long time ... ever, actually. And after everything we'd gone through—mostly my efforts to stay away from him—there was a tangible sense of finality in the air. Either something would happen now, or it never would.

I stared at CJ and felt myself leaning forward, toward the smooth skin and golden stubble, toward those deep chocolate eyes, toward those full amazing lips most of all. And within seconds, I'd lost control. I gave into everything I wanted, pressing my lips against his and tightening my arms around his neck until it felt like everything I needed in the world would come from that kiss.

He reacted immediately, his lips parting to allow my tongue to find its way in, to taste him. And his mouth was as sweet as it had been in my dreams each night since I'd kissed him last. He kissed me back, his hands pulling me toward him, his body curving around mine as I pressed myself into him. Sounds escaped my lips that I didn't know a kiss could evoke, and I would have been embarrassed, were I not so tipsy, or so completely in love with the man I was kissing.

Moments passed, maybe lifetimes. We kissed for all the days that we'd missed being together and for all of the unknowns that lay ahead of us. And finally, the intensity waned for just a second —long enough for CJ to pull away. When his lips left mine, the spell broke.

"Natalie, I ..."

"No. Don't do that." I kissed him again, harder, trying to prove a point.

He held me close to him, and never stopped kissing me back as he stood, placing me on my feet in front of him.

"My room is right here," I breathed, slipping the key card from my purse as we fumbled down the hall, walking, kissing.

He pushed me against the door and I thought that his hesitation had vanished. His mouth was urgent on mine, his tongue demanding and fervent. I groped behind me, trying to fit the key card into the lock.

"Let me," CJ said, breaking away for a moment. He tried several times, shoving the key in and pulling it back out, but the light flashed red each time. "What the ... ?"

Suddenly the door pulled open, and I practically fell into the room, at the feet of a grizzled bald man wearing only boxer shorts.

"What the hell?" he asked us, clearly having been roused from sleep.

"S-sorry," I stuttered, pulling the door shut again as I scampered back into the hallway, regaining my feet.

"So, I'm guessing that's not your room," CJ said, smiling.

"Maybe not," I conceded.

"Do you know your room number?"

"Of course I do," I said. "It isn't this one. It's that one!" I pointed to the next door. "You got me all confused."

"Right." CJ laughed and then inserted the key card into the next door's lock. The light turned green and he pushed the door open, waving me inside.

I walked past him, pretending to be annoyed instead of drunk, and then realized that he was not following me. "Aren't you coming in?"

He shook his head and remained at the threshold.

"But ... " Everything that had just happened ... what was that to him? Was he just taking advantage of the fact that I was drunk? I thought he was waiting for me. Now here I was and he was just standing there? I cursed myself for being stupid, for thinking that CJ would be at my beck and call. I was a selfish idiot. But what had that all kissing meant, then?

"But," CJ said, his voice low and soft. "You're drunk. And that's not the way I want to start things."

"So ... ?" I was confused. What did that mean?

"So, I'll see you in the morning, beautiful girl. And we'll figure everything out then."

"We will?" I asked him, still confused.

"We will." He smiled, the dimples charming me into submission. "Now get some sleep. And Natalie? Drink some water, and take a couple ibuprofen, please. You'll be glad in the morning."

"No, CJ, I've been trying to talk to you forever." I was whining. I couldn't help it. He couldn't walk away from me now.

"We'll have time to talk tomorrow," he said.

"No we won't," I said. "You'll be busy having breakfast with Justine." I knew I was being petulant, but I couldn't help it.

"What about Justine?"

"You like her."

"I like her?"

"Yeah, you know. Like, like." I sounded like a high school

freshman. Wonderful. I changed my tone. "Do you like her?"

CJ walked back to me, wrapping his arms around my waist and pulling me against his hard chest. "What the hell are you talking about?"

His breath was warm and set off little alarms all through my body. I wanted to wrap myself around him. "I'm talking about you. And Justine. And how maybe you've finally given up on me and how maybe she likes you, and how ... " I was interrupted by CJ's mouth on mine. His lips were soft but insistent, and his tongue teased at the tip of mine before thrusting against it, sending electricity shooting up and down my limbs. A wet warmth developed between my legs and I felt like if he walked away I might actually die. "Oh God," I moaned.

CJ stopped, and stepped back, still holding me. "I'll talk to you tomorrow, okay?"

"Why don't you just stay?" I whispered. Where was the line between sexy and desperate, I wondered.

"I'd love to, but it wouldn't be right. We'll have plenty of time for that," CJ said. And we'll figure everything out tomorrow. Go to bed, beautiful."

"Okay," I said.

CJ pulled my door shut and I pressed my eye against the peephole, to watch him as he turned to walk away. When he threw a fist into the air and jumped, quietly yelling, "Yeah!" I almost collapsed. I watched him walk his sexy walk down the hall and then practically passed out, deliriously happy and fairly drunk.

When the alarm sounded, I woke with a headache and a tongue that felt like it was coated in lawn clippings. But I was feeling happy and optimistic. I felt like things with CJ were on the right track again, finally. Not only that, but I felt like I'd finally managed to get out of my own way. My friends were right—it was an easy enough choice to make. I would be with CJ, and everything else would work itself out.

I showered and got dressed, thoughts of CJ never far from my mind, and went down to the hotel restaurant for breakfast. Justine and CJ were there already, at a small table near the wall. The smile CJ let loose when he saw me was almost enough to knock me off my feet.

"Hey," he said as I approached.

"Morning!" Justine chirped.

"Hey guys," I said. "I'll go grab some food and be right back."

The hotel buffet was plentiful, and I filled my plate with fruit, yogurt, muffins, and sausage. Only as I sat did I realize that I'd gotten enough food for a small army.

"Thanks," CJ said, as he pulled a muffin off my plate, grinning.

"Go ahead. My eyes are way bigger than my stomach."

"Seriously," he said. "Is this the lumberjack special?"

"Shut up."

Justine giggled.

"I have back-to-back meetings today," CJ said. "You guys have fun in the booth."

"Okay," I said, disappointment making my buzz lighten just a shade. "You'll be around for dinner?"

"Client meetings," CJ said. He met my eye as he said it, and I could see the same disappointment there that I felt. He gave my shoulder a friendly squeeze, and stood. "I'll see you after."

I knew that he had to be discreet since Justine was with us, but the girly part of me had hoped for a taste of the connection we'd remade the night before.

"Have a good day, CJ!" Justine trilled as he walked away. "God, he's cute."

"He is," I said, my voice low. I wanted to add, "and he's mine," but thought better of it.

I didn't see CJ all day. I tried to stay up, renting a movie on TV and propping myself up on the bed, but at some point I passed out from exhaustion. The last thing I remembered was looking at the clock and seeing that it was almost 10:00 p.m.

There was a note, along with my hotel bill, under my door in the morning. It said, "Sleep tight, beautiful. — CJ"

Short and sweet, and enough to reignite the hope and optimism that I'd had the previous day.

The three of us spent the morning in the booth, until the show ended at noon. CJ helped us break down and label our boxes for shipping, and then we headed to the airport, and back home. This time CJ didn't switch seats with Justine, and we finally had time to talk.

"I've been a complete idiot," I told him.

"You are not an idiot." CJ held my hand as we talked, and it felt like we were in our own little cocoon, the outside world finally kept at bay by the hum of the plane and the tight space around us.

"I want to make things work with us."

"And what about dating people you work with?"

"I don't care anymore. Jobs come and go, right? But I've never felt this way about anyone before." I found it hard to look into those deep eyes when I said this, but I knew that this was my opportunity. "I don't want to miss a chance with you."

CJ's smile could have lit the whole plane. He squeezed my hand and put his arm around my shoulders. His voice was a thick whisper, "I haven't felt this way about anyone before either." He watched me for a minute, and looked like he was thinking about what to say next. "I tried so hard to forget about this, Natalie. I seriously tried to give up ... but you're in my heart. I couldn't do it."

I leaned forward and kissed him then, tears standing in my eyes. I had everything I wanted. Right here. Right next to me.

I spent five hours holding CJ's hand and sleeping with my

head on his shoulder. It was the best five hours of my life.

CJ kissed me softly after the plane landed. "I can't wait to see you."

"I'm right here." I smiled at him.

"I know. I mean, I can't wait to take you out. On an actual date."

I couldn't help the silly grin that smeared itself across my face.

"After work tomorrow night?"

"That sounds great."

"I guess we shouldn't go straight from work. I'll pick you up at your place."

"You don't have to do that."

"I want to. Let's do this right. We've waited long enough." He was rubbing circles on my palm with his thumb, and my powers of coherent speech were fading.

"Okay," I said.

I went to work the next day feeling as if everything had changed—clicked into place. The city seemed cleaner, the people on the subway friendlier. I halfway expected Lanie Bill to do a sudden about-face and maybe even remember my name for a change.

"Nicole, can you come see me?" she said, sticking her head in my door almost as soon as I'd arrived.

"Sure." I put down my things and followed her to her office.

"Door." She slouched into her seat and pointed to the door.

I closed it behind me and took a seat across from her desk.

Lanie steepled her fingers and leaned on her elbows. I got the sense she was playing the role of troubled executive for this encounter and wondered what was up. "How was the windy city?"

"Uh, I think that's Chicago. We were in San Francisco."

"I know where you were. Let me ask you this. Was it windy?"

"Yeah, actually. It was."

"And there you have it." She stared at me, a strange expression making her jowls sag lower than normal. "As you can see, you are not always right."

"Okay," I said. "Well, the show went great. The All Night name was everywhere, and a few of the sites that CJ met up with dropped by to chat, sounding like they were on board ... "

Lanie cut me off. "I'm not interested in that."

Strange. That was why we went in the first place. I waited. Close to the vest was not Lanie's usual style.

"Listen. I have heard some rumors, and I gotta tell you, they make me uncomfortable."

"Rumors?" My blood chilled. What the hell was this?

"About you. About some people on staff. About some fraternization."

Did someone see me kissing CJ? My face must have shown my guilt, because Lanie continued, looking grim.

"I don't allow any fraternization from members of my staff," she began. I couldn't help but think of the numerous times she'd discussed Damon as if he were leaving her bed each morning to come to the office. I doubted that she had any such rules for herself. I wondered how much of this was coming from her frustration at his disinterest. "And I think you're smart enough to know that workplace dalliances are never secret, and that they can only end badly."

"Okay." My voice was quiet. I did know. Hadn't I been saying that exact same thing for months? Why did this have to come up now, now that I'd finally gotten over this issue?

"Well, I know that this was in the past, so I'm going to let it go."

"In the past?" I blurted. Holy crap, had she found out about Damon somehow?

"Unless there's something going on now," she said, her eyebrow arching and her entire body seeming to rise with her growing interest. "And if I find out that there is ... well, your prior indiscretions will come to light. The whole company will inevitably find out, and that could be very embarrassing for you."

Was she threatening me? "No, I just ... "

"Don't deny anything, okay? Just accept this warning and move forward." She shook her head, her lank curls rustling on her shoulders. "You know, I had to give Damon a similar warning. He wants to date me now, but I just don't date people I work with. I told him to back off."

It was my turn to look surprised. I doubted very much that she had told Damon any such thing. And I was ninety-nine percent sure that this "rule" had arisen from some realization on Lanie's part that her chance of dating Damon was about as good as her chance of ever getting my name right.

"Anyway, that can all be in the past. But if I find out that there's anything going on, whether it's you, or Justine, or anyone else, frankly ... well, I'll need to talk to David, but the policy at All Night is clear. You'll be asked to leave."

"I didn't know we had an official policy on this."

"All good companies do." She leaned back in her chair. It seemed we were done.

"Okay," I said, rising. I turned and walked back to my office, my brain chasing itself in endless loops. How did she find out about Damon? Did he tell her? Why? Did it matter? She'd been perfectly clear.

I sat back down at my desk, disappointment working its way through me, replacing every ounce of optimism I'd found for what might be possible with CJ. The timing was ridiculous. And the worst thing was I knew she was probably right.

I holed up in my office for the rest of the day, trying to figure out what to do. I'd already decided ... in San Francisco. I was going to quit being timid and go after what I wanted. But now ... I needed to get perspective. I called Lulu. She had a knack for seeing things as they were—stripping away all the bullshit.

"Hey," I said when she answered.

"Hi." She sounded awful.

"Lu, are you okay? What's wrong?"

"Andrew's not speaking to me."

"Why not? What happened?"

"I was sick."

I waited for more explanation, but it didn't come. "What do you mean?"

"At his parents' house, at dinner. I had to use the bathroom and it was loud and horrible and they all heard it, and his mother is a beast who hates me, and now he does, too."

"Wow." I hadn't heard Lulu like this before. I'd thought of her as very much in control—it seemed that the men in her life did what she wanted or she cut them loose. It was surprising to hear her so upset. There was something childlike in her hurt, something so bewildered and innocent.

"Yes, wow." She was silent a minute. "I'm sorry. That is not why you called. What's up?"

"I don't want to add to your load," I said.

"Go ahead. It will distract me from the complete silence."

"I'm looking for advice. CJ and I hooked up on our trip."

"Oh, that's good. I knew you'd come to your senses."

"Okay, right, well, it was good. But then we got back. And my boss said that she knows I've been 'fraternizing' at the office, and that if she finds out that it's still going on she'll fire me!"

"'Fraternizing?' Oh, like getting close with your brothers? How does she know?"

"I don't think that's the exact translation. But you get the gist—messing around with co-workers. And I have no idea. She knows about Damon, somehow."

"Did Damon tell her?"

"Why would he tell her?"

"Why does he do anything? He's a man ditz." Lulu had also dated Damon.

"Huh. Well, it doesn't matter. She knows. And if she finds out about CJ, I'll lose my job, and CJ will find out about Damon. And then I'll be screwed. I won't have a job or CJ."

"Why would CJ care about Damon?"

"You don't think it would bother him to find out that I'd been with someone else that we work with?"

"You barely kissed him."

"But I did. And Lanie knows about it, and she's basically threatening me. God, I hate her."

"Me too. Oh, wow!" She sounded surprised suddenly.

"What?"

"You made me forget about Andrew for a while. That was the best part of my whole day."

"I'm glad my misery brought you such relief."

"What will you do?"

"I guess I'll tell CJ we have to wait."

"Wait for what?"

"I don't know ... " I put my head on my desk. I felt miserable. "Shit. I just don't know."

"I think you should ignore your ridiculous boss and just do what feels right."

"I'd love to do that. But suddenly it feels like the stakes are higher somehow, like the chance of this screwing up work just got more real."

"You need a plan B."

"I don't have a plan A, let alone a plan B!" She was right. I needed some time to think.

"Well, good luck, Pepper."

"Thanks." I hung up, feeling no better than I had before. CJ chose that minute to rap lightly on my door, his smile radiating through the narrow pane of glass next to the door.

"Hey," he said, as he entered. "Uh oh, what's wrong?"

"CJ," I moaned. I was about to tell him everything that Lanie had said to me, but then my brain stilled my tongue. If I told him what Lanie had said, he might pursue it, and if he went digging around, there was a good chance that my indiscretion with Damon would come up. And if it did, I'd surely lose CJ anyway.

"What's wrong, Natalie?"

"I just ... " I couldn't tell him. I needed more time to figure out what to do. But I didn't want to screw up the possibility of being with him. I looked into those beautiful eyes and saw the hope that I'd shared with him for us until a few hours ago. "I ... uh, I'm feeling terrible."

"Oh no," he said, genuine concern wrinkling his brow.

The guilt I felt at lying was eons better than breaking CJ's heart, even if my own was in shards. "Yeah, I think I better just go home tonight."

His face fell as he realized I was canceling our date. "Oh," he said. "Of course. You should take it easy. Want me to come by? Bring you some soup?"

I shook my head. "No, it's my stomach," I lied. "I'm just going to go to bed."

"Okay," he said. "Will you call me tomorrow?"

Lanie Bill walked by just as he uttered this line, and her massive head turned my way through the open door.

"We can talk about it all next week at the office," I said, too loud.

CJ looked confused, then hurt.

Lanie moved on.

"I'll call you," I said.

"Natalie, is there something ... "

I shook my head and put a hand over my mouth as if I might vomit at any moment. "I better go," I said.

"Okay. Feel better." CJ stood and walked out of my office, a look of concentration on his face. At least he didn't hate me ... yet.

Chapter Fourteen

PLAYING HOMELESS

Lulu

IT HAD BEEN a week since the dinner at Andrew's parents' house, and I had heard nothing. I knew that I could not wander around my apartment any longer waiting for him to call. I could not leave him another message, and I definitely could not page him at work again. It was becoming apparent that he had broken up with me.

And I deserved to know why.

Waiting outside the hospital may not have been the most mature thing to do, but I didn't know how else to catch him. I was able to check his schedule with the ER attendant inside, telling her that I'd hoped to schedule a follow-up about my ankle. I had worn my brace for this purpose, though my ankle was almost healed.

Andrew did not appear on schedule. I ended up sitting outside the main entrance, my back against the wall and my new Diesel jeans on the dirty sidewalk. There was a man sitting in the same position about five feet away from me, his scraggly beard and dirty face turning in my direction at regular intervals.

"You don't look like you do this much," he finally said. His voice was like a key pulling through the paint on the side of a car. "You need a sign or something. And you're too clean." He held up his cardboard sign, which read, "Anything helps. God bless."

"Oh, no. I'm not ... " Was "homeless" a slur? Would that hurt his feelings? "I am not trying to raise money."

He nodded and turned away, but then scooted himself closer and began offering tips on how to make the most from a few hours spent panhandling.

After two hours of being coached on raising money by appearing more slovenly, Andrew appeared, his golden-brown hair blazing in the afternoon light. Stubble covered his neck and chin, and there were dark circles under his eyes. He looked awful.

"Andrew!" I stood and took his arm.

He looked surprised, but then the familiar warmth came back to his eyes. He smiled. "Lulu," he said. He pulled me into his arms and buried his face in my neck.

I pushed him back. "What is wrong with you?" I was furious now that he was in front of me. "How can you ignore me for a week and then hug me like we've never been apart? How can you be angry at me for being sick, and make me feel so small in front of your family, and then stand here smiling at me?"

"He's mad that you're sick? Ain't he a doctor?" My homeless friend chimed in.

I pulled Andrew farther down the sidewalk.

"I'm so sorry, Lulu. I was just going to come to your place. I couldn't go another minute without talking to you."

"You went a whole week," I told him. I didn't believe him at all.

"It was an awful week. I fought with my family, I fought with myself."

"You fought with Tippy? About me?" It was a shock—not so

much that Andrew fought with his mother over me, but that she really did hate me enough to necessitate a fight. "I'm sorry to have brought trouble to paradise, then." I pulled away.

Andrew didn't let go of my arm. "I did fight with her. All week. I told her that she treated you unfairly and that I didn't care what she thought because I really am falling for you." His eyes were bright as he said it. He looked sincere, and almost desperate.

I pulled my hand from his grasp. "You didn't return any of my messages."

"I'm so sorry. I didn't know how to apologize for my family."

"'I'm sorry my mother is a bitch' would be a good start."

Andrew looked shocked. "That's a little harsh."

I turned and began walking away.

"Lulu!" He was right next to me, taking my hand again. "Please don't walk away. Please give me another chance."

I stopped to face him. "I don't deserve to be treated like that."

"No, you don't. That's what I told her. And she didn't realize how horrible she had been. She wants you to give her another chance."

"No." I was so angry I was shaking. "How could she not realize how horrible she was? And how could you let her?"

"I'm so sorry. I wasn't the man you deserve. But things will be different ..."

I stared at him, trying to decide what to do. The hurt part of me wanted to walk away and forget about all of this. But Andrew looked so sincere. And the softer side of me really did want to forgive him, even though he'd been an idiot. He was back, wasn't he? He was apologizing. He was saying all the things I needed to hear. What more could I ask of him?

"My mother agrees that she didn't give you a chance. She suggested that you come to the Hamptons house this weekend. Will you come? I won't leave your side the whole time." A wicked gleam came into the blue eyes then. "And there are plenty of bathrooms in the house. I'll show you the secret back wing one."

I stared at him. Was he making fun of me? "No." I said. My heart was screaming "yes" but I did not feel that I should give in so easily. He couldn't treat people this way. I pretended I was going to walk away, thankful to feel his hand on my arm as I fled.

"Lulu, please. Give me another chance. I love you."

Shock slammed through me. Love? He had not said "love" before. And if I were truthful, I hadn't heard the word many times in my life. Not directed at me. I stared at him.

"I do, Lulu. I realized it when I didn't talk to you all week. I realized that I don't want to go without you like that again. I was miserable. Please forgive me. Please give my family another chance. Come to the Hamptons."

I felt my anger melting in the face of his words. "I will come. But I am still mad at you."

"Okay. Can I work on making it up to you?"

"All right. You can start right now." I took his hand in mine and turned toward home.

We walked together toward my apartment, where Tom handed me a box as we entered. Andrew carried it upstairs, where I opened it.

"What is this?" I asked, holding a Betsy Johnson bikini.

"An invitation," he said, smiling.

"This is from you?"

"From Tippy. See the card."

There was a pink card tucked in with the suit, which read: *Please join us at our house in Sag Harbor this weekend. We will expect you from Saturday morning until Monday.*

"My parents will go today, but we can take the Jitney together tomorrow morning." Andrew looked excited. His face glowed and he was almost bouncing. It reminded me of a little boy. I couldn't help but forgive him.

I threw my arms around his neck and walked him to the bed,

pushing him down. "I'll go with you, but first you have a whole week to make up to me."

"My pleasure," he said, pulling his shirt off over his head.

I smiled as my hands found the smooth planes of his chest and my mouth found his. The world clicked back into place as he slowly made me believe that he really had missed me.

———

Andrew helped me pack my bag that evening and we went together to his apartment.

"I'm closer to the Jitney stop," he explained. "We can get a nice dinner tonight and be out there first thing tomorrow."

"Fine, but first you explain something to me."

"Okay," he looked worried. We'd rehashed the week of silence several times so far, and he didn't seem eager to talk about it again.

"What is a 'Jitney'?"

"The Jitney?" He laughed.

"Don't laugh at me. I was not born here. I don't know what this is."

"I'm not laughing at you," he said. "I bet there are plenty of Americans who wouldn't know what the Jitney is."

"Oh. Well, what is it?"

"It's a bus! It runs a route from the Upper East Side to the Hamptons during the summer. It's a regular thing for people who live in the city, but if you weren't from here, you wouldn't know that."

"I've never been to the Hamptons," I said, in my defense.

"So there's no reason you'd know about the Jitney," he said, smiling. The eyes were dancing again.

My heart softened. "Okay. So we take this Jitney in the morning."

"Yes, I'll show you," he said, pulling me against him. "But right now, let me take you to dinner." His fingers threaded through my hair and his other hand held me firmly as he pressed his forehead to mine. "Do you know how cute you are when you're confused and trying to be angry?"

"I wasn't trying. I was angry."

"Right. Well, you're very cute when you're angry."

"You haven't seen me really angry."

"Scary."

"Very."

"I'll try to be on my best behavior, then."

"You'd better." I kissed him, then, pressing his lips open with my tongue and surprising him with the force of it. He grunted and his arms tightened around me.

"Maybe we don't go to dinner quite yet," he breathed, pushing me down on the couch.

"Maybe not yet," I agreed.

Eventually we did go to dinner, and the next day found us standing on 40th Street near Third with a few other people who stood looking bored with expensive luggage at their feet. Andrew stood next to me in the late morning light with one arm over my shoulders. He looked down at me constantly, smiling the smile that made his eyes crinkle. It helped calm my nerves a bit, but I was not excited to see Tippy again.

It had been my experience in life that women generally did not like me on first meeting me. One might think this would make me more talented at second meetings, but that was not usually the case. I could only hope that whatever natural charm I possessed might win the cold papery woman over. And that she would stop asking questions about my family. Detailing my history would surely confirm her suspicions that I was not qualified to hold Andrew's hand.

The Jitney was a bus, exactly as Andrew had described. It pulled to the curb and everyone boarded and found their seats. Most people appeared to do this often, and came prepared with magazines, headphones, and books. Andrew and I settled toward the back.

"About two hours," he told me.

"I was about to ask."

"I can read your mind," he said, smiling.

"No you can't."

"Sure I can. You're worried about seeing Tippy again. You're wondering what the house will be like, and you are hoping that the suit fits since you didn't try it on and didn't bring another."

I gasped, and put my hand over my mouth. "I didn't even think about that!" We'd be in bathing suits all weekend, at the beach and the pool at the house. I'd packed the gift from Tippy and moved on. He was right; it might not fit. "I can't think of anything worse than parading around in a suit that looks terrible on me in front of your mother ... or that doesn't cover ... things."

"It'll be fine."

"How do you know?"

"I'll take you shopping if it doesn't fit."

"Okay," I said, settling in.

The bus ride was long. We stopped many times before arriving at the Sag Harbor stop in front of a quaint old movie theater.

"Art films," Andrew said, without me asking a question. I raised an eyebrow.

"Mr. Barton," Sheldon said, appearing from a dark car parked near the curb.

We followed him to the car and rode a few minutes to a long driveway that wound across a grassy lawn facing the main road and the beach. Set back from the road was a large white house that looked like a small castle. It had several turrets topped with sloping grey roofs, and a huge wraparound porch with columns descending into carefully tended bushes. There was another small house at the end of the driveway that looked similar, and as the car pulled down the drive, we could see behind the main house to where the pool and several other small buildings were scattered across a sprawling back lawn.

"It's beautiful," I told Andrew. I was not blown over by the obvious wealth that the home displayed. I'd seen many big houses and lived in a few myself. Money did not especially impress me. If anything, I had learned to be wary of people who have too much. They often get bored with expensive material toys and turn to playing with people.

"Andrew, darling!" Tippy's reedy voice came from the pool area, where she appeared wearing a thin white robe that wrapped around her skeletal form as the breeze lifted it and wrapped around her skinny legs. She wore a floppy white hat and overlarge sunglasses.

I cringed without meaning to, and was glad that Tippy was paying no attention to me whatever. She certainly didn't see my disgust at seeing her so revealed.

"Andrew, Lulu!" Cherry came bounding around the side of the house, wearing a red two-piece suit that pulled tight across her small flat chest. She seemed to be blooming on the later side, given that she was thirteen and still had a childish body. Something about that realization made me feel closer to the girl, since I had been very much the same. She threw her arms around me, nearly knocking me over.

"Hi," I said, grinning back at her.

"I'm so glad you came out! We'll have so much fun!" She hugged her brother while Tippy stepped back and extended a hand toward me.

Unsure what to do, I grasped it and shook in the American style, which seemed not to be Tippy's intent, as her face showed surprise as I waved her frail arm up and down.

"Yes, Lulu. Nice to see you again, dear," she said. "So glad you could take a break from your activities to join us."

"Thank you for having me," I said. "And for the suit."

"Oh, think nothing of it," she said, turning to walk to the house. "I'll show you where I've put you both."

We followed her into the house, Andrew grinning at me with dancing eyes as we climbed the steps to the back porch.

"Sheldon will bring your bags in," Tippy called back at us. "Andrew, darling. You'll have your favorite room." We followed her through the back door of the house, which was essentially a wall of glass, the sliding doors opened to the sun for the day. The living area was oriented to enjoy the back yard with couches and chairs positioned in small conversation areas around the large room. Tippy led us toward a narrow stairway, which I guessed was one of at least two, and had probably been a servants' stair originally. "Here we are," she said at the top, waving us into a large room that sat to the left of the stair.

It was two rooms, actually. The bedroom overlooked the back yard and pool, and the front sitting room had a large window on the front of the house, where it looked out over the beach. The room was almost completely white, the king-sized bed covered in numerous pillows with various kinds of lace and frills. Everything about the room made me think of fresh air, the ocean, and peace. A calm settled over me, broken by Tippy's high-pitched voice.

"Lulu, you'll be down here." She began to leave the room.

"Mom, Lulu will stay with me," Andrew said.

She stopped and turned, stepping back into the doorway. "Not under my roof, Andrew Elliott Bancroft Barton." Her drawn-on eyebrow was raised and her eyes blazed. "You might be a grown-up and a doctor, but you're my son and you're unmarried."

I laughed without thinking about it. How ridiculous! Surely, Andrew would remind her that he was twenty-eight years old and could decide upon his sleeping arrangements.

"Lulu, follow me," Tippy said.

I turned to look at Andrew, who simply shrugged. Irritation flooded me. Wasn't he going to stand up to her?

I narrowed my eyes at him and we followed Tippy past a seemingly endless hallway of doors, each one open to a beautiful bedroom. She didn't stop until we reached the other end of the hallway. It seemed she wanted to keep us as far apart as possible. I was not surprised. She showed me to a small tight room that had clearly been a maid's quarters at some point. There was a twin bed against the far wall and two small windows facing the driveway. The room also enjoyed one small chair and a pole across one of the windows that had several hangers on it. This would serve as a closet, I guessed. Compared to all the other rooms I'd seen, this was essentially a cubbyhole.

"Your bathroom will be down the hall here," Tippy said, leading me back down the hallway about halfway to a bathroom covered in white marble. The bathroom was bigger than my bedroom.

"Thank you," I said, my voice tight.

"I'll see you both downstairs shortly," Tippy said lightly. She turned and left me fuming, standing in the glowing bathroom.

Andrew smiled at me again, as if everything was perfect.

"Seriously?" I asked him.

"What?" he said, shrugging again.

I was learning that when Andrew shrugged, it meant that Tippy was winning. I pushed past him to unpack my bag in my maid's room.

"Lulu," he began. Then I heard him turn away, following his mother. "Mom, can't we put Lulu in a different room? Something ... "

"No, dear. Cherry's got a friend coming too. This isn't a hotel. We only have so much space!"

I stood and stared at Andrew as he returned to the doorway of my tiny room. "You won't really be in here anyway," he said. "You'll sleep with me, and we'll be out all day. You'll just be in here for dressing. Think of it as a big walk-in closet."

"Andrew. That's what it is."

He shrugged again.

"I'll see you downstairs," I told him, rustling in my bag as I pretended to look for something. I needed a minute to calm down.

"Put on your suit!" he called as he disappeared back to his luxurious room.

Chapter Fifteen

PARTY PANTS

Natalie

I HAD three messages from CJ when I woke on Saturday morning, all equally concerned. I had turned my phone off Friday night, afraid that if I actually spoke to CJ I might end up telling him everything. I didn't want to let Lanie win—that was the last thing I wanted. But I also didn't want her telling CJ about my past mistake with Damon, either. I'd bought some time, now I needed to figure out what to do with it.

Tory was standing in the hallway when I came out of my bedroom. I couldn't tell if she'd been waiting for me or if she'd just come out of the bathroom.

"Oh, hey, Natalie," she said.

"Hey." I smiled at her. I liked Tory. I just didn't want to live with her anymore. We didn't have much in common, and it just didn't feel like a great match.

"I wasn't sure you were here."

"Oh, yeah, I was in San Francisco this week, but I'm back

now." Our schedules were so different that we rarely saw each other. I was sure I'd left her a note about my travel plans, though.

"Oh, fun," she said. "Sometimes I wish I got to travel a bit." Tory was an elementary school teacher. She was overworked, underpaid, and always tired. She often got to school while it was still dark and went to bed pretty early. I didn't envy her. But sometimes I didn't envy me, either.

"It was fun," I said, starting to wish she'd move so I could go pee. I stood there in my T-shirt and boxers, shifting from one leg to the next. "So, uh ... " I motioned toward the bathroom door, but she didn't make any moves.

"Do you think you'll have rent in the next day or two?"

Oh, shit. Rent. Moving. The new apartment. I'd celebrated signing the lease, and then had left town, thinking it was all taken care of. But it wasn't. One huge detail was standing in front of me. "Oh God, Tory. I'm sorry."

"What?"

"No, I mean ... I've been so crazed. Listen," God, I needed to pee. "So, an opportunity came up to take this really amazing apartment ... "

"You want to move?" Her face fell, the blue eyes suddenly looking more shadowed and tired than they had before, her shoulders slouching noticeably.

"No! I mean. Well, yeah, but not because of you or anything. It's a studio, and I just kinda want to try living on my own." Watching her face made me feel like I was abandoning her.

"Natalie, I can't pay for this place myself," she said, her voice quiet.

"I know. And I really don't want to screw you. I'm going to give you this month's rent and then you have my last month's rent from when I first moved in, right?"

She nodded, the short, blonde hair falling across her chin.

"So that's two full months before you'd need rent again." I smiled, hoping she'd follow suit.

She just looked at me, no clear emotion on her face. "Okay," she said. "I guess I couldn't really ask for more notice than that."

I shifted my weight again, my feet crossed as I squeezed for all I was worth. This was not the best way to have this conversation. "I'm sorry to spring it on you, Tory. I've loved living here, I just … "

"It's fine, Natalie. I hope the new place is great."

"It … okay," I said. "Thanks."

Tory walked down the narrow hallway toward the kitchen and I bolted into the bathroom. Despite feeling crappy about leaving Tory, I felt lighter. I couldn't wait to move.

The phone rang as I finished my walk around the reservoir in Central Park. I'd thought that some fresh air might clear my head, but I was just as confused as I'd been Friday, and dread was building in my stomach over seeing CJ again on Monday.

"We're going out tonight!" Candace shrieked into the phone.

"Hello," I said.

"Hear me? Put on your party pants!"

"The plastic ones?"

"No, I told you to burn those. It's a figure of speech."

"I don't think it is." I'd never heard anyone say party pants before.

"Well, it is now. What's got your panties all bunched up?"

"Nothing." I didn't feel like getting into all the details of my messed up love life with Miss perfect job, perfect guy.

"Sure," she said, clearly not believing me. "Fine, don't tell. You'll tell us tonight."

"Where are we going?"

"Pre-party at Maggie's. Then to the Webhead awards after party. HellCat won in our category."

"Cool. When were the awards?"

"Last night."

"How come we didn't go to that?"

"We did. I called you. You didn't pick up."

"Oh. Why wasn't the after party last night?"

"Why would it be?" She sounded annoyed now.

"Because the awards were last night." I crossed Park Drive and followed the path out of the Park at 81st Street. "Should the after party be, you know, *after* the awards?"

"Why not have two parties?" she asked. "If it'd been last night, then what would we do tonight?"

"Uh, okay. Where?"

"It's at the Bowery Bar."

"What time to Maggie's?"

"Be there by eight or so. We're starting early."

"Okay, see ya." I hung up, glad to have plans.

Going to Maggie's meant seeing Catalina, which was not my favorite weekend activity. She also made me insecure, so I spent more time getting dressed than I might have otherwise. I settled on a black tank dress with knee boots and a pink clutch purse. I climbed carefully down the six flights to my apartment's front door and went out into the warm night air. Amsterdam—at least the stretch where I lived—was dominated by sports bars and cheap little restaurants, and I felt oddly vulnerable in my high heels among the college guys and girls in jeans who wandered the sidewalks. I flagged the first cab I could get.

"Cross the Park, please," I told him. "Second Avenue and 73rd."

Maggie and Catalina shared a nice two bedroom in a doorman building on 73rd. The place looked like it had been decorated for an IKEA catalog shoot, all sparse clean lines and bright colors.

"Hey!" Maggie cooed as I entered. "You look fantastic!"

"Thanks." I hugged her and smiled as Candace sauntered over with a drink to put into my hand.

"I made Manhattans," she said with a wink.

"What's in a Manhattan?" I looked at the martini glass suspiciously. There was a cherry at the bottom and the rest of the glass was reddish-brown in color.

"Taste it first."

"Never a good sign," I said, walking to sit next to Tamara on the couch.

"It's fine," she said. "You'll like it. It's part of Candace's new life philosophy."

"A drink that mirrors your life philosophy?" I looked to Candace to explain.

"Again?" Catalina moaned from her spot at the end of the coffee table where she sat with her legs pulled under her and to one side. She had the dark cat eye makeup on again, making her brown eyes more startling.

"This isn't a drink for the faint-hearted, Pepper," Candace said, standing in front of us as if she addressed a crowd of more than just four girls. "It's a metaphor for life, really. It starts with the tough stuff—whiskey. It tests your mettle, shows you what you're made of."

"How many of these have you had?" I asked.

"She's on her third or fourth," Tamara said.

"It's got some sweet vermouth—because life isn't all rough ... " She swayed in front of us, staring into her uplifted glass. "And some bitters, because things can be bitter. But, it all ends with a cherry." She smiled a triumphant smile, her red lips revealing her bright white teeth. The speech over, she plopped down on the floor across from me. The mood lightened. "See, Pepper? Doesn't that totally make sense? You fight through the tough stuff to get the reward. The cherry!"

"Sure," I told her. "I think I'm still fighting the tough stuff. In the drink and in life." I was trying to swallow my second sip of the drink, but I ended up putting it down on the table.

"What's up?" Maggie asked, leaning in.

"Same crap. Not worth discussing," I told them. I was lying. I would have loved to go into detail about CJ's amazing kissing, about Lanie's threats ... but not in front of Catalina.

Maggie winked at me, as if she'd read my mind. "We heard you got a new place, though."

I turned to smile at Tamara. "Thanks to Tam," I said. "Yeah, I just told Tory today."

"How'd that go?" Catalina asked, smiling as if she anticipated me describing a fight.

"Great, actually. I felt a little bit bad, but she's got two months to find someone else."

"Who'd want to live there?" Catalina said, evidently unable to keep her talons sheathed for more than five minutes in my presence.

"I guess I would," I told her, picking up the drink and taking a big swallow. One day I hoped to have a good reason to actually punch Catalina.

"I guess you wouldn't," she spat back. "Since you're moving."

"Tory will find someone with no problem," Maggie said. "It's totally affordable."

"Six flights of stairs," Candace said. "They should pay you to live there."

"We all know what New York real estate's like," Tamara said. "It'll be fine."

After two or three more of Candace's life-mimicking Manhattans, we headed out to the party down in the Bowery. We took two cabs, and I was able to talk to Maggie on the way down since the other girls went together. Maggie always managed to make me feel better.

The bar was full of dot-com types—twenty-somethings congratulating each other and themselves, mostly on managing to be in the right place at the right time. I spotted Todd Fraser across the room, wearing a plastic crown and a cape. His company had enjoyed the largest first day gain of any IPO in history the past fall, and he'd evidently been named the king of the internet IPO at the awards the night before.

Candace found her boss, Marc, in the crowd and within minutes, there were shots in all our hands.

"To HellCat!" Shouted Marc.

Candace glowed and we all tossed back the shot.

There were many more shots that night, and I remembered just a few of them. What I didn't remember as clearly was at what point exactly I went outside to call CJ.

"Hello?" His voice was warm, perfect.

"Hey," I said, trying not to slur.

"Natalie. Are you feeling better? I called you a couple times."

"I know. I'm sorry. I'm fine."

"Are you out?"

CJ was out, too. I could hear a crowd in the background. "Yeah, I'm down at Bowery."

"I'm not far," he said. "Karma."

"Cool," I said.

Karma was a hookah joint down in the East Village.

"Wanna meet up?" CJ asked. He sounded timid. Like he wasn't sure I would say yes.

"Yes!" I said, maybe too enthusiastically.

"I'll come up," he said. "Stay there?"

"I'll wait for you and we'll figure it out," I told him.

"See you soon, Natalie."

"Bye."

I went back inside, the din louder than I remembered it being when I'd stepped out. There was a girl lying over the bar top, her head flung back as a bartender shot something into her mouth from a dark bottle, and several people were chanting some kind of frat-boy drinking verse. I looked around, feeling crowded and jostled, until I found my friends in a corner toward the back. I pushed through the crowd and waited near them, not talking to anyone and trying to pretend I wasn't watching the door. I had at least one more beer before CJ's golden head appeared toward the front.

I watched him look around, his dark eyes scanning the crowd as several women nearby watched him and stood a bit taller. He wore a dark short-sleeved shirt, and even when he was by himself, he wore a faint smile. After a moment, he spotted me, and the dimples appeared. Even across a crowd, I could feel the draw to CJ, my skin tingled and my heart beat faster. We pushed through the crowd toward each other and met in the middle.

With people pushing at us from all sides, it was almost like being alone. CJ's strong arms went around me, and I laced mine around his neck.

"Hey, beautiful," he said into my ear. His breath was warm on my neck and sent shivers through me.

"Hey," I said back. "I missed you."

"Me too. You wanna stay here?"

"Not at all."

"Need to say goodbye?"

I didn't want to fight my way back through the crowd to my friends, and I didn't want to see Catalina. Or more specifically, I didn't want her to see CJ. "I'll call Maggie from outside."

"Okay."

We stepped out and I realized that the world was spinning slightly. As we walked down the sidewalk, it got worse, and the sidewalk seemed to slope and move under my feet.

"Maybe I should take my shoes off," I said, as CJ caught me the second time I tripped over nothing.

"Or maybe you just had a bit too much to drink." He laughed.

He was right. I was starting to feel more than just a bit tipsy and worried that maybe I would vomit. I might have moaned a bit.

"Let's go home," CJ said.

As soon as we got into a cab, I leaned my head into the warmth of CJ's strong shoulder. He pulled me close, and I could feel his lips against the top of my head. As the glaring lights of the city streaked past our windows, I put everything else aside and decided to exist in that moment. It was one I would pull up later throughout my life when I needed to find my center. A quiet cab with CJ. I didn't know how, but CJ always managed to bring me peace.

The comfort of CJ's arms must have put me to sleep, because the next thing I remembered was being shaken gently and pulled from the cab.

"Natalie, come on," CJ was saying. He was leaning over me, sliding his arms beneath me, and preparing to carry me like a child.

"No, no," I said. "I'm awake." I slid out the curbside door and the cab took off. Standing felt like too much effort, and I decided that sitting might be easier. As I slid to the ground, CJ let out a low chuckle.

"Okay, Natalie," he said, pulling me up by the armpits. He leaned forward, wrapping his arms beneath my knees and around my back and then lifted me into the air. He held me close against him, and I automatically wrapped my arms around his neck and laid my head against his shoulder again.

"CJ," I said in a small voice. I was just reassuring myself that it was he who carried me, that he was really there. I might've been drunk, but I was happy.

"Come on," he said, laughing. He turned and walked us into a tall building. In the lobby he stopped, turning with me in his arms to talk to a doorman behind the low counter.

"Allen, this is Natalie," he said.

"Hi Natalie," the doorman smiled. He had a short salt-and-pepper afro and a warm smile.

"Hi," I said. Were I not drunk, it would have occurred to me that meeting people while being physically carried was not ideal.

CJ took me upstairs to his apartment, and I felt my stomach roiling—with either nerves or nausea. I wasn't sure which and began to seriously regret the shots I'd done.

CJ set me on a low dark leather couch and placed a soft brown blanket over my lap.

"Be right back," he winked. He reappeared a moment later with two tall glasses of water and sat beside me. "You doing okay?"

"I'm okay," I said, trying to pronounce the words carefully so I didn't slur. It didn't work.

"Long night." He laughed.

"Yeah. It's been a long week," I said. "Everything with Lanie, and now I'm moving and you're here, and there's so much to figure out."

"Is there? You're moving?" he asked.

"Just down to Chelsea," I reassured him.

CJ looked thoughtful, and not completely happy, which was unusual. "Natalie, I need to tell you some things, but first—what's going on at work? Did something happen after we got back?" He was sitting close to me, his arm over the back of the couch behind me, and worry making his dark eyes impossibly deep. A tiny furrow appeared above his eyebrows.

I reached two fingers up to smooth the worry I saw on his forehead. I traced the lines away, then let my fingers run down the side of his face, lingering over the soft stubble I felt along his jaw. Finally, I traced his lips, letting my fingers linger on the soft fullness of his bottom lip. CJ closed his eyes, and I could hear his breath quicken. I leaned in to kiss him, but he stopped me, opening his eyes, and putting a strong hand on my shoulder.

"What's going on at work, Natalie?"

"Oh," I half-moaned. "It's a mess. I was so ready to forget all my stupid rules and then Lanie Bill told me that there's a new 'no fraternization' rule and that if I fraternize than she'll tell everyone about the fraternization and then she'll fire me, and it's all because she wants to fraternize with Damon, but I don't think he wants to fraternize her back, and she's completely psycho to start with so now she's a lovesick psycho and she's taking it out on us." The effort of delivering that sentence—and my new fixation with the word "fraternize"—was exhausting. I slumped back on the couch, remembering why I wasn't supposed to be sitting on CJ's couch, in CJ's apartment on a Saturday night after midnight.

"That's a lot of fraternizing," CJ said softly.

"Or really, it's not," I told him, my eyes pulling shut.

"Right," he said. "Well, if we just hold off a bit, maybe it won't matter."

I wasn't sure what he was talking about, but my eyelids felt like concrete. "What?"

"Drink your water, Natalie," he said, holding the glass to my lips.

I drank. "Love you, CJ," I said, not thinking. I was caught in the warmth and tenderness of his actions and his eyes. I was wrapped in a warm blanket, he was taking care of me, and I felt like I was floating in a happy place. A happy place that was spinning a little too fast, but happy nonetheless.

I awoke in a soft warm bed with light filtering through cellular shades, giving the room a soft gray cast. At first, I wasn't sure where I was. As I stretched and looked around, realization dawned. The biggest tip off was the golden head resting on the pillow beside me, CJ's strong back bare under the light duvet. One arm rested above the covers, and I stared at the carved muscles of his shoulder and bicep as I tried to piece together the time between leaving the bar and coming here.

Quietly, I slipped out of the bed and found the bathroom. I was surprised to find myself in an unfamiliar T-shirt, and realized it must be CJ's. And that CJ must have helped me put it on. I wished I could remember that. I washed my face and brushed my teeth, hoping CJ wouldn't mind too much that I used his toothbrush. I also spent just a second looking over all the manly products in his medicine cabinet—and reassuring myself that there were no signs of frequent female guests, before turning off the light and climbing back into the queen-sized bed.

Wow. I was in CJ's bed. I was fairly certain that nothing had happened. Had CJ even kissed me? I couldn't remember, but I didn't feel like he had. Instead, I felt a coil of tension within me, a mixture of things said and unsaid, my desire for the man beside me driving me forward despite the potential consequences.

I laid a hand on CJ's smooth tanned shoulder. His skin was warm, soft. I let my palm trail down the exposed arm, loving the way the muscles felt, bulging and firm beneath my fingers. As I traced the same line back up, CJ rolled over onto his back and turned his head toward me. One dark lash-fringed eye opened slowly and a sexy smile spread across his face.

"Good morning, beautiful."

"Hi," I said, my hand on his bare chest now. There was a tiny tuft of golden hair just in the center of the line between his pecs.

"I can't think of anything better than waking up with Natalie Pepper in my bed," he said, his voice thick with sleep.

My heart lunged and I scooted closer to him, my leg pressing between his beneath the sheets and my stomach touching his hip. I laid my head in the crook of his neck, keeping my hand on his chest, and letting it move slowly downward. "I can," I whispered.

CJ stopped my hand before it reached its destination.

"Natalie," he said, his voice a low moan. "I don't think we're there yet," he said.

"We could be," I told him, taking his earlobe between my teeth gently.

"Oh, God," he moaned, rolling to face me. "Trust me, I'd like that. But we need to talk first. There are some things we need to talk about sober."

Uncertainty did little to quell the nervous fire of arousal inside me, but it dampened it enough that I stilled my hand on CJ's hard flat stomach.

"What things?"

"Do you remember what you said last night?" he asked.

"Not really."

He smiled at me. "Okay. I'll remind you. You told me about the threat that Lanie made at work Friday. You used the word 'fraternization' quite a lot."

The word sounded very familiar and I had a vague memory of repeating it to him on his couch. "Okay." I didn't know exactly what I'd told him. Had I mentioned my kiss with Damon? Did I tell him that I hadn't wanted to mention the conversation with Lanie because of the mistake with Damon?

"And you seemed pretty worried about losing your job," CJ continued.

"I am," I said.

"But there's something else I need to tell you." CJ's dark eyes were serious.

Worry sprouted between the swirling clouds of desire inside me. "What?" I whispered.

"How do you feel about long distance?"

"Running? Travel? What do you mean?"

"Relationships." CJ looked grim.

"What?" What was he telling me? Shock trickled through me. CJ couldn't be leaving.

"I have a job offer," he said. "Back home in Buffalo."

"What?" Incredulity made my voice harsh. "No! You can't leave!"

CJ smiled sadly. "It's a good offer, Natalie, and my parents could use a hand closer to home. They're getting older and having a tough time getting some things done around the house. I could help out a lot. I started talking to the company up there when I was pretty sure things were never going to work with us. I didn't think I could be near you and not be with you, so this was an alternative. And now it seems like it might actually be a great job."

I didn't say anything, but I could feel the tears welling at the thought of CJ leaving me. The city around us started to loom in my mind, menacing and cold.

"Plus, then we wouldn't be fraternizing," he said, his voice falling to a whisper.

"CJ," I said into his neck. "Is this already decided?"

"Not completely."

"Can't I convince you not to go? We've barely gotten a chance."

"We've had one, Natalie ... we've had a few."

I looked into his brown eyes, guilt adding to the load of emotions threatening to push the tears down my cheeks. I was the one who'd denied us our chance. We could have been together all this time.

"I need to talk to Irene about terms," he said, his voice louder as he discussed specifics. "None of that has been mentioned and I don't know what she's thinking of besides the salary. I want to be sure it's a good opportunity, too—not just an excuse to get home."

"Irene?" I asked.

He gave me an odd look, his eyes searching my face. "She runs a small investment firm in Buffalo. I met her when I was still in school."

I decided that I probably didn't like Irene.

"CJ, I don't know if I have any influence here or not, but I'm just going to say this ... please don't go." My voice dropped. "I don't want you to go."

"You have a lot of influence, Natalie. But I also know how important your job is to you. Maybe this is the best thing."

"I don't care about my job." My voice was small. We both knew it wasn't true.

CJ's arms went around me then, and we kissed for a while, but there was a sadness between us that had not been there before. And even as his lips pushed most thoughts from my mind, I couldn't help turning the past few weeks over and around, looking for the exact point where I'd pushed him away hard enough to make him actually decide to leave me.

Chapter Sixteen

NANTUCKET REDS

Lulu

I SAT on the end of my tiny bed and thought about my options. Clearly, Tippy was trying to upset me. And it was working, but I could not let her see that. On the other hand, Andrew was allowing it, and I wanted him to know I was upset. Then again, appearing at odds in front of Tippy would show her that she was succeeding in her plans to upset whatever existed between Andrew and me. I wasn't sure how to behave, but decided that my best course of action was probably the tried and true. I would pretend to be wonderfully happy in front of Tippy while simultaneously withholding all sexual affection from her clueless son. I hoped he would get the idea and stand up to his tyrannical mother before I lost all respect for him.

The bikini fit perfectly. Even if I left this entire situation humiliated and heartbroken, at least I'd have a gorgeous Betsy Johnson suit to show for it. I tied a sarong around my waist and ventured down to the pool, pulling my hair into a high knot as I went.

Andrew sat on the diving board at the end of a long sparkling blue pool. Cherry was in the water at his feet, teasing him.

"But do you loo-oove her?" she sang.

"I might," Andrew said, laughing as Cherry splashed him.

"Andrew's in lo-ove," Cherry sang.

"That's very childish," Tippy called from her lounge chair, clearly annoyed.

My heart lurched at the use of that word again, and at the fact that he'd allow his sister and mother to believe that he loved me. But I didn't want them to know I'd overheard, so I called out as I came down the steps on the patio. "How's the water, Cherry?"

"Come in!" she called, paddling over to the shallow end. "It's perfect!"

I untied my sarong, taking my time letting it fall from my hips. I looked over my shoulder to see Andrew watching me. Perfect. I locked eyes with him and squirted suntan lotion into my palm. Never losing his gaze, I smeared it over my shoulders and arms, breaking the stare only to drop one thin strap down my shoulder to apply lotion to my shoulder and the top of my breast. I closed my eyes and tilted my head back while I did this, as if my own touch had me nearly over the edge. I finished applying lotion, catching Andrew's eye once more. He was practically drooling. I knew that if he stood, we'd all see exactly how interested he was in my lotion show. I glanced at Tippy to see if she'd noticed my questionable behavior, but she seemed to be at least pretending to read her magazine. She despised me anyway, and I was no longer very worried about her opinion.

"Are you planning to sit there all day?" I asked Andrew, climbing to the diving board behind him. I nudged him with my foot. "Scoot," I said.

His face reddened and he cast a guilty glance at Tippy, who was pretending not to watch us over the top of her New Yorker.

He scooted forward and leaned over into the pool, swimming to the side in the shallow end and turning back to face me, his chest shining as the water ran off him. He did look amazing in his black swim trunks, his perfect arms and chest just the right color of golden as he pushed the water from his wavy hair.

I walked quickly up the board and dove, executing the perfect jackknife that I had learned in my teens. I found the bottom of the pool with my hands and then turned, pushing off to come back up.

"Can you teach me how to do that?" Cherry asked the second my head broke the surface.

"Sure," I said.

"I bet you could teach me a few things," Andrew said quietly, swimming over to put his arms around me.

I ducked from his hold and took Cherry by the hand.

"Lesson one," I began, taking her to stand next to me beside the pool.

We spent the rest of the afternoon perfecting our dives while Andrew slowly seemed to understand that I was angry with him. Tippy, for her part, seemed to ignore us almost completely. In the late afternoon, as the sun began to slide back down the endless blue sky, she stood.

"Neal should be here soon," she announced. "Cocktails will be at six o'clock on the verandah." She picked her way back into the house, the floppy hat bouncing with every step.

"Shall we go up and shower?" Andrew asked, swimming to my side to put his arms around me.

Cherry was reading a magazine in the sun.

Even though I was angry, it was hard not to be swayed by the sparkling blue eyes and Andrew's warm hands on my skin under the water. I wrapped my legs around him and pressed myself against him.

"Or we could stay in the pool for a while," he murmured, his lips finding mine.

I cursed myself for being unable to remain angry, but I was so ridiculously attracted to this man. I kissed him for a long minute and then pulled away. "You need to stand up to your mother," I told him in a whisper.

"I know," he said, a boyish grin on his sexy face. He pulled me closer and I could feel the firmness of his erection pressed against me. "I will, Lu. I promise."

I glanced up to see Cherry lying on her back with her eyes closed as Andrew guided me toward the edge of the pool. Even if she'd looked up, she'd see only our heads. I grasped the sides of the pool on either side of Andrew's head as he slipped his fingers beneath the thin fabric of my suit. In a few minutes, I had much more than his fingers inside my suit and I couldn't help but glance around to make sure no one was watching us. That was when I saw a ghostly white face appear in the glass between the fluttering curtains on the second floor of the Barton's palatial home. I blinked to clear my vision. Was it Tippy? I opened my eyes again to find her gone, and soon after I found myself beyond caring as Andrew lifted me slowly up and down, the lapping of the pool water matching our movements.

———

It turned out that cocktails meant that Tippy had invited forty people over to wander the yard and sip drinks on her patio. Sheldon evidently played the role of waiter as well, and he wandered the crowd offering a platter of appetizers on his outstretched hand.

Mr. Barton arrived in the midst of the party, and crossed the lawn to greet me where I sat with Cherry on a lounge chair.

"Lulu, it's wonderful that you could come," he said. He seemed genuine.

I wondered how he'd ended up with someone as cold and stiff as Tippy. "Thank you for having me," I said.

"I see that you've got a drink. Is Andrew taking care of you?" he looked around for his son.

"He's doing fine," I said.

"I'm keeping her company," Cherry said, taking my hand.

"Thanks," I told her.

"You know," she said, leaning in. "You're not the first girl that Andrew has brought out here, but I like you best."

I couldn't help but swivel my head to gape at her, and had to remind myself that she was only thirteen and this was probably not meant to hurt my feelings. "Oh? How many others?"

"Oh, not many. Mom scares most of them away before they can get this far," she said. "But there've been a few. Mom thinks that most women only date Andrew for his money." She flipped her long blonde hair and looked around her, sipping her pink soda. She seemed to be practicing for the years to come, when she would be sipping real drinks and seducing the linen-clad men around us. "You're different, though," she said.

"Really? How?"

"Well, the other two girls that have been here spent all their time trying to get in good with my mom. Or hanging all over my brother. You're actually fun." She grinned.

I thought about that and watched the people circulate around us.

It reminded me of parties at my Uncle Jorge's house, where I sat unnoticed in a corner while the adults drank and put on false faces for one another to enjoy. It made me feel sick then—the efforts that adults seemed willing to go to in order to impress one another—and it made me feel slightly ill now. I smiled at Cherry, feeling a little bit sorry for her for the family into which she was born. Maybe I should be feeling sorry for Andrew; if only I could see past how attracted I was to him.

"So I'm just one in a parade?" I asked.

"Oh no," Cherry said, bobbing her head. "Mom thinks you're different, too."

"What does that mean?"

"She says you're an 'unknown.' That's why she wanted you to come—so she could figure you out. She does think you're after his money, though." Cherry said this last part offhandedly, then quickly covered her mouth with her manicured hand. "Ooh," she gasped. "I'm sorry. I'm so bad at this."

"It's fine," I told her. "I figured that."

Cherry blushed and looked up from under the same dark lashes that fringed Andrew's blue eyes. "You are different though, Lulu. I really like you."

"Thanks," I said, pulling her into a quick hug. "I'd better go find Andrew."

"Hey gorgeous," Andrew said as I approached. He was standing with a small cluster of men who were all smoking cigars. One of them was wearing pants in an audacious salmon color.

"I love your pink pants," I told the man.

He stood with his mouth open for a moment, then corrected me. "They're Nantucket Red."

"Well, the color is wonderful," I told him. "Whatever they're called. I have a skirt that color, and I always get compliments on it."

He huffed and then elbowed the man next to him, who was laughing. I did not feel that I was in on whatever joke I'd made, and chose to let it go.

Andrew stayed by my side for the rest of the evening, and when we finally settled for dinner—with only a few of the guests still present—I felt more relaxed, though Cherry's words were still in my mind.

Dinner was better than the last I'd had with his family, only in that I wasn't ill. Tippy was in rare form. As we sat, she announced that she'd had several "highballs" and wasn't sure what her appetite might be like. I began to see why Tippy might be so thin. And perhaps why she was called Tippy.

Neal and the man in the pink pants bantered over salad while

Andrew's hand rested on my upper thigh. As the lobster was served, I found Tippy staring at me down the length of the table. Every time I glanced up, she seemed to be regarding me with her wide watery eyes.

"Your mother is staring at me," I whispered to Andrew finally.

"Because you're beautiful."

"I doubt that's it," I said.

As if our whispering was a cue, Tippy announced to the table, "I hope everyone has had time to meet Andrew's friend, Lulu."

There were nods and murmurs around the table as a blush climbed my cheeks. I smiled and returned to my food, hoping she was done. She was not.

"Lulu is from a small town in Brazil. She," here she paused dramatically, "is an orphan!" She emphasized the last word and then smiled triumphantly at me. "Isn't that sad?"

"It's fine," I told her, hoping she'd stop.

"Mother!" Andrew said, his voice harsh.

"That's enough, dear." Neal stared down the length of the table at his wife.

Tippy waved her hand in front of her, dismissing their concerns. "Lucky for her, she had an uncle with money to save her. Perhaps she's always just looking for a wealthy man to save her from her sad circumstances. For some of us, patterns repeat, you know."

I whipped my head to look at Andrew, who was staring at me with a strange look on his face. I hadn't told him anything about my past, and this was not the way I wanted him to learn of it. His hand had tightened on my thigh, and I knew that he was trying to decide how to handle his mother's inappropriate comments. He was angry. He was going to stand up to her.

Other guests looked uncomfortable, and Andrew's father chuckled and then chimed in, "That's my wife, always making drama when there's none to be had!"

"Oh, no, Neal," she said. "It's like a soap opera. She was in an orphanage for years, but when her rich uncle suddenly took an interest, she became heir to one of the largest fortunes in Florianopolis. Makes you wonder what she did for her 'uncle,' doesn't it? Did he come with plans to adopt you, dear, or did you have to *convince* him?"

I was shaking in anger, waiting for Andrew to say something. Anything.

"She's pretty enough," Tippy said to the man next to her, "I'm sure most men might be willing to give up quite a lot depending on what she was willing to ... "

"Tippy!" Mr. Barton said, silencing her.

"Mother," Andrew said, finally. "That's more than enough." His voice was icy.

"Don't scold me at my table, Andrew." Tippy lifted her glass to her lips, looking quite merry. She shot a look of hatred at her husband.

"Don't make assumptions about things you can't possibly know," he said, his words full of venom. He put an arm around my shoulders, looking into my eyes with obvious concern.

"Oh, I do know. I had Lucien look into it." She addressed the woman just down the table from her, another overly made up, reed-thin socialite. "Lucien is the absolute best investigator. If you ever need his number ... " At least the woman she spoke to had the grace to look shocked.

I'd had enough. "Excuse me," I said, pushing my chair back from the table. I gave a thin smile to the table and turned for the stairs to my room. I could hear low murmurs behind me, and Andrew's angry voice echoing as he spoke to his mother. My head was spinning and the words he said were muffled by the sound of my angry blood rushing.

I pulled my bag together, marched back down the stairs, and let myself out the front door, hurrying toward the street in the gathering darkness. I cared about Andrew, but if he was willing to let his family speak to me—about me—that way, then I was not going to stay.

I walked toward the main part of town, where the Jitney had dropped us off, with no real plan in mind. I'd get myself back to the city, I figured, even if it meant paying a cab to take me. After all, I had my uncle's fortune, didn't I?

The tears rolling down my cheeks irritated me, and I wiped them away angrily as I walked. As I came to a main street, I saw several bars and restaurants, and decided that maybe one drink and some time alone would allow me to figure out what to do.

"Lu!" I could hear Andrew running to catch up with me.

I stopped, wheeling around. "Why are you following me?"

"Because ... Lu, look, I'm so sorry. About what my mom said, about those things ... "

"Those things are true," I told him, my voice thick with tears.

Andrew looked surprised, but then his face softened. "Lu, you never told me. You won't talk about your family."

"Because I don't have a family!" I said. "And sometimes I think maybe it's better that way. Look at yours!" I turned and marched into the nearest bar, climbing onto a stool.

"What can I get you, miss?" The bartender had grey hair protruding from his ears and nose, but none on his head. He looked like a sweet man all the same.

In my anger and confusion, I couldn't think of what to order, and Tippy was forefront in my mind. Her signature drink tumbled from my lips since I'd heard her order it several times that night. "Whiskey highball with ginger and a twist."

Andrew had claimed the stool next to me and was watching me as if I might turn and attack him suddenly like a caged jaguar. "Lu, are you all right?"

"No!" I shouted at him. "Why did you wait so long to say anything? I don't talk about my family, and now an entire town full of strangers knows more than most of my friends!"

"But why don't you talk about it?" he asked.

"Because ... " I cringed. Shame flooded me and mingled with the fury piping within me. I felt like I might explode. I carefully controlled my voice. "Your mother is right."

"What do you mean?" Andrew asked. "About what? Not about your uncle making you ... ?"

"God, no!" How could he think that? "But the truth is bad enough. I was eight when my uncle came to get me. Eight! He let me live in the orphanage for five years by myself. My family was killed when I was three years old, and he was the only family I had that knew I even existed."

"How ... how did they ... "

"My mother was kidnapped from our home one day while I was with the nanny on a walk." I stared into Andrew's face as I spoke. I had never discussed this with anyone, and didn't know how to tell it. The only way to get it out was to hold my voice emotionless, colorless, and just tell him. His eyes widened as I spoke, and he took one of my hands. I let him, but I could barely feel the touch of his skin on mine. "They took my brother, too. He was an infant, just born." I shut my eyes, remembering what little I could of my mother, of the chubby arms and legs that were my little brother. Kidnappings were not uncommon where I grew up. For some, it was a primary source of income. I looked down for a moment, then took a sip of my drink. Tippy's drink. It tasted like poison.

Andrew sat waiting, holding my hand.

"They called my father at work. They asked for money. They told him they had his whole family. My father took them the money they asked for, but they killed him anyway. They killed them all."

"Oh Lulu," Andrew said, a tear rolling down his cheek. "Oh God."

I stared at him. There was nothing else to say.

"And my mother made it out like ... God, I'm so sorry." He

took a sip of my drink. "But didn't you have family? Grandparents?"

"No. My mother's family did not approve of the match she had made, and they disowned her when she married my father. Her parents and her brother lived far away, in a city in the north. They never heard about her children. And my father's parents were gone. There was only his brother, Jorge."

"Why didn't he come get you right away? Why did you ever go to an orphanage?"

"He knew of me, but he didn't want me. He took my father's money. I wasn't the heir—he was. And only when he became sick I became important. He could not have children, and he wanted to leave his money to a blood relative. He didn't trust his wife."

"I see." Andrew was looking at me with pity now, and I despised it. "Was he good to you?"

"He let me rot in an orphanage for five years. What do you think?"

"Lu," he said, his voice soft. He tried to take me in his arms, but I pushed him away.

"This," I said, "is why I do not tell people about this."

"So the apartment on Grove?" Andrew asked. "It's your uncle's, right?"

"My mother's brother."

"Jorge was your father's brother? So how did this other uncle find you?"

"Through Jorge's wife. Once Jorge was gone, she helped me find what was left of my mother's family. While Jorge was alive, he wouldn't allow it. My uncle Esteban owns the Grove apartment. He moved to New York when I was in high school and brought me here with him. I've been back to Brazil only a year since then, after college."

We drank in silence for a bit, Andrew rubbing my hands as we sat side by side. He ordered some food for us, a bottle of wine. After a while, I felt less angry, and realized that I was exhausted.

"My mother's been calling," Andrew said, checking his phone. "Lulu, do you think you can forgive her? Can you forgive me for allowing her to go on like that?"

"I don't know," I said honestly.

"Will you come back to the house?"

I looked around us. It was late and the street was full of young people wandering in groups. Their voices rose and fell in the night air as they called to each other. I wished I were with them, carefree and happy.

"I won't sleep in that closet. I won't follow her ridiculous rules."

"Sleep in my room. We'll move your things."

I pointed to my bag at my feet.

"It will be easy, then." Andrew smiled, the crinkles appearing at the corners of his eyes. "I'm so sorry Lu, for everything. Come back. It will be different, I promise."

I was too tired to argue.

The next day I woke in Andrew's arms, in the beautiful room overlooking the beach and the yard. The sunlight caught dust particles as they floated on its rays, and the world felt happy again. I decided that I could stay one more day and just avoid Tippy as much as possible.

"Let's go to the beach today," Andrew said, his voice sleepy as he pulled himself on top of me, our bodies pressed together and his elbows on either side of my head.

"But not yet," I said, arching into him.

"Not yet," he agreed.

We spent another hour in bed, and finally put on bathing suits and found our way downstairs. Tippy sat in a wicker chair in the living room, dressed in light blue capri pants and a light blue top, reading the paper. I had the feeling she was waiting for us.

"Good morning," she chirped, looking only at Andrew.

"Mother," Andrew said, his voice cold.

I smiled triumphantly and followed him to the kitchen. We packed a picnic, eating breakfast as we worked, and then made our way out the side door of the house.

We spread a blanket in the sand, and Andrew put up an umbrella for shade. The sun was warm, and the dense muggy air enveloped us like a soggy sweater. The gentle waves were a relief when we wandered into the surf, holding hands.

As we lounged in the sun later, I felt that maybe telling Andrew everything had been the right thing. Maybe Tippy dragging everything out would turn out to be for the best. I felt closer to him now, and he was treating me just a little bit more gently, more lovingly.

He was rubbing lotion onto my shoulders when Tippy and Cherry appeared, dragging chairs and a tall blonde woman with very large breasts behind them.

"You remember Isabella," Tippy told her son.

"Hello, Andrew," the blonde girl said. Something about the way she eyed him made me feel that I needed to put my guard up.

Andrew's hands stilled on my shoulders.

"Isabella," he returned.

The tone of his voice chilled me. Who was this?

"I'm Lulu," I told her, sitting up. I couldn't stop the impulse to pull my dark hair over one shoulder and sit straighter.

"Sorry, yes," Andrew said, recovering himself. "Isabella, this is my girlfriend, Lulu."

"Lovely to meet you," she said, taking a seat on the other side of Andrew.

I noticed Tippy trying to catch my eye with an evil smile on her face, and I purposely ignored her.

"Will you swim with me, Lu?" Cherry asked. She bounced in front of me and made her eyes into sad puppy eyes.

"Of course," I said. As I followed her toward the water, I glanced back to see the blonde with a hand on Andrew's arm.

I had no doubt that Isabella's presence was some kind of Tippy-initiated plot. I was getting tired of fighting her.

I swam with Cherry, bobbing in the waves as I watched the beach. Isabella had stretched out next to Andrew and they appeared to be deep in conversation, their heads close together.

"Who is that?" I asked Cherry.

"Oh, Isabella?" She looked worried for a second, but seemed to put it aside. "That's Andrew's old fiancée."

"Fianceé?" I repeated. "He was engaged?"

"Only for a little while," Cherry said quickly.

"What happened?" I asked. Clearly, they were still close.

"Tippy threatened to disown him if he married her." Cherry said this and then bobbed under an oncoming wave. I was so busy watching the shore that I didn't see or hear it, and the wave caught me sideways, knocking me down and forcing me under its churn. I came back up sputtering, and wiped my eyes, annoyed to see Andrew and Isabella walking together toward the small ice cream cart down the beach.

When Cherry and I came back to the sand, Andrew handed me an ice cream cone and patted the spot beside him. Isabella offered a false smile and then turned away, her face falling. Tippy watched with open interest.

"So," I said. "You were engaged?"

Andrew looked guilty, then seemed to recover himself. "Yes, for a bit. We agreed that it wouldn't work out."

"Right," Isabella said, sounding less than certain.

"I see."

"My family has a house just down the beach," Isabella said.

"Sounds as if your credentials are in order, then. What was the problem?" I was talking mostly to Tippy.

Andrew's jaw dropped.

"Nothing, it just ... didn't work out," Isabella said.

"Lulu," Andrew said.

I shot him a fierce look and whatever he'd been planning to say died in his throat.

Back at the house that evening, Andrew was quiet as we dressed for dinner.

"You're angry with me now?" I asked him.

"I don't know what to think. You're as bad as Tippy. You didn't need to be rude to Isabella."

"Seriously?" I sat on the edge of the bed and watched him as he pulled on a pair of light linen khakis over the red boxer briefs he wore. He moved to a whitewashed dresser and pulled a pair of socks from it, purposely avoiding my gaze. "Andrew. Your mother is plotting to keep us apart. Surely you see that?"

He didn't answer.

"It sounds like she did the same with Isabella. Your sister told me that Tippy called her a 'money grubber' because her family isn't 'old money'—whatever that means."

"Tippy wants what's best for me," Andrew said. "I'm her only son."

"You're an adult. You decide what's best for you."

Andrew stopped moving around the room and knelt in front of me, taking my hands. "Lulu, you can't possibly understand what it's like. This is just part of our family. We're very protective of our ... "

"Of your money!" I cried. He didn't seem to see the truth that was right in front of him. This behavior of his mother's was clearly a repeating pattern. And if he was blind to it, then he wasn't going to put a stop to it.

"No, it isn't that, it's ... "

"It's all about money, Andrew! And it's so ridiculous because I don't care about money! I have more money than I'll ever be able to spend. And I don't care at all about it. I'd rather be poor and have a real family, but I don't. And the last thing I want is to part of a family that cares about nothing else. You don't even see how lucky you are to have each other. Instead, you're all acting like you're on some kind of soap opera, plotting and scheming!

"Your mother hates me for no reason at all, and you don't have the balls to defend me. It's ludicrous. You're twenty-eight years old. Either stand up to your mother or go fuck yourself!"

Andrew just stared at me. But the thing that gave me resolve was that he didn't bother to deny it. I believed that he saw the truth in my words, and if I was right, then we had no future at all —even if he did actually love me.

I stood and stormed around, packing my things as my loose white dress flowed around me in a way that was totally at odds with the sharp edges of my anger. I left the house for the second time that weekend, and this time I didn't wait for Andrew to stop me, though I could hear him calling me from the driveway. I practically ran into town and stepped directly into a cab that was waiting in front of a restaurant on the main street.

"Manhattan!" I barked at the driver.

"Lady, that's gonna be ..."

"I don't care. Why is everything about money?"

"Well, because it's gonna be a lot of money," he said.

"It's fine. Just stop by an ATM on our way into the village and I'll pay you double what you want. Just get me back to the city, please."

The guy let out a low whistle and I laid my head against the seat and watched the Hamptons slide by as tears slipped down my face.

Chapter Seventeen

BUFFALO BECKONS

Natalie

Monday at work, CJ stopped by at lunchtime. I felt my entire mood lift as his broad form appeared in my doorway. God, he made a tie look good.

"Hey Natalie," he said.

His smile was missing and it was jarring. He looked worried.

"What's up?" I asked.

"Just wanted to let you know that I'm headed out overnight."

"Okay," I said slowly. "To ... ?"

"Buffalo. The thing I told you about. I'm going to go talk to Irene, see my parents."

My heart fell. I knew he was pursuing the job, but while I sat in his apartment, it just hadn't felt possible that he would leave. Now it seemed all too real.

"Oh," I said. I could think of nothing to add to that.

"I'll call you when I get back."

"Oh." Full of creativity.

He turned and a cloud settled over my desk. I swung my chair around and stared out the window at the sun glistening off the metallic sides of the Empire State Building. Up close, the windows were all edged with a thin red line. In pictures or from the street, you really never noticed that. I stared at the tower and thought about how there was always more than what you could see—even when you believed you knew something well. CJ had said he would wait. He told me that he'd wait as long as it took. I remembered staring at him in the biting cold as we'd stood inches apart in Union Square just a few months ago. And he'd promised to wait.

But CJ was young, smart, and good looking. How long would a guy like that wait for me? I was nothing special. Just a California transplant with daddy issues. Maybe I shouldn't be surprised that he was giving up on us. I'd never given him a reason to believe that waiting would result in anything but more waiting. Even the other night when I'd finally told him about everything at work and tried to tell him that I was ready to take a chance, I'd blown it.

And now he was going to leave.

I was an idiot.

I was pulled from my misery by the ring of my office phone.

"Natalie Pepper."

"Pepper. Ready for the big move?" It was Tamara. I'd told her that I'd move this weekend. Of course, I'd done nothing to prepare for that to happen.

"I need to book a truck," I told her.

"I've got one for you. I'll call them. What time?"

"First thing, I guess. Saturday?"

"Sounds good. I'll help."

"Okay."

"What's wrong? You sound terrible."

"Thanks."

"Meet me for lunch?"

"Okay. Where?"

"Just come to my office," Tamara said.

I was too morose to think of anything more creative.

As I was on my way out, Lanie called my name down the hall. Actually, she called a name that was meant for me.

"Natalia!"

I walked to her office door. "Close that time," I said.

"Did you tell Jessica what I told you Friday?"

"Who is Jessica?"

"You know, the marketing coordinator." Lanie waved her hands as if she were too busy to be bothered with correct names.

"Justine?"

"Whoever! Just make sure that little vixen knows that I'm watching her, too. No dating at the office. This isn't a fraternity party."

"Um. Okay." I turned and shook my head as I walked away. I wondered what it took to have people actually committed. Lanie Bill was undoubtedly off her rocker.

"Justine," I said, walking into Justine's cube.

She turned, her adorable bangs bouncing as she smiled at me. "Natalie, are you okay?" Her eyes widened.

"Yeah, just tired. Listen," I said. "Lanie's on the warpath about weird stuff right now. She has it in for anyone dating around the office. I know you're not, but just wanted to put it out there. She's being really weird about it."

Justine actually blushed. "Oh," she stuttered. "I ... "

I leaned forward. This was interesting. "Are you seeing someone here?" I asked, my voice hushed.

Her eyes darted around. "I know you told me ... but, well ... I'm sleeping with Damon," she blurted. She put her hand over her eyes, she just couldn't bear to look at me.

I laughed without meaning to. "Of course you are," I said, giggling.

"What?"

"Look," I told her. "I seriously don't care. Just be careful with that one ... and don't let Lanie find out. I think he's actually the origin of this tirade."

"What?"

"She has a thing for him."

"Oh, that."

"So be careful, okay?"

Justine looked miserable and nodded.

"I'm headed out. I might not come back today."

"Got it."

"Hey," Tamara said as I got out of a cab in front of her building.

"Where to?" I asked.

"Not feeling creative," she said. "Let's just go in here."

We found ourselves back in the same bar where we'd had drinks before. "They serve food?" I asked.

"They serve drinks," Tamara smiled.

"How are things?" I asked her.

"Do you mean 'The Hair?'" She smiled, clearly desperate to tell me something.

"Tell me about The Hair."

"Oh my God, Pepper. He's so fucking hot."

"I know that part. Have you made any progress?"

"Yes! Oh, I thought you knew. We've been out a couple times, and the last time, I got to go to the apartment. In Irving Place."

Location meant a lot to Tamara. "And?"

"He will no longer be called 'The Hair,'" she said.

"Because?"

"He will now be called 'The Bed.'"

"So you slept with him?"

"No, but I'm desperate to. You have to understand the bed that this man has in his apartment!"

"You're getting desperate about his bed?"

"He's also really fucking hot, remember?" She winked over her martini glass.

"Right."

"But the bed just clinches it. It's this huge cherry sleigh bed. It's like four feet off the floor. It looks like something from a fairytale, like something a king would sleep in."

"Tell me it's not draped with velvet curtains or anything."

"Ew. No. That'd be creepy."

"Yes it would."

"Anyway, I must get into that bed. With that man and his amazing hair."

"Anything else you're interested in about this guy? Is he nice? Funny?"

"Oh, sure. Yeah, he's amazing. Not like 'I'm gonna marry this guy' amazing, but definitely worth sticking around for a while. Especially when you consider the—"

"The hair and the bed," I finished for her.

"Right."

The bar did turn out to serve food, so we had some burgers and then agreed not to go back to work. We called Lulu and invited her to join us, since she should have gotten home from the Hamptons that morning.

She arrived wearing a bright yellow tank dress and glowing pink pumps.

"I thought bright colors would help my mood," she explained.

"Working?" Tamara asked.

"Not at all." Lulu ordered a drink and then slouched in her seat. "Andrew is a little pansy mommy's boy."

Tamara and I looked at each other with raised eyebrows.

"What does that mean?" I asked.

"It means that I have terrible taste in men. And I do not want to see him anymore. And that I am in love with him even though he's an ass."

"Okay," Tamara said.

Lulu explained what had happened over the weekend, and we tried to console her.

"I have no good advice," I said. "I've basically chased away the guy I'm in love with."

"CJ?" Lulu asked, seeming happy to forget her issues for a moment.

"Yes. He's on a job interview right now."

"But that'd be good, right? If he didn't work with you, you wouldn't have an issue!" Tamara looked pleased, as if she'd solved the problem herself. Lulu nodded her agreement.

"The job is in Buffalo," I said.

"Oh."

"Yeah, oh."

"Well that is less good," Lulu said.

"Yes. Right. Much less good," I said.

"Sorry, Pepper," she moaned.

"I'm sorry for you, too," I moaned back.

CJ was back at work by mid-week. I had no idea how the interview went, though I was rooting for "terribly." Knowing CJ, it went well. I watched him anytime he was near me at the office, looking for hints, but nothing in his cheerful demeanor was giving anything away, and he wasn't making any special effort to fill me in. He did stop in when he first got back to say hello, but Lanie chose that moment to swing through and discuss something pointless, so we didn't get to talk.

By Thursday afternoon, I was a simmering mess. I needed to know what he was going to do. I couldn't imagine my life without

CJ in it, and he needed to know that. I went to his office and was glad to catch him alone, the golden head bent over some papers on his desk. He looked up as I stepped in, as if he could sense me there in his doorway.

"Hey, beautiful," he said.

"Hi." I was nervous. I should have planned what I was going to say. I had no clue what was going to come out of my mouth next, and that usually resulted in me sputtering the most awkward and embarrassing things possible. "Have a minute?"

"Sure," he said, sitting back in his chair and hitting me with the smile that filled my dreams each night.

I stepped in to sit, but then thought better of it and went back to push the door shut behind me. Taking the seat across the desk, I gave CJ a weak smile. "I was just wondering how things went up in Buffalo," I told him.

His smile faded a bit and he leaned forward. "They went really well actually." His voice was quiet as if he believed that if he told me he was leaving very quietly, it might hurt less. "The offer is pretty incredible, considering the firm isn't in the city. The pay is really competitive with what I'm getting here, and there are a lot of incentives."

"It sounds like you've taken the job." I knew I looked like a forlorn child, but I couldn't help it. My chest literally ached.

"I haven't. It hasn't officially been offered. They're talking to another candidate, too."

"Oh."

"I have one more interview. I'll go back up on Monday."

"Oh."

"Natalie."

"Congratulations?"

"Natalie."

I stood. Then I sat back down. I couldn't keep walking away from CJ. I needed to let him know that if he left, my heart would break. I needed to let him know that I loved him. But something in his face was making it hard for me. He looked excited about the job.

Finally, I said, "I don't know what to say, CJ. I want to be happy for you, if you're happy, but I don't want you to leave. Like, at all. I can't imagine being here and you not being here. I can't imagine not seeing you."

"If I go, it doesn't mean we can't see each other," he said. "Maybe it would actually make things easier for you."

"No!" I yelped. "I mean, it would be terrible not seeing you. Not easy."

He looked thoughtful. And confused. "Natalie, look. I feel like I've been really clear about how I feel about you. I think you know that I'd like more than friendship, that I have strong feelings for you. And I know that you care about me, too. But I also know that you're conflicted and confused about it.

"To me, things are pretty clear. You won't let anything happen between us as long as we work together."

I felt tears bubbling beneath the surface and hoped they would wait until I wasn't sitting in CJ's office. "But ... " I stammered. "No, I mean, it's just Lanie, and it's not what I want ... " I wasn't making sense.

CJ smiled. "Okay, but if I don't work here, at least that eliminates that roadblock. And this is a really incredible opportunity for me."

"You're right," I said.

He looked disappointed.

I realized that I'd just told him that he should go. "I mean, no. You're right about me, how I've messed everything up and made things so complicated. But not about leaving. CJ, you can't leave ... " I could not manage to find the words that I needed to say to make him see that staying was the only way to give us a chance.

"Natalie, I think that me leaving is the only shot I have at ever getting to see what it'd be like to be more than just a guy you work with. And I'll be near my family. And it's a great job." He sounded a little bit like he was convincing himself.

The office door opened abruptly, and a blast of air-conditioned air from the hallway followed the robust form of Lanie Bill into the office.

"CJ," she boomed. "Oh, hey Nellie." She looked between us, an eyebrow raised dramatically. "This is rather cozy."

"If you don't have anything else," I said, trying to sound businesslike.

"No," CJ said, his dark eyes sad. "I think we've covered everything."

"CJ," Lanie began, settling herself in the chair I'd just vacated. "I've got some affiliate ideas for you."

I walked out, unable to figure out how that had gone so wrong, yet again.

Chapter Eighteen

TEAM TIPPY

Lulu

ANDREW CALLED several times from the Hamptons, and I answered late Sunday night.

"Lulu," he sounded relieved. "Where are you?"

"At home," I told him.

"I can't believe you actually left!"

"Really? You were there when I went."

"I just didn't think you'd really go."

"Andrew, I'd had enough."

"I know. Lulu, I'm so sorry. Please don't be angry. My mother, she's ... "

"If you think this is about your mother, then we are finished. There is no point in continuing this conversation." A tear rolled down my cheek. My heart was breaking. How could he be so amazing, and still so clueless?

"But the things she said ... "

"I don't care about her. It wasn't the things she said. It was the things you didn't say. You and Tippy are a team, and no one will ever come between you. There's no room for anyone else there."

"Lulu, I have a long shift tomorrow, but I'd like to come by when I'm done. Will you let me talk to you?"

"I honestly don't see the purpose." I wanted to say, "Yes," but I was still angry.

"Please."

"I don't think it is a good idea."

"Then ... "

"Andrew, I think we are through."

"No, Lu ... let me—"

"There's nothing else to be done, Andrew. But I hope that the next girl you bring to Tippy will get a bit more protection from you." I cringed. It hurt my heart to think of another girl at Andrew's side, touching him, smiling at him. "Stand beside her, hold her hand, and tell your mother that she is important to you. Don't bow down and allow Tippy to humiliate and demean her like some worthless toy. Be a man, Andrew. You're too old to be Tippy's little boy. Maybe even she will respect you more for it."

"Lu ... " his voice was in shreds. Was he crying?

"Goodbye, Andrew." I turned off my phone and walked to the bedroom. I stared at Andrew's pile of clothes in the corner and then turned my gaze to the bed where we'd spent long days and wonderful nights.

I wanted to be strong, but figured one day of weakness could be allowed for all that I'd just said goodbye to. I picked up a T-shirt where Andrew had slung it over the back of the chair and crawled into bed, holding it to me. I lay down and buried my face in it, in his scent—cinnamon and salt, warm sand and vanilla. The smell of him overwhelmed me and I cried. Deep wracking sobs wrenched from my throat, and I felt hopeless and alone. Again.

The next day arrived with a sore throat and puffy eyes. And nothing to do.

I folded all of Andrew's things and carried them downstairs in a pillowcase.

"Tom," I said as I approached the doorman. "Can you have a messenger return these things to this address?" I handed him a slip of paper with Andrew's address and a twenty.

"Sure, Lulu." He took the bundle from my arms. "How are you doing?"

"I'm well," I lied.

His wrinkled face gathered into a smile, and the kind grey eyes smiled, too. "I hope you're telling me the truth," he said. "You know, your uncle Esteban calls me now and then to check in on you."

"He does?" I was surprised. Uncle Esteban rarely even called me.

"He does. And I tell him that you have lots of friends and that you seem happy. But today you don't seem happy."

"I'll be fine, Tom. Not every day can be a happy day."

"That's true," he agreed.

"Thanks," I said, pulling my headphones from around my neck. "I'm going out for a run."

"Okay, Lulu."

My ankle felt nearly perfect—just a little weak—and I was dying to clear my head. Even if I couldn't run, I could walk and get some air.

The day was hot and swampy. Summer in the city was always overwhelming. Now I knew why people went out to the Hamptons to catch the ocean breezes that made the air feel less suffocating. Despite the heat, there were plenty of people moving quickly along the path next to the River. I stretched on a vacant bench for a few minutes and then took off at a slow jog, being careful with my newly-healed ankle.

Soon, the soft warm breeze across the water and the open path before me began to push away the thoughts that had plagued me since meeting Tippy. She had reminded me of things I hadn't felt in many years. Things I had tried desperately not to think about since the days when I went to bed each night in a creaky metal cot to the sounds of other children crying. I did not remember much about the years I spent in the orphanage. I didn't remember how I spent my days, or if I had any friends there. I didn't remember the grown-ups who were in charge, or what we ate. But I remembered how I felt every single day of those five years. Alone, abandoned, and hopelessly sad. And when I was old enough to look back and understand that it had not been my fault, I began working to build a life in which I would never feel any of those things again.

So I ran. I ran faster and faster to escape the too-familiar feelings of disappointment and shame.

And when I turned back to head home, I believed that maybe I'd outrun my past again. I felt like maybe I could start fresh. Again.

Until I returned home to find Andrew sitting in my lobby, looking a lot like the dejected child I once was.

"Andrew," I said, my breath still short from running home. "What are you doing here?"

"You won't talk to me on the phone."

"And I told you not to come by."

"I know." Andrew stood and walked toward me, his face pale and golden stubble covering his usually clean-shaven jaw. He wore scrubs in a light green color, so I guessed he must have come straight from an all-night shift at work. "I just ... Lulu, I screwed up."

"Yes," I agreed. "Andrew, it was hard for me to say goodbye. It will only be harder if you don't allow me to walk away."

"At least you tell me that it was hard. It didn't seem like it."

"Think about how this all happened, Andrew. It was hard. It

still is. And I just want to move forward." I turned toward the elevator. "Please go away."

The bright blue eyes were tearful and the laugh lines at their corners just looked sad. Every molecule that made up my body struggled to push me toward him, to take him in my arms and tell him that it was okay. I hated that I had made him look so sad and vulnerable, but I reminded myself that he had hurt me first. And then again.

I punched the elevator button and then watched the man I loved shrink down to a narrow sliver as the doors closed.

All the freedom and grace I had recovered on my run slipped away as the elevator car ascended.

Inside my apartment, I crawled back into bed and cried. One more day of wallowing, I told myself. And then I would figure out how to move on.

Chapter Nineteen

CHASING CABS

Natalie

When I got to work Monday, I waited eagerly for CJ to appear. I'd spent the weekend moving into my new apartment, with Tamara's help. Once my belongings were settled, I had realized a few things. For one, I really needed to buy some furniture. Tamara had suggested that I get a mattress and futon couch right off the bat, and she'd helped me arrange delivery, so that was taken care of. But the rest of the small apartment was basically empty and I relished the idea of decorating a place completely to my tastes. Cheaply, of course.

But I'd also realized that anyone living by herself, in her own apartment, should be making her own decisions. I'd moved to New York City six months ago, unsure what would be waiting for me. And I'd found a good job, amazing girlfriends, and the man I wanted to be with. I'd been incredibly successful, and the only thing standing in my way was me. And my own fear.

I woke up for work Monday morning and promised myself

that I'd allow myself to take the steps that I'd been so afraid to take for too long. I had vowed to talk to CJ first thing, to tell him everything. I was going to tell him how I felt when he looked at me, how my mind scattered when he smiled. I was going to tell him how it felt when he kissed me and how everything else in the world fell away while I was in his arms. I went to work that morning ready to tell him that the thought of him with Justine—or anyone else—shattered me into a pile of jagged girl shards, and how much it meant to me that he'd never been anything but open with me about how he felt. I went to work ready to say, "screw Lanie Bill." And while I wasn't ready to say "screw my dad," I did realize that I couldn't live my life for him anymore, or in fear of how he'd feel if he didn't like my choices. Or afraid of how I would feel if my choices didn't work out. I would live for me, for today. And that meant talking to CJ first thing.

But CJ wasn't at the office.

I checked email and found that he'd sent something late the night before. He must have been at work over the weekend.

Natalie: I'm headed to Buffalo again around noon Monday for my last meeting tomorrow morning. I'll know everything for sure by tomorrow afternoon. Call you then.

Oh God, he was already on his way to seal the deal! But his email said "around noon." Maybe I could catch him at home before he left.

I stood abruptly, grabbing my purse from the back of the door and heading straight for the lobby. As the elevator doors closed, I might've heard Lanie's voice calling me, or calling someone with a name that kind of sounded like mine ... "Natasha!"

But I didn't have time for her madness. I was in a hell of a hurry.

I raced to the subway and lucked into an express train from 34th to 72nd. CJ lived on 73rd, so I ran as fast as my black pumps would allow, dodging strollers and shoppers on Broadway as I ran.

At the curb outside CJ's building was a black town car. A familiar blond head was just ducking inside.

"CJ!" I screamed.

The door began to close just as I came to a halt next to the car. I knocked on the tinted window, and the car door reopened.

"Natalie?" CJ turned to the driver. "Just a second, sorry." He closed the door and took my forearms, leading me into the shade of the building as I panted and coughed.

"Did you run here from the office?"

I gasped and coughed, and decided at that moment that maybe I needed to get more cardio. Sweat was trickling down my face. "No," I wheezed. "From the subway."

"66th?"

"72nd."

"Oh." Then CJ seemed to stop contemplating my exhaustion after a mere block and a half sprint and realize that there was probably a reason for my presence. "Why?"

"CJ, don't leave."

"I have an interview, Natalie, I have to."

"No." I stared into his dark deep eyes. "No, you don't."

"I'll miss my flight."

"Then miss it. Don't go to Buffalo at all. Don't leave the city. Don't leave me."

CJ looked around as if he thought maybe someone nearby could explain to me that we'd been all through this. He sighed, and I saw at that moment that it was our last. If I didn't drop every last wall at that second, he would be finished with me. We'd run in this exact circle so many times, it felt like a rutted and craggy path with muddy walls high enough to trap us forever. He was looking for an escape.

"CJ," I said it in a low voice, and he looked at me then, a question in his eyes. "I'm so sorry that I've made you wait so long." I took a steadying breath. "I have known that I wanted to get to know you from the first moment I met you, when you interviewed me for the job. I've known I wanted to spend more time with you since the first time you touched my arm. I've known that I wanted to kiss you since the first time we ever talked. And I've known that I wanted to be with you since the first time we kissed."

A smile was breaking across CJ's face, the dimples appearing on either side of his full lips as his dark eyes watched my face.

"CJ, I've been an idiot. That day in Union Square? I should have said yes. I should have said that I'd do anything to be with you and that I'd figure out the rest later. And I know my timing is terrible and maybe it's just too late, but I—"

"It's not too late," CJ said quietly.

"It's not?"

"I doubt it would have ever been too late." CJ's eyes were taking in my face, moving from my sweat-drenched brow to my lips. "But the distance ... I mean, you're so worried about your job, and Lanie, and ... we can still be together if I'm in Buffalo. You can visit, I can come back to the city ... " He searched my face as he spoke.

"Is that what you really want?"

"All I've really wanted for as long as I've known you is to figure out a way to convince you to be with me." He looked suddenly shy, like a golden-haired little boy peering at me from under those dark lashes. "That's really all I want."

"Then please don't go. I'm not worried about work. Or Lanie. I'll figure it all out later."

"Are you sure?"

I didn't blame him for doubting me. How many times had I waffled already?

"I'm sure." What more could I say to convince him?

He stood there for a moment, watching me, his hands still on my forearms in an awkward half-embrace. Then he dropped my arms. "But Natalie, I have to ... " he walked back to the town car and I felt my heart begin to crack. Was he still leaving? How could he still go?

CJ opened the door and leaned into the car, as I began to feel like the ground was slipping from beneath me. How could he just walk away?

But CJ didn't get in. The trunk popped open and he walked around to retrieve an overnight bag. "Guess I won't be going to Buffalo after all," he told the driver, putting his bag on the curb and handing him several bills across the seat back before shutting the door.

"You won't?" I asked, my whole body shaking.

"Definitely not," CJ said, crossing the sidewalk to take me in his arms. One hand threaded into my hair as the other slid across my back. And finally, after what seemed like a lifetime, CJ's lips pressed against mine once again, warm and soft and perfect.

And as his tongue gently traced my lips and finally met my own, one word flitted into my mind and repeated itself. *Home. Home. Home.*

CJ walked me into his building, holding my hand and glancing at me repeatedly, like he was trying to be sure I wasn't going anywhere. There was a beautiful smile plastered across his face, which I didn't get to see much of once we'd gotten into the elevator. That was because once the doors were shut, it seemed that all hesitation was gone. For both of us.

CJ's bag hit the floor and I dropped my purse. His mouth was on me, not rough, but not as tentative as it had been outside. His tongue was persistent and soft, equally demanding and teasing, and his hands were everywhere. The air around us seemed to buzz and snap with electricity, and I wouldn't have even known that the elevator had stopped moving had CJ not stopped kissing me abruptly.

"Come on," he said, pulling me toward his apartment. His voice was gruff and low. He stopped outside his door, pressing me against it. "Did you need to get back to work today?"

"Probably," I said, my voice a whisper.

"That's too bad," he said, an evil grin replacing the signature CJ smile.

I'd never seen the sexy bad boy glint in his eye before. He might as well have ripped my clothes off right there in the hallway. I knew CJ was sweet. I thought he was sexy. He was undeniably handsome. I knew he was a great kisser. But it appeared that CJ also had some other moves. I couldn't wait to find out what else I didn't know about him.

He pulled me into the apartment and shut the door behind us. He dropped his bag and lifted me to wrap my legs around his waist. He set me on the counter separating the living room from the kitchen. I lost track of time as his hands and his tongue went exploring. At some point, we ended up in CJ's bed. I'd had sex before, but I could honestly say that it had never been like that. CJ had secrets that were just not apparent in the work environment.

I drifted to sleep in CJ's arms in the early afternoon light, feeling like everything had finally fallen into place.

CJ and I stayed in bed all afternoon. There were things we probably should have talked about, but we didn't talk much. By the time the light began to fade, leaving his bedroom awash in a filtered light that cast everything in muted shades, I was starving.

"Delivery?" CJ asked when I mentioned it.

"I feel like we should rejoin the world."

"You want to go out? Together?" CJ was grinning at me. "It'd be like a date. You know, someone might see us. You ready for that?"

He was teasing me, and it was deserved. I'd kept us in the dark far too long. I was ready to walk down the street holding CJ's hand, and I didn't care who saw us. "Yes," I said.

I pulled my work clothes back on as CJ dressed in dark jeans and a T-shirt that hugged his firm chest and cut abs. We brushed our teeth, and I tried to calm my wild hair. Frustrated with the tangles, knots, and general disarray of the long, blonde waves sticking out everywhere, I made a face in the mirror.

"I might as well just wear a sign that says, 'I had sex all day.'"

CJ smiled at me in the mirror. "I can make you one if you like. I have some markers here somewhere."

"No thanks." I pulled it into a loose knot on the back of my head and stuck a pencil from CJ's dresser into it. "That might hold."

"I like it," CJ said, pulling me close and kissing my forehead. "It's very 'sexy librarian.'"

"That's totally my signature look," I said.

"Not quite," he said, narrowing his eyes to consider this.

"No? What is, then?" I stepped back and did a quick turn for him while he thought about it.

"You've got this whole innocent sexy thing happening."

"Innocent sexy, huh? Think that's why Candace always tells people I'm from the Midwest?"

"Yeah, it's kind of a 'corn-fed farm girl meets the big city' sort of appeal."

"Oh really?" I pushed him in the chest playfully, laughing. "I guess that works. Especially with you pulling off that 'all-American golden boy football player' thing so well."

"Really? Football, huh?"

"Is there no football in your past?"

"Lacrosse, actually. A little soccer."

He took my hand as I picked up my bag and we headed for the elevator. I had a sensation that felt like being on vacation, like all the rules had changed. It definitely didn't feel like a Monday evening. I didn't even consider the fact that we would have to go back to work the next day.

We found our way to a little Italian place on Columbus called Pomodoro Rosso and settled into a sidewalk table. The waiter was friendly and sweet, and the wine he brought was the perfect compliment to the soft comfortable feeling I had as I sat across the table from CJ. The world wandered by in the late summer warmth and I felt ridiculously happy.

"Did you play Lacrosse at school?"

"I did," he said, smiling at me.

"Were you any good?"

"I don't think they'll let you play varsity unless you have a vague amount of talent for the sport."

"Depends on the school, I think." I winked at CJ.

"Yeah, you're right. Mine wasn't too discriminating."

"Those Ivy Leagues are notoriously lax about things like that." I laughed. CJ had gone to Harvard, but he was too humble to mention it unless someone forced it out of him.

"Did you play sports?" CJ leaned in. "And why don't I already know this?"

"The answers are, 'kind of' and 'because we never get to just sit and talk like this.'"

"How do you kind of play sports? And you're right ... " CJ leaned back in his chair and stretched his arms overhead, looking around at the darkening street, the people wandering by. The muscles on his arms bulged and his t-shirt pulled enticingly against his chest. "It's nice to get to see you in the real world."

"I was a dancer when I was young, until I went to college. Then I rebelled from ballet and started playing volleyball. But I only ever played IM."

"A dancer?" CJ raised an eyebrow and a hint of the sexy evil grin returned as he turned that over in his mind. "I could see that. I bet you were great at volleyball. You've got the height."

"Turns out that you have to do more than be tall and stand on the court. I'm bad at actually returning the ball. No one's throwing balls at you in ballet. I didn't develop those kinds of reflexes growing up."

"Aha."

We talked for hours and finished off dinner and two bottles of wine. Eventually, we found ourselves standing in the glow of streetlights outside CJ's apartment building.

"I should get home. We've got work tomorrow." I didn't make a single move to leave.

"Or you could stay over," CJ said, looking adorably hopeful.

"I don't have any of my stuff. I can't wear these clothes to work tomorrow." I was rumpled and felt dirty. "But," I said, thinking. "I live by myself now ... you could come to my place. Grab some stuff for work, and come stay with me. We'll go in together in the morning."

"Yeah?" CJ looked uncertain. He was waiting for me to change my mind. He'd certainly had experience with me doing just that. But I was never going to waffle where CJ was concerned again.

"Yeah," I said.

We went upstairs quickly and then caught the train down to 15th Street, where CJ made a nice addition to my sparsely-furnished apartment.

Chapter Twenty

THE RABBIT RIDES AGAIN

Lulu

I NEEDED A GIRLS' night. It was an emergency. I had huddled in my apartment most of the week. By the time Thursday rolled around, I couldn't face another long stretch of time alone. I needed the girls to distract me and encourage me.

"Pepper, I need a night out." Natalie was at work, and she'd been strangely silent all week.

"Me too," she said. "When? Tonight?"

"As soon as possible."

"You sound so sad, Lulu. I'm not used to sad Lulu."

"I'll be fine," I told her. "Just need a distraction."

"Well, we'll distract you tonight then. I'll call the girls. Let's meet at my place."

"Oh, that's right, you moved!" I had forgotten about Pepper's new apartment. "Where is it?"

Pepper gave me the address and I hung up feeling hopeful.

Besides having a night with my best friends, I had shopping to do for a housewarming gift.

I pulled on some leggings, a tank top, and my leopard print flats. I felt brighter than I had in days. With my hair piled on top of my head and my favorite Dior sunglasses, I walked out into the bright sunshine. I was moving on. I could do this. It almost felt good.

I had a successful day of shopping and headed to Natalie's new apartment at eight, ready for a night out. We hadn't been drinking and dancing in what much too long, and it was definitely time.

I buzzed apartment 2F as Pepper had directed, stepping back to look at the squatty dark brown building. It was not very attractive. I prepared myself for squalor. As I gazed at the dirty facade, a dark, bobbed head popped over the railing of the fire escape on the second floor.

"Hello!" she called down.

"Candace!"

"Come on up, the verandah is amazing!"

The door buzzed and I pushed into the vestibule and then through the second door, climbing the stairs. The front door of 2F stood ajar, so I let myself in.

"Lulu!" Pepper called, crossing a mostly empty apartment to hug me.

Candace was stepping in through the open window. "Isn't this fabulous?" she gushed, opening her arms to the space around us.

It was empty, but bright and clean, with windows everywhere. By New York standards, it was amazing. The verandah Candace had mentioned turned out to be the fire escape, where you could sit and watch New York go by beneath you.

"This is incredible," I said, looking around. I walked into the bathroom, peeked into the refrigerator, opened and inspected the closet, and finally sat on Natalie's bed. "You'll be so happy here."

Natalie beamed at us both.

"She'd be happy in a closet right now," Candace said.

"Why?" I asked. Natalie did seem to be glowing. She was always pretty, with her long legs and straight blonde hair, the deep blue eyes. But her skin was flushed and her smile seemed permanently glued to her face.

"She finally sealed the deal with CJ."

"Seriously? Oh, that's wonderful!" I was honestly happy for her. "Took you long enough. I told you that you needed to have sex with him like six months ago."

"You were right," she said. "I should have listened."

"Sometimes sex can solve everything," I told them. It might not have been completely genuine, but I played the role of sexual adventurer with my friends, and I loved that they saw me that way.

"Well, in this case, that was true," Pepper said.

"And not to rain on your parade," Candace said, moving to the kitchen where a very large bottle of vodka sat on the counter. "But now you just have to figure out what to do when you lose your job because of it."

"What?" I said.

Natalie's face fell a bit, but the buzzer rang just then and she flounced to the door to open it.

Maggie and Tamara arrived a few minutes later, Tamara making an extraordinary amount of noise coming up the stairs. When she came through the door, the reason was apparent. She was wearing the biggest pair of chocolate suede platform boots I had ever seen.

"Aren't they amazing?" Tamara said, spinning in the middle of the room, showing off her boots.

"They're big," I said.

Candace handed us each a drink. We all stared at Tamara's boots.

Pepper took a sip of her martini. "They do have a certain Chewbacca appeal."

"What the fuck is that supposed to mean?" Tamara said, her entire body stiffening.

"No, I mean, they're ... " Pepper couldn't backpedal fast enough.

"She means that the best thing about us is that we each have our own sense of style," Candace said smoothly. "And yours is assertive. I love it."

"Nicely put," Maggie said, the worried look leaving her face.

We raised our glasses to toast Pepper's new apartment and then sat wherever we could find something to sit on.

"You might consider some furniture at some point," Candace said.

"I'm considering it." Pepper laughed. "I did buy a stereo." She pointed at a huge stereo resting on a small folding table near her bed. "It holds three hundred CDs!" She walked over and picked up a remote control, and soon Madonna's Ray of Light was blasting through the space.

"That's really all you need," Tamara shouted over the music.

We laughed and drank and danced. Soon it was after ten o'clock. A loud knocking came at the door.

Pepper turned the music down and went to open it. I couldn't see who was on the other side, but the male voice didn't sound happy.

"I just haven't gotten any furniture or anything yet," Pepper was saying. "I'm so sorry."

Tamara and Candace went to the door to stand next to Pepper.

"Want a martini?" Candace asked whoever stood on the other side.

Soon, a short stocky guy in a very tight shirt and lounge pants was sitting between Tamara and Candace, holding a martini glass.

"This is Lulu," Candace told him, pointing at me as I sat on Pepper's bed, "and that's Maggie. Girls, this is Tom. He lives downstairs, and he thinks that Tamara's boots are too big for indoor wear."

Tamara scowled, but her smile returned when Tom put an arm around her.

"No, sweetheart, they're fabulous. Natalie just needs to get some rugs on this floor."

Something about the way he emphasized the first syllable of the word "fabulous" made me think that Tom was probably gay. I couldn't help but be a little excited by the idea. Every girl needed a good gay friend. They were the perfect bridge between the sexes—they could consult on outfits and give practical male perspective on life and relationship stuff. Depending on the guy, of course.

Just then I remembered the gift I'd brought. "Pepper!" I shrieked, seeing my gift bag still sitting next to the door where I'd dropped it. "I forgot to give you your housewarming gift!" I ran across the room to get it, bounding back to where Natalie stood in the kitchen.

"Good thing I'm not down there right now, FloJo." Tom laughed. "That was athletic."

I smiled at him and handed Natalie her gift.

"Open it now?" she asked.

"Of course!" I said. I pushed her toward the group on the futon. She put the package on the milk crate that was acting as a coffee table and knelt down to open it.

"What the ... ?" She pulled all the tissue off and stared into the bag, then looked at me with a question in her eyes.

"Well, I didn't know that you'd finally gotten CJ into bed when I bought it," I said. "But every girl needs one anyway."

She pulled my gift from the bag, and eyes got wide all around.

"What is it?" she said.

"It's the rabbit!" Tom said, grinning. "You've got good taste," he told me.

I winked at him.

"Um. Thanks?" Natalie still looked confused.

"Let me see it," Candace said, reaching for the box. She proceeded to remove the giant purple vibrator from its packaging and switch it on. Three different parts of the hefty device began to hum and rotate or vibrate.

"Oh my God," Maggie breathed.

"Isn't it amazing?" I said.

"It's terrifying," Tamara said. "Where can I get one?"

"The Pleasure Chest," I told them.

"On Seventh." Tom confirmed.

I smiled at him. I was so happy to have a new friend. It almost dampened the sharp pain I felt whenever I thought about what I had lost in the past few days.

We talked Tom into joining us out, and he went downstairs to dress.

"Isn't anyone going to ask me about John?" Tamara said, fake pouting as she poured herself another drink.

"Who is John?" I asked. Had Tamara met someone new?

"The Bed!" she cried.

"Oh, right. The Bed." I had been very self-absorbed. I smiled at Tamara in apology.

"Tell us about John," Candace said in a patronizing voice.

"Even though I don't think you really deserve to know, since you asked like that," Tamara said, pointing at Candace, "I will tell you. Because an important milestone has been reached."

"Did you get into the bed?" Pepper asked.

By then we'd all heard how John had morphed from "The Hair" to "The Bed."

"I did," Tamara said, nodding dramatically with a twinkle in her eye as she stood before us all. She knelt down to put her drink on the crate, drawing out the moment.

"And?" Maggie asked.

"Was it amazing? Are we going to call him 'The Orgasm' now?" I asked.

"Afraid not," Tamara said. There was still a gleam in her eye, so whatever happened must not have been too disappointing.

"I'm aging," Candace said. "Just tell us."

"So I was over at John's a few nights ago. We ordered delivery, had some wine. We were watching Dr. Quinn, Medicine Woman, and—"

"Wait, what? You were watching what?" Candace said.

Pepper was trying not to spit her drink out, her hand over her mouth.

"Let her tell the story," Maggie chided.

"We weren't really watching it. You know, it was on. It was just on."

"Oh, I see," said Pepper. "So you're on the couch, getting hot and heavy with Dr. Quinn ... go on."

"Okay, so we move the action into the bedroom, and finally, *finally* I get up onto The Bed."

We all shared enthusiastic looks. Here came the good stuff.

"So things are getting hot, right? Clothes are coming off, John's saying super sexy things to me ... "

"Like what?" I asked.

"What?" Tamara looked annoyed. "That's not important, stop interrupting me."

"It would be a better story if we knew exactly what he was saying." I pouted.

Tom had stepped back in, wearing some tight black pants and a shiny short-sleeved shirt with a collar. It wasn't quite metallic, but had a gleam to it that made me want to investigate. He walked over to us and I motioned for him to join me on the couch and then proceeded to run a hand over the fabric. It was soft. "It's like magic," I told him.

Tom smiled at me and then turned to Tamara. "So I just heard the end of that. Someone's saying sexy things, right?"

"Right. He was. Thank you," she said. "So it's getting hot. There are hands, fingers, tongues ... you know." Tamara's face was animated as she spoke, her eyes lighting up, her cheeks flushing. "And finally we're in The Bed, and we're totally naked, and things are happening. And I swear, I was more excited than I think I've ever been, between all the buildup and—Tom," Tamara interrupted herself. "You just met us, so you haven't heard about all this, but this guy has the *perfect* hair, and he's amazingly hot and he has a fantastic one bedroom at Irving Place, and this bed ... I swear to you, it's like straight out of an Ethan Allen display. It's this huge cherry sleigh bed that's like eight feet off the floor, and it's piled high with this amazing duvet and these uber-masculine pillows, and—"

"Is he gay?" Tom asked.

"No, why?"

"Just wondering. He doesn't sound super straight."

"No, he's straight."

"Then he's got a girlfriend."

Tamara shot him a look that said *go to hell and die there*. "Well," she said dramatically, "she can have him."

"Why, honey? What happened?" Maggie put a hand on Tamara's arm.

Tom looked amused by everything.

"So, it's all happening, right? And then we're doing the deed, and things are moving along, and they're escalating, right? And then just as I'm hitting the edge, he ruined everything."

"How? What happened?" Pepper asked.

Tamara's voice dropped to a near-whisper. "He came like a little girl."

"What?" Candace shrieked. "What does that mean?"

Everyone else was laughing hysterically, so Tamara waited until it was quiet again.

"He clung to me and whimpered when he came. Like a little girl."

"That's spectacular," Tom said in a dry voice.

We were all giggling, and after a minute, Tamara joined in. "It was so disappointing!"

"So you are through with The Hair?" I asked.

"I don't know. Probably. There's not much to look forward to."

"Are we going out, or not?" Tom asked. "I put on a shiny shirt. Let's find a party."

"I want to dance," Tamara said.

"Those boots were made for dancing," Tom told her. "Just not on my ceiling."

"Yeah," she said to Pepper. "And Chewbacca has some serious moves."

"I know where we should go," Candace said as we gathered our things and moved toward the door. "Hogs and Heifers."

"Ohhhh, really?" Maggie said, seeming to think about this.

"Definitely," Candace said.

"I could get into that tonight," Tom agreed.

"What's Hogs and Heifers?" Pepper asked.

I'd been there once before, so I just smiled. "You'll love it. And we can walk from here."

"Come on, Chewbacca," Candace said, linking her arm with Tamara's as we reached the sidewalk.

Hogs and Heifers was a well-known motorcycle bar on the West side of the village where the female bartenders wore very little and danced on the bar regularly. It was rowdy and gaudy, and for some reason, it felt like the perfect place to go that night.

Pepper and Tamara's faces were hilarious as they walked in to the small space to see bras hanging from the walls and the ceiling all around us.

"What the fuck?" Tamara asked.

"Yours'll be up there by the end of the night if you do it right," said Tom. He'd clearly been here before.

We walked to the bar and I ordered a round of shots. Pepper leaned forward and asked the bartender if she could also give us some water.

"No problem," she answered with a sweet smile. She wore a gingham print bikini top and cut off denim shorts, showing off a very cut midsection. She lined up the shots and then asked Pepper, "water, right?"

Pepper smiled and nodded, and then the bartender held up the soda gun she used to add mixers to drinks and shot Pepper in the chest with a stream of water. Pepper screamed and jumped backwards, as the bartender laughed.

Candace cackled loudly and the rest of the group looked nervous. After getting over her initial shock, Pepper began laughing and wiping at her chest and chin. "Did you seriously just do that?" she asked.

The bartender winked and moved on to another customer.

"Don't order water," Tom told her.

"Yeah, I got the memo," Pepper said.

The bar filled up quickly as the hour got later, and soon we were dancing to Lynyrd Skynyrd and Guns N' Roses in a tightly packed sea of drunk men and women. When "The Devil Went Down to Georgia" came on, all four bartenders jumped on the bar and danced, their feet stomping along and their hips turning to the beat.

Tamara looked especially impressed as she pushed near them and screamed encouragement. The bartender who had shot Pepper with water looked down at her and reached down a hand, pulling Tamara up to dance. She jumped up eagerly, and we all cheered as her blonde curls bounced around her and her huge boots stomped along the bar top. As the song ended, the other bartenders all applauded her, and the one that had served us grabbed her and gave her a kiss on the lips before hopping back down, leaving Tamara on the bar by herself. She looked surprised for one second before Van Morrison starting singing Brown Eyed Girl, and she forgot that she was dancing by herself, on top of a bar in front of at least fifty strangers. Vodka will do that to some people.

We spilled out onto the sidewalk somewhere after two, heading our separate directions and staggering off down the vacant sidewalks.

I walked all the way home—which wasn't too far, except that my ankle had begun to feel the effects of my run and a long night of dancing. I went to bed feeling as if I was turning a corner. Andrew's name hadn't crossed my lips once all night.

Chapter Twenty-One

A SUSHI SITUATION

Natalie

I WOKE Friday with a pounding head and an apartment full of half-empty glasses. The sight of the mostly empty vodka bottle turned my stomach, and the closest I could get to breakfast was a swallow of water in the shower while I got ready for work. I pulled my wet hair into a knot and threw on a dress, hoping Friday casual would stretch to include my hungover look.

I'd just slid into my seat when a familiar shape filled my doorway, a sexy smile on his face and an even sexier cup of coffee in his hand.

"How was the night with the girls?" he asked, taking the seat across from me. "Looks like it was a good time." He chuckled and put the coffee in front of me.

"First of all, thanks for the coffee. I'm not sure I'd be able to actually get myself any. All my energy was used up just getting here." I sipped at the cup. "Ooh, and it's a latte."

"Thought you might need it."

"I do, thanks." CJ was the best. I was nearly convinced he could read my mind. "And secondly, saying that it 'looks like I had a good night' could be construed as an insult."

"It's not."

"But it could be. It means that I look like I feel. Which is not good."

"The price we pay for fun," he said, leaning back and grinning at me.

"I think you're enjoying my misery too much."

"Maybe."

I told him about the night out, and about my downstairs neighbor, Tom, who had walked me home.

"Not sure how to feel about some other dude walking you home."

"You should feel happy that I have a friend in the building, who is big and strong and protective, and who is not at all interested in sleeping with me."

"Good point."

We talked some more, CJ telling me about his exciting night of PS2 with his buddy, James. I hadn't met the guy yet, but he and CJ had gone to college together, and he sounded like a good friend. After a while, CJ rose and walked to the door, turning back around.

"Hey, you wanna get something to eat tonight? Go see a movie or something?"

"How about delivery and a couch movie? I'm feeling immobile."

"Sounds good." CJ turned and walked away, the smile he'd shot at me before leaving still making my nerves tingle.

Just as he disappeared, Lanie Bill appeared.

"Nikki," she said, walking slowly into my office. She looked over her shoulder at CJ walking away and shook her head slowly back and forth. "I don't think I'd kick that one out of bed," she said.

Between her comment and my nausea, I nearly threw up. "Okay," I coughed out.

"But I don't think you would either, huh?" She raised an eyebrow and sat across from me.

What was she getting at? Did she know something? Or was she just testing me?

I decided that silence was my friend.

"So ... do you remember the conversation we had last week? In my office?"

She could only mean the one about fraternization. I nodded, guilt pooling with dread in my stomach. Here it came. I was about to lose my job.

"Well, I need you to get on that, like now."

"What?"

"You just said you remembered."

"I thought you meant something else. What do you need me to do?"

"God, it's like working with monkeys," she rolled her eyes and leaned forward. "No, sorry. I shouldn't have said that. I'm just really hung over right now. Late night, you know?"

"Sure," I said, careful not to agree to anything.

"Anyway, we talked about getting the meeting set up with the investors and Andy, making sure the packets are all prepared for them. Everything's in your email. I just need it printed in color, collated, and put into binders. We need twenty of them. And the presentation needs proofing. I've been through it a thousand times, so I'm sure it's perfect, but it never hurts to have someone who doesn't know what they're looking at take a look."

"Okay," I said, ignoring the insult as relief flooded me. "I'll get those all put together by end of day Monday."

"Good. Perfect. And stay away from that golden god of business development, Naomi. I saw the look on your face when he walked away."

I didn't respond, but hoped I didn't look surprised. What the hell were we going to do? Could we keep our relationship a secret forever?

"See ya. I may take off in a few. Gotta go get some sleep."

"Okay," I said, feeling relieved as she left.

I worked tirelessly that day, mostly because I was too hungover to actually get up from my desk and do much else.

CJ swung by somewhere around five, and whispered, "I know we said delivery, but I'm starving. Wanna go find something now?"

"Yes!" I said, eager to get out of the office. I was beginning to feel glued to my chair.

"Let's go."

I gathered my things and followed CJ out to the elevators and into the warm air blowing down 37th Street.

"Where should we go?" he asked.

"You wanna go home and drop our stuff and then go, or go from here?"

"I'm too hungry to wait. Let's go around here."

We were standing apart from one another on the sidewalk, conscious that people from work could be around us. "Let's just walk. We'll find something," he said.

We did. We found a little sushi place on 31st that I would never have known was there. It was perfect. It was dark and private, and it felt like we were worlds away from work. Two bottles of sake and lots of sashimi had us leaning close across the table, our fingers linked as we talked. My hangover was gone, my heart was light, and it was easy to forget that we were just a few blocks from the office.

At least it was easy until Lanie Bill walked in.

She doesn't do anything quietly, so her arrival naturally pulled our attention. She huffed in the entrance as if she'd just run a marathon to get there and then tapped impatiently on the empty hostess stand, looking around. She turned her head and spotted us, just as CJ dropped my hand to take his water glass.

Unfortunately, she'd already seen enough to spike her suspicions.

"Isn't this a cozy little dinner you're having?" she asked us, weaving through two other tables of closely seated diners to get to us. "This place is very romantic, isn't it?" Her grin was pure evil, her eyes sparkling with the knowledge that she had something on us.

"Hi Lanie, how are you? Care to join us?" CJ did his best to play it off.

"Oh, I wouldn't want to intrude," she said. "I live just around the corner. This is my local sushi spot." She winked at me then and something about it made me very uncomfortable. "I'm just here to pick up my order. Don't let me interrupt your date, you two!" She smiled sweetly and turned away, meeting the hostess at the podium by the door.

"Shit," I said. "Shit. Shit. Shit."

"It's okay," CJ said. "She doesn't know anything. She only suspects."

"I think that's probably enough," I said.

I spent most of the weekend at CJ's apartment. Luckily, he was quite good at distracting me from thoughts of Lanie and the bad things that might happen at the office on Monday. And despite my discomfort at what I suspected might be coming, I wasn't about to give up everything I had now. I would just have to wait and see what would come.

Sunday night, I went back to my place, full of trepidation for what Monday morning would bring. CJ and I had agreed that showing up to the office together Monday morning might not be the best recipe for success, but the goodbye we shared after our first official weekend together as a couple was pretty phenomenal.

I'd been back in my empty apartment all of five minutes when there was a knock at the door. Since the buzzer hadn't rung, either someone had slipped in as a resident came through the doors, or it was someone who lived here. I peeked through the peephole to see Tom standing before my door.

"Hey," I said, pulling the heavy door open.

"Hey yourself," he said, grabbing me and hugging me quickly.

"Come on in."

"I heard you come home. Honey, can we go rug shopping this week?"

"Is that a euphemism?"

"Definitely not." Tom smiled and seated himself on the futon. "This is sad. You need furniture. Or a television at least."

"I know. I'm working on it. We have an IPO coming up next month. I have a ton of options. If we do well, I can cash some in and get some furniture."

"Can you ask for a loan from your parents until then or something?"

"I could. I probably won't, though."

"Because ... "

"Because I don't want my dad to think I can't do things myself."

"Oh, I see."

"I don't want to give him any reason to be disappointed with me. This is the first time he's ever been proud of me. You know, with all my wild success out here in the big city." I held up a Diet Coke in Tom's direction and raised an eyebrow.

"Not this close to bedtime, thanks."

"Me too," I said. Caffeine always bothered me. "Decaf tea?"

"Lovely," he said.

"So little girl makes good in the big city and solves her daddy dilemma, huh?"

"Not quite," I moaned as I put the water on to boil.

"Oh oh. What's up?"

I told Tom about everything going on at work. I told him about the months of getting in my own way when it came to admitting how crazy I was about CJ. I told him about San Francisco, about CJ's job offer, and about our recent happiness together. Then I told him about Lanie Bill.

"So she saw you having dinner, big whoop."

"She's also seen us chatting a lot at the office, and made very specific threats about this stuff."

"Why does she care? Doesn't she have more important things to worry about with an IPO coming up?" Tom stretched his arms overhead, his chest muscles bulging through his shirt. Tom was a good-looking guy—all lean muscle in designer clothes. His blond hair was perfectly mussed at all times, it seemed, and he had a good day's growth of stubble.

"You'd think. But she cares mostly because she's certifiable, I guess." I handed him a mug of tea and sat next to him on the couch. "And I'm pretty sure that tomorrow I'm going to be looking for a new job."

"Oh, Pepper," he said. His dark eyes were sympathetic. "I'm sorry." He sipped his tea, and looked around. "Let's see. Marketing types, Internet savvy ... who do I know?"

Tom pulled out his phone and began punching numbers.

"Who are you calling?" I hissed.

"Patience is not on the resume, I see," he whispered back. Then his face came alive as whomever he'd called picked up. "Allen, hey it's Tom. I'm sitting here with someone you're gonna want to meet."

He was quiet a second.

"She's the marketing director at an Internet company—"

I whispered the name of my company.

"All Night Media? And she's going to be popping by your office this week."

His eyebrows went up and a smile lit his face.

"Oh really?" he said. "Well, I will let her know that. Thanks, Allen! We'll be in touch."

He put down the phone and grinned at me. "You've made quite the name for yourself, I see."

"What do you mean?"

"Allen knows who you are. He said that he's been trying to woo you for a while now."

My mind turned until I found the conversation I'd had a few weeks ago with a headhunter who'd randomly called my office. "Allen Page?" I asked.

"The one and only."

"That's so weird. Yeah, he called me a while ago out of the blue."

"Well, it's time to call him back. He said he'd love to meet with you and that he has a couple opportunities for you to think about."

"Oh my God," I said. "I can't believe I'm going to get fired before the IPO. There goes my furniture."

"Um, Pepper? You work in the Internet industry. You can write your own rules. Ask for a signing bonus at your next gig."

"A signing bonus?"

"It's not unheard of."

"That'd be awesome." I smiled at him and leaned into his firm shoulder. "Thanks, Tom."

"I'm the best."

"I think you might be."

We finished our tea and Tom said goodnight, leaving me Allen's number. I went to bed feeling both excited and afraid about what Monday might hold.

Chapter Twenty-Two

TIPPY GOES DOWNTOWN

Lulu

I RAN AGAIN on Monday morning. I was beginning to think I needed to begin looking for a job. I enjoyed my free time, but too many empty minutes had me believing I was lonely, and gave me too much time to think about a certain Upper East Side doctor whom I had been doing my best to banish.

Of course, having that doctor show up in my lobby every few days was making it hard to banish him completely. I arrived home from my run to find not just Andrew, but Tippy, sitting on the small couch in the seating area of my lobby.

My face must have shown my surprise as I looked between them, and then back to the doorman. He shrugged and mouthed, "Sorry."

"Lu," Andrew said, his voice tight. "Do you have a few minutes?" He stood and walked toward me. Tippy stayed perched on the edge of the couch, looking around herself as if she were surrounded by filthy farm animals who might paw her Chanel skirt at any moment.

"No," I told him. "What are you doing here? What is she doing here?"

Andrew seemed to glow in the soft morning light coming in through the front doors of my building. The diffuse light brightened his hair, his blue eyes. He wore slim-fitting jeans and a polo shirt that hugged just enough of his chest to make me want to run my hands over it. The worry on his face was apparent. I fought the urge to smooth the lines around his beautiful eyes. Didn't he know that my heart broke all over again every time I had to see him?

"Just five minutes, Lulu, please." He looked down at his feet, and then tentatively took one of my hands and held my fingertips, rubbing his thumb across them. "Lu, please. I'm a mess without you."

I looked into his eyes—which was probably a mistake—and I felt my shattered heart soften. "Five minutes. Down here. I don't want her in my apartment." I pulled my hand from his grasp and we sat in the wing chairs facing the couch where Tippy waited.

"Lulu," she said, her voice terse, but softer than I'd heard it before. She seemed smaller, less fearsome.

"Hello," I told her. Then I sat back in the chair and waited.

"Lulu," Andrew said. "I brought my mother here today because I needed her to tell you what she told me this week. I've been home a lot since we broke up ... whenever I'm not at work. I can't seem to manage to do much on my own besides work and sleep, and my mother is nice enough to make sure that I eat and shower."

I raised an eyebrow. I was certain Tippy loved having him back home under her roof. Under her control.

"My heart is broken, Lulu." Andrew looked at me and then at the floor. "I love you," he said, looking up again. "I know I behaved terribly, and I am here to ask for another chance." He turned to Tippy then, staring at her pointedly.

She cleared her throat and sat up straighter. "I am here to tell you that I am sorry," she said, her voice almost robotic. Clearly, she hadn't done this often. "Andrew has made me see that my behavior was appallingly rude, and that if I truly want him to be happy, then I need to step back."

I couldn't help but nod.

"Andrew loves you, Lulu," she said, spreading her thin fingers across her knees. "And I cannot bear to see him this unhappy." She looked at her son, and the first genuine emotion I'd ever seen from her crossed her face. "I came here today to make a grand gesture of sorts. I know that I was the problem between you, and I wanted to tell you that if you give Andrew another chance, I will be a problem no more." She seemed to deflate, her little speech over.

I looked between them, not certain what to say. I wanted to take Andrew back, but I had done that already. He was inextricably tied to his family, and I did not believe that we would ever be left alone where they were concerned.

"Would we have to stay indoors?" I asked. "I would hate for you to be embarrassed by any more photographs." I didn't care, which I'm sure was obvious by my tone.

"Of course not," Tippy said. "I'd have our publicists briefed on your involvement, and they would take care of that sort of thing." She said "involvement" like it was a dirty word.

"I see."

"Lulu, it's not as complicated as it seems." Andrew stood and took my hand again, pulling me to my feet. He walked me across the lobby, out of his mother's earshot. "I know this feels like a mess. And it has been, and I'm sorry I let my mother and my family become so involved in what should have been just between us. But I need you to forget all of that if you can. This is just you and me. And I'm just a guy, hopelessly in love with a beautiful girl, asking for one more chance." Andrew's eyes glistened, the dark blue looking more intense as he stared at me.

He was beautiful, and my heart lurched as he spoke. Could it ever be that simple with Andrew?

"I don't know," I told him. "Let me think about this."

His face fell, but then he seemed to realize that I hadn't said 'no.'

"Can I call you later?"

I nodded, my fingers tingling where he still held them.

He smiled at me, his eyes lightening. He kissed my cheek and then released my hand. "I love you, Lu," he said.

I went upstairs without another glance at Tippy, letting the weight of her presence sink in as I rode in the elevator to my apartment.

After a shower, I sat on my couch and stared into the air around me. I wanted to take Andrew back. Despite my better judgment, my heart had leapt when I'd seen him sitting in my lobby. When he touched me, other parts seemed to join in trying to convince me that we were meant to be together.

But there was no avoiding the fact that his family would always be involved, no matter how distant Tippy promised to be, and I wasn't sure if he would be up to the task of choosing me over her as time went on. I could only imagine the complexities that we would face if we ever decided to get married or have children. I didn't think Tippy was a woman who could stand by and let a member of her family choose their own entrée, let alone name children or buy a house.

I could not work this out entirely on my own. I called Maggie, who was always a good listener. "Is there any chance you could meet for lunch today?"

"Sure, hon," she said, her voice bright. "Anything wrong?"

"No. Not really. I just need to bounce some ideas off you."

"Oh, that sounds fun," she said. "What kind of ideas?"

"Andrew-related ideas."

"Oh," her voice fell slightly. "Okay."

"What time?"

"I can be free around noon. Can you come up this way? How about the Bryant Park Grill?"

"Sounds good," I said.

With nothing to do between then and noon, I selected my clothes slowly and then decided to walk. It would take at least forty-five minutes for me to walk to 40th Street if I didn't hurry. Then I'd only have a few minutes to wait. It was almost ten-thirty.

The sky was damp and grey as I walked, and I hoped that the thick muggy air didn't decide to relieve itself by raining—the Bryant Park Grill was outdoors. I meandered around the park for a while, watching people come and go. It made me feel less aimless to see how many other people were not sitting behind a desk in one of the famously tall buildings around us. I knew that I needed to work at some point. Maybe soon. But not today.

When my watch showed noon, I approached the hostess stand at the Grill.

"I'm meeting someone," I told the petite brunette holding menus. Then I spotted Maggie waving across the patio. "There she is," I said.

"Hi!" Maggie stood and hugged me.

We ordered iced tea and I was ready to talk.

"So, what's going on?" she asked. Maggie had a way about her that made you want to tell her things. She was very open and nonjudgmental, and I knew that I could say anything to her. It was strange that I had met her through Candace at school, when Candace was the complete opposite of Maggie in almost every way.

I explained what had been going on at the end of my time

with Andrew—the coverage in the paper, the details of Tippy's efforts to split us up in the Hamptons.

"So Tippy must be happy now," she said, sipping her tea.

"Well, maybe not. That's why I called. Andrew showed up this morning. With Tippy. In my lobby."

"You're kidding," Maggie said. "I don't know why, but from your descriptions, I see her riding around in limos, or horse-drawn carriages! I can't imagine her in regular places where people like us go!"

"Exactly," I said. "That's why it was so startling that he brought her—that she allowed herself to be brought."

"So you think he's really sincere because of that?"

"That, and the way he looked and talked to me. I believe he is sincere. And I don't doubt that he's sorry."

"So are you willing to take him back?"

"That's what I can't decide."

The waitress arrived and we placed our order. The question remained, and Maggie leaned forward, waiting for my explanation.

"I guess I see now how completely tied Andrew is to his family. With other men I've dated it hasn't been an issue. So many of us are on our own here. But he is not. He is part of something old and traditional, and something that I'm not sure I want to be part of. Or maybe I can't be."

"Just because you didn't 'come out' at a deb ball doesn't mean you can't be with him."

"Maybe not, but it makes things harder."

"This isn't exactly interracial or anything, Lu. It's not that controversial, you know."

"But it is exactly like that. It's two people from two distinct cultures. The color of our skin isn't important here; it's what is normal to us. And my normal is not the same as Andrew's normal."

"So are you willing to accept his normal?"

"I don't know if he can accept mine."

"Good point."

We ate in silence after our food came, though I couldn't do more than pick at the chicken salad that sat before me.

"So what would he have to do to get you to give him another chance?"

"I guess he did it. He acknowledged that Tippy was the problem. He made her acknowledge it."

"But that might not change anything."

"No. I can't guarantee him that we won't be on Page Six again, with nasty things written about us."

"But you can guarantee him that you'll love him and be kind to him. That's all any of us can really offer someone else, right?"

I thought about that. I couldn't control the circumstances of our relationship. But that didn't mean it shouldn't happen.

"I think you should give him another chance," she said around a French fry.

I snatched one off her plate and smiled. "I think I will. Why didn't I get fries?"

"You didn't order them."

"I thought they came." French fries came with everything.

"They didn't."

"I'll just eat yours."

Maggie rolled her eyes and let me eat her fries. When she went back to work, I felt better. I called Andrew and left a message at his apartment.

"Andrew, it's Lulu. I have thought about what you said, and I am willing to give things one more chance. Call me."

When the phone woke me from a nap at three in the afternoon, I was groggy and disoriented. "Hello?"

"Hey, sleepy!" Andrew.

“Hi,” I said.

“I got your message.”

“You did?” I smiled. Even though he couldn’t see me, it made me happy to believe that things were back on track, and I couldn’t help the grin that overtook my face. Plus, he sounded happy.

“So ... do you like tennis?”

“To play?”

“To watch.”

“I guess it depends. Watch who?”

“The world’s best? At the U.S. Open?”

“Oh, that could be fun.”

“Let’s go! I have courtside tickets this afternoon.”

“And you’re free?”

“I can be.”

“Okay, that sounds good.”

“I’ll swing by in a half hour. No fancy car, though. The best way to get out there is the subway.”

“That’s fine,” I said. I didn’t mind the subway at all.

We hung up and I searched for appropriate tennis match attire. I settled on a sequined tank top and black short shorts with wedge sandals. I had a pink visor that seemed perfect for the occasion.

Andrew buzzed and I headed down to the lobby to meet him.

“You look fantastic,” he said, kissing me on the cheek.

Tom, the doorman, gave us a happy smile as we left.

The subway was packed, and the occasional jolt had me leaning into Andrew’s body as we stood near the sliding doors. It wasn’t a short ride to the stadium, and it was loud enough that it was hard to talk. I let myself mold against his body and inhaled the vanilla scent of him as we stood pressed together. His hand was on my low back, and whenever the train jumped, he pulled me closer. By the time we finally arrived, I was almost straddling one of his legs, and I would rather have headed straight home than out to see a tennis match.

"This way," he said, guiding me out of the train. The venue was packed, and crowds moved all around us, but Andrew clearly knew where he was going. He led me through several entrance gates and past various personnel, flashing our tickets. Finally, we emerged into the very lowest courtside seating, and took seats in the second row, practically on the court.

"Wow," I said. "These are fantastic seats!"

Andrew smiled at me, then leaned forward and kissed me on the lips—just a sweet peck.

A voice interrupted us, coming from beside us where a man held a huge camera and had it aimed right at us. My heart sunk. Here we went again.

"One more kiss, Mr. Barton?" the photographer asked.

"Sure," Andrew said, his voice happy as he grinned at me. He wrapped his arm around me, leaning me back slightly, and kissed me slowly, his tongue teasing my lips. At first, I was very self-conscious—there was a photographer snapping photos as we kissed! But as Andrew's mouth claimed mine, his tongue becoming more insistent until I finally parted my lips to allow him in, I forgot about everything around us. My heart swelled, and I felt my pulse accelerate. As Andrew broke off the kiss, he smiled at me.

"This is Lulu Rossi," he told the photographer. "My girlfriend."

The photographer jotted notes and smiled at us. "You make a great couple," he said. "Thanks."

We waved as he moved on to find other people to surprise, and I turned to Andrew.

"Will your mother be upset? Are you upset?"

"No," he said, laughing. "She'll live. And I'm many things right now, but I'm not upset. I just wanted to make sure they get your name right," he said. "And that they know that you're my girlfriend. Those papers have a habit of going for a juicy story if they don't know the truth."

We held hands and watched a few matches, wandering back out toward the train once the sun had set.

"Dinner?" Andrew asked.

I wanted to say yes. I wanted to fall back into the habit of just being with Andrew. But if I was fearful, too. This man had hurt me. And I didn't want to be hurt again.

"Maybe we should call it an evening," I said.

Andrew's face fell. "Oh," he said.

I stopped to face him. "I am happy to spend time with you again, Andrew. And I've had such a nice time here." I looked around us, at the stadium, the orange sky colored by the setting sun. "But I need to take things slowly."

He nodded, but he still didn't look happy.

"I have a habit of jumping in so fast. I always want to be there —at the destination. I forget to enjoy the journey. And sometimes I end up surprised when the journey doesn't take me where I had thought it would. Does that make sense?"

"I guess it does." He sounded unsure.

"I don't mean to talk in riddle. I just ... I am learning myself. And I am learning you. And I want to give us both more time, okay?"

He nodded, and reached a finger up to trace my jaw. "Okay, Lu. I understand. You take all the time you need."

"And Andrew?" I said, stepping closer to him.

He waited for me to speak, his eyes on my lips.

"I'm in no hurry to have dinner with your parents again anytime soon."

Andrew smiled. "Understood."

I kissed him then, just a light teasing kiss. We took the subway back to my apartment and Andrew walked me to the door. "I'll call you tomorrow?"

"Please do," I said.

"Goodnight, Lu." Andrew kissed me softly and then watched as I walked into my building. I turned to see him walking away, his hands in his pockets and a smile on his face.

I smiled at Tom.

"Everything okay, Miss Rossi?"

"Everything is good, Tom. Very good."

"I'm glad."

I waved at Tom as the elevator doors closed and went upstairs feeling proud of myself for maintaining some distance, and also hopeful for the time ahead—when maybe I wouldn't have to.

Chapter Twenty-Three

HUNTING FOR HEADS

Natalie

I ARRIVED to work Monday morning feeling as if I were about to cross a minefield. I was probably tiptoeing through the lobby, because I felt like if I could just sneak through the reception area and down the hall to my office without running into a certain VP of marketing, then I'd be safe.

Just as I slid into my office, pushing the door shut to a crack behind me, Lanie burst through it, practically knocking me down.

"Just getting in?" she asked, glancing at her wrist. She was not wearing a watch.

"It's seven-thirty," I told her. I definitely wasn't late. In fact, if she did not plan to fire me this morning, I was going to begin a transformation into model employee. No more three-hour lunches that ended in martinis and morphed straight into happy hour. No more personal chats on the office phone. No more extended mental breaks in the developers' lounge. I was turning over a new early-arriving, late-departing hard-working leaf.

"Well make yourself comfortable," she said. It was possible that she spoke to herself, because she settled into one of the chairs across from my desk just after saying this.

I hung my purse and sat down at my desk, switching the computer on, then bringing my eyes fearfully to Lanie's face.

"So," she said. She didn't seem to have a solid plan for what would follow that, and we both sat in uncomfortable silence for a few minutes. She tried again. "So look. I have a thing for Damon, right? That's not a secret."

"Okay," I said slowly.

"But I've had to deny myself. Because, Natalie, Damon and I are colleagues. We are professionals."

She paused and I wondered what it meant that she'd gotten my name right for perhaps the first time ever.

"And I know that you understand this," she said. "And that is why it's so hard for me to let you go."

Shock spiked in my brain and turned my blood to ice. I'd known this could happen, but hadn't really believed that it would.

"I am disappointed in your lack of self-restraint, frankly." She stared at me then, and the tiniest hint of a smile seemed to play around her eyes and the corners of her mouth. I could only imagine what my own face looked like.

Should I try to deny it? Ask what she was talking about? I decided that making sure David was on board with her irrationality was the best plan. David was our CEO and the person who initially approved my hiring.

"Have you spoken to David about this?" I asked her.

Surprise crossed her face, but she covered it quickly with a condescending head tilt. "It's not exactly a secret, now is it?"

"That doesn't exactly answer my question."

"I'm going to speak to him this morning."

"I'd like to be present when you do."

"That won't be necessary."

"No, but it would be courteous, considering my professionalism is in question. It would be *professional*, I think, to include me in a meeting where you accuse me of something," I said.

"Maybe we should just part ways amicably," she said suddenly. "I know you never wanted me here, that you felt like I stepped on your toes a lot. But maybe it's just a personality conflict that we have, and it's for the best if you go."

"Maybe," I said, "If you ever bothered to learn my name, you might be just a little bit easier for me to work for. And maybe you should be the one to go."

"That was rude." She actually looked offended. "And I know your name, Natalie. I just don't like it."

"I see."

"Well, I think we're done here." She stood. "Please clean out your desk."

"Not before I speak to David."

"He's very busy. In case you haven't noticed, we're preparing for an initial public offering!"

"I'm aware of that."

Our voices had grown in volume, and Andy, the CFO stepped around the wall between his office and mine to raise his eyebrows at us. "Everything good in here?" he asked.

"Fine," Lanie said quickly. "I'll speak with you later," she hissed at me. "Today is your last day."

I followed her from the office and toward David's secretary's cube, just outside his door.

"Can I help you, Lanie?" Alannah, his receptionist, asked.

Lanie shifted her weight from foot to foot, appearing to search for the right thing to say.

"Is David in this morning?" I asked.

"He's out until Wednesday, actually," Alannah replied.

"Thank you," I told her. Turning to Lanie, I said, "I'll be emailing him today, and nothing can be officially decided until he returns."

"If you make this difficult, you'll regret it," she said in a low voice.

"I'll take that chance." I walked away from her and straight to CJ's office. I closed the door and collapsed onto his couch.

"What happened?" he asked. "You look like you're all worked up."

"Oh, I am," I told him. "Lanie just tried to fire me."

"Tried to?"

"Yeah, I told her she couldn't until David said so. And he's not in until Wednesday."

"Wow, nice move." CJ smiled. "I'm proud of you."

"I'm actually kind of proud of me too. Usually, I'm so confrontation averse that I totally back down. But I'm so sick of her bullshit."

"Can't blame you. And we kinda knew this was coming, right?" CJ rose and came to sit next to me on the couch, putting an arm over my shoulders. "Natalie, you're shaking."

"I'm a little amped up," I said, my voice trembling.

CJ put his other arm around me and scooted closer to me on the couch until our foreheads were touching. "Just take some deep breaths," he said quietly, his dark eyes gazing into mine.

The adrenaline that rushed through me as a result of my confrontation with Lanie began to morph into something else, something very CJ-specific.

"If I'm already being fired, do you suppose it would hurt things to have a quickie in your office?" I asked, smiling and pressing myself against him, one hand dropping down to his lap.

CJ inhaled sharply as I touched him, but then scooted away. "Actually, yeah, I think it might hurt things. You're not officially fired yet, as much as I'd like to lay you down right here." A dark look passed through his eyes as he seemed to consider it. "I don't think it's a good idea."

I pulled my hand away. "You're right." I pouted for just a moment, then scooted close again, missing his warm arms.

"So I didn't tell you what happened when I got home last

night," I said. I told him about Tom and the headhunter friend he knew.

"Time to go make some calls, I think," CJ said.

"Yeah, I guess you're right. I'm probably leaving either way."

"I'll check in after a bit," he said, giving me a quick kiss.

I headed back to my office, ready to start the hunt for a new job.

When I called Tom's friend, Allen, he acted as if he'd been waiting his whole life for my call.

"What are you doing this evening after work?" he asked.

I felt strangely like I was already committing to something. "Uh, nothing?"

"Will you meet me for a drink? We can just talk? See what you're looking for?"

"Okay?" It was a conversation of questions.

"Cool. Dewey's? They have a nice lounge area on the second floor. I'll see you there at five?"

"Okay."

The rest of the day passed without my having to speak to Lanie Bill again. I did send a quick email to David, letting him know that I needed to speak with him when he returned to the office Wednesday. I doubted that Lanie would get in touch with him if she hadn't already. I suspected she was mostly blowing smoke, but I wasn't going to let myself believe that my job was safe.

Allen was waiting, as promised, at Dewey's. He rose to greet me as I ascended the stairs to the second level.

"Natalie?" he said, shooting a hand out to shake.

"Yup," I said. He had a friendly smile, which helped calm my nerves.

"Have a seat," he said, motioning to an armchair next to a low table. "Let's talk a bit."

A waitress took our drink order and Allen asked me some questions about where I'd grown up and gone to school.

"I have a few opportunities that I think you'd be a great fit for," he said.

I felt a bit like I had when CJ had told me that they were hiring me to be the Director of Marketing at All Night—totally underqualified.

"Um, hey, hate to interrupt," I said. "You do know that I've been at All Night only for about six months, right?"

"Yes, but I think ... "

"And that before that I really didn't even work in marketing exactly?"

"Right, but Natalie ... "

"And ... "

"Let me stop you for a second," he said, still smiling. "You do know that you're kind of supposed to be selling yourself here, right? Not telling me how you're not qualified." He laughed a bit, which put me at ease.

"I guess I'm just surprised to find myself pursued when I have so little experience," I admitted. I took a big gulp of my beer, feeling awkward.

"I know," he said. He had a sincere face, and his light blue eyes were open and clear. "I know. It's a new world, it really is. And there's so much demand for smart young people now that experience isn't the only thing these companies are looking for. You've demonstrated flexibility and had some success at All Night. Your name is attached to some successful ad placements; you've pulled off a major level sponsorship and a pretty impressive launch party. Natalie, companies know you now. This industry moves fast. Really fast. Six months working in the Internet industry is like ten years in some older industries."

"Seriously?" I still found this very hard to believe.

"Seriously. But you have to play the game, and that means presenting yourself as a confident and seasoned Internet exec at any interviews that I set you up for."

"Right."

"Can you do that?"

"Yeah," I said, convincing myself. "I think I can."

"Good. Let's talk numbers."

Allen and I talked for an hour. He had three companies he wanted to send me to, and thought that each of them would be willing to pay me more than I was making now, and one of them he was sure would offer a signing bonus.

I walked home, wanting the time and open space to think. It was amazing to me that I was in the position I was in—choosing a new job, potentially being pursued by multiple companies. But I allowed a new confidence to wash over me. I could do this. Maybe getting fired by Lanie Bill would be the best thing I ever did.

Besides dating CJ.

When Allen said the industry moved fast, he wasn't kidding. I had two interviews on Tuesday, and another one scheduled for lunch Wednesday. By Wednesday afternoon, I actually had two offers at other companies. The third company wanted to set up a second interview, which would take place on Friday. By the following week, I could actually have a new job.

David was back in the office Wednesday. He stopped by that morning to tell me he was swamped, but that he would have time for me late in the day.

Lanie, oddly, had been avoiding me, which was fine with me.

"Hey hotshot," CJ said as I wandered into his office after my lunchtime interview. "How did it go?" His warm smile washed over me, and as usual, I felt immediately at ease in his presence.

"I think it went well. They set up a second interview right there during the first, so that seems like a good thing, right?"

"It's not a bad thing."

"It's going to be so weird not working with you." I felt sad thinking about it. CJ had been one of the first people I'd met in

New York. He represented so much comfort and familiarity to me that it was hard to think of not seeing him every day.

"No, it's going to be fine," he said. "We can meet for lunch like other couples do. We won't have to hide our relationship—"

"Because we're so good at that." I laughed.

"Right," he said, the dimples distracting me as he laughed. "And we'll see each other after work when we want to. It'll be fine. And you won't be under the thumb of the Internet industry's most notoriously insane VP anymore."

"That is a bonus," I said, thinking about escaping the insanity that was Lanie. I felt a twinge of guilt at the thought of leaving Justine to deal with her alone, but there wasn't much I could do about that. As I was learning in a variety of ways lately, we were all grown-ups, and we all had to look out for ourselves.

As I got up to head back to my office, David caught me in the hallway. "I have time to talk now, Natalie," he said.

I tried to force down the guilty blush that was creeping up my chest as a result of being caught coming out of CJ's office. I didn't know what David did or didn't know, and hoped I hadn't just proved Lanie's case for her.

"Sure," I said, following him to the corner office past mine.

"Close the door," he said. "You know, I got a strange message from Lanie while I was traveling, too. What exactly is going on?" He steepled his fingers and gave me the fatherly look that he'd probably perfected with his teenagers at home.

Lanie burst through the closed door then, throwing herself into the chair next to me. "So much for professionalism, I guess," she said, accusing me.

"I guess," I responded, raising an eyebrow at her entrance.

"Ladies, please tell me my marketing department isn't imploding a month before the IPO." David looked tired.

Lanie's face was red, like she'd been running to get here. I wondered how she even knew we were meeting. "David, Natalie and some of her office mates have been engaging in some rather unprofessional behavior," Lanie said. She nodded slowly and looked back and forth between us.

"Which means?" David said.

"David," I said. "I have a relationship with CJ. It's fairly new, but it's serious. And I don't want this to be a problem here at work. I don't want it to cause any conflicts."

"Which it clearly does," Lanie interjected.

"Right, well, I disagree," I said. "But I wanted to let you know that I'll be leaving All Night Media. I thought it would be best to give you my notice in person."

"You'll stay through the IPO?" he asked hopefully.

"I'd like to," I said. "But I'm not sure that's the best idea."

Lanie was practically foaming at the mouth. She was huffing and shifting in her chair, her head zinging back and forth as if our conversation were a tennis match.

"I'd like that, too," he said. "I'm sure you realize that your options won't vest if you leave. You'll be able to exercise a few of them immediately, but the rest ... you'll have done all that work for nothing."

"I know."

"Are you sure this is the right choice?"

"I don't know if you can ever be sure," I said.

He smiled then, leaning forward. "I'm gonna be sorry to see you go, Natalie."

"Thanks," I said. I stood and walked out, casting a quick glance back at Lanie, who looked like she'd just heard a joke she didn't get the punchline for. Her mouth was turned down in a comical frown and her eyes were wide and wild.

As I walked away, I heard David say, "Anything else, Lanie?"

I didn't hear her answer, as I was already halfway back to CJ's office to tell him that I'd quit. I felt nervous and giddy, scared, and happy all at once. But more than anything, I felt like I'd finally taken a step forward, a step through the door that led to the future ... my future. I couldn't help but smile.

Chapter Twenty-Four

PAGE SIX CAN SUCK IT

Lulu

AFTER OUR TENNIS DATE, Andrew ended up working almost three full days in a row. We chatted on the phone when he had breaks, and he sent flowers once again. But he didn't push to see me, and he didn't drop by in the middle of the night, which felt like a healthy change.

I no longer felt lost in my own apartment. I felt like I had done something healthy and smart in accepting Andrew back on my own terms. It was something a grownup would do. My head was clear, and I was ready to approach other parts of my life that I had been neglecting.

I called Natalie at work at the end of the week.

"Pepper," I said when she picked up.

"Lu! How are you?"

"Good. Really good."

"Why so good?"

"Andrew and I are back together. We've worked things out." I felt happier just saying it out loud.

"That's wonderful," she said. "But it's not really news, you know. I mean, the Post beat you to it."

"What are you talking about?"

"Check out Page Six this morning. Nice visor by the way."

"Oh my God," I moaned. "Page Six is what started things going wrong in the first place." I remembered the photographer at the Open, and Andrew's easy reaction to him this time. "Is it a good picture at least?"

"Adorable. Not sure about the visor, though."

"We were at the Open!"

"It does say that here. I guess you're okay then."

"Until Tippy sees this. Oh well. This is not actually why I called." I hoped Andrew had already prepared his mother for the photo.

"Oh? What's up?"

"Can I get the number of the head seeker you talked about?"

"Head seeker?"

"I want to look for a job!"

"Wow," Pepper said, laughing. "And I think you mean 'headhunter.'"

"Okay, yes, whatever."

"Sure," she said. "I've actually been talking to him a lot this week. I just gave notice here at work."

"You are leaving?"

"Not the city. Just the company. CJ and I can't officially date if I stay. Or maybe we could, but it's way too complicated."

"Wow. That is a big deal."

"I think it is, yeah."

She gave me the number for someone named Allen, and I set it on my desk. I would call him later. First, I needed to find a copy of the Post. I put on my shoes, and Tom stopped me in the lobby.

"Miss Lu," he called as I headed out. "Something just arrived for you." He handed me a vase of flowers and a copy of the Post with a card taped to it.

"Thanks," I said. I took the items to the low table in front of the couch where Tippy had sat. It still made me feel odd to think of her in my lobby. Or in the village at all.

I opened the card, recognizing Tippy's tight handwriting immediately from the other card she'd sent with the bathing suit.

This is a wonderful photograph. I didn't know if you had a copy yet. We hope to see you at the house soon. Cherry misses you. — Tippy

I re-read the note three times, but it still said the same thing and I could not find any hidden meaning. I decided to accept that Tippy really was trying.

I pulled the paper open to the page that had a Post-it sticking out, and was surprised to see that the photo of Andrew and me took up half the page. It was a good picture I had to admit. And I thought my visor looked cute. The photo showed us kissing at the Open. It was sweet, no tongue or rolling eyes. Looking at it made me smile. And there was a headline above it that read, "UES Prince Courts Princess."

I glanced at Tom, who was watching me with interest. I showed him the page.

"It's a good shot," he said. "I didn't know you were a princess." He winked at me.

"I'm not." I laughed. "I'm a lonely Brazilian girl who got lucky. But every girl wants to be a princess, Tom."

"You deserve it, Lu."

"Thanks."

I took the flowers and vase back upstairs and laid the paper open on my nightstand.

Then I sat down to call the headhunter.

"What did he say?" Andrew asked, when I told him about my phone call that night. Andrew had come over after his long shift and was practically asleep on his feet when he arrived at my doorstep. Though we had planned to go to dinner, he looked so exhausted I just put him to bed and sat next to him.

"He thinks I can find something in sales," I said, stroking the golden hair away from his forehead as he lay next to me. "I'll tell you about it tomorrow after my first interview."

One blue eye popped open. "You have an interview tomorrow? Good luck, honey. That's great." He smiled and within seconds his breathing became deep and even. We hadn't even talked about the picture or Tippy's note yet. Oh well. That could all wait.

I turned out the light and then slid into the cool sheets next to Andrew. I pressed myself against his warm back, hugging one arm up his solid chest and nestling my head against the nape of his neck.

"My prince," I whispered.

It was funny. When I'd been little and alone, I had the same fantasy that so many girls did—a prince would sweep into the orphanage, rescue me, and banish all my fears. That didn't happen when I was little, but honestly, I wouldn't have known what to do with a prince anyway when I was eight. Now though, my prince was right here beside me. I tightened my arm around him. I wasn't going to let him go again.

Chapter Twenty-Five

ALIVE AT TWENTY-FIVE

Natalie

STARTING a new job had been exciting. Between the new apartment and the gig, I felt like I'd reinvented myself. I'd done it once before, leaving behind everything I knew to come to New York City from California. And now I was doing it again. New York, it seemed, was a city that moved and shifted as you needed it to. I could be whatever I wanted to be here. My mother had told me that before she died—that the world was at my fingertips—but I'd never really believed her. New York made me believe she was right.

As I settled into the first real work I had to do as the marketing director for a small online software company called AdTrack.com, my desk phone rang.

"AdTrack, Natalie Pepper."

"Hey, beautiful."

"CJ." Just saying his name made me smile. I missed seeing his broad shoulders and hot backside moving past my office door every day and knowing that he was just down the hall, but he'd been right—in my first week of work, we'd still seen each other almost every day. And the time we spent together was no longer colored by the threats spewed by Lanie Bill.

"Can I take you to an early dinner?" he asked.

"Of course you can. What's up?"

"Nothing special," he said. "I'll pick you up at six-thirty. Will you still be at work?"

"No, I'll go home and change first. Dress up or down?"

"Dress up."

"Oh, fun. Okay. Where are we going?"

"It's a secret." There was a grin in his voice, making it low and sexy like a promise.

I went home at the end of the day and found a tight short red dress in my closet that I'd never had the nerve to wear in California. I'd lost a bit of weight since moving—all the walking, I guessed—and the dress fit better than I remembered.

CJ was right on time, and I ran down to the curb when he declined to come up. There was a limousine there, idling, with CJ standing next to the open door.

"Oh my," I said. "I've actually never been in a limo!"

"Happy birthday, Natalie," he said, laughing.

"It's not my ... " It wasn't my birthday. But in a week, it would be.

"Just a little early," he said. "It's much easier to surprise you that way."

I grinned and my insides did a little jig. "Okay!" I said, kissing him quickly and then sliding into the dark interior.

The limo was lit with neon lights in tubes around the interior. There was a bottle of champagne chilling in a built-in ice bucket in the long seat running down the side. CJ sat next to me in back, and turned on the CD player built into the wall. He pressed another button and the lights began to shimmer and dance. As

David Gray's voice filled the space, CJ popped the cork on the champagne and poured me a glass.

"Happy birthday, Natalie," he said, handing it to me.

We toasted and drank. "Where are we going?" I asked.

"For now, here," he said, a gleam in his eye. "We do have plans at eight, but we're just going to tour the city for a bit in our limo."

I grinned. I couldn't help it. I was so excited to be in a limo. With CJ. On my way to secret birthday plans.

We drank most of the bottle and thanks to my very short skirt, we managed to accomplish a few other goals during our limo ride, too. It turned out that all the space could be put to a wide range of uses.

CJ poured the last of the champagne into my glass and smiled at me, his face flushed and gorgeous.

"Ready for the next part?"

"I can't believe there's more," I said. It had already been the best birthday celebration I'd had. My body still hummed with happiness and arousal.

CJ knocked on the glass separating the driver from the back and they exchanged words.

Fifteen minutes later, we pulled up outside an innocuous building in the meatpacking district.

There were a few people roaming the streets, but for the most part, this side of town was dark and not too busy.

"Where are we going?" I asked.

"To your party," CJ said.

The driver opened the door for us and I stood on wobbly legs, thanks to the champagne and CJ's magic hands.

"This way," CJ said, pulling me toward a dark door with a single red light glowing over it.

We went into a space lit with hidden lights behind the thin walls, making it glow.

"Careful," CJ said, as he led me down a narrow staircase. As we got lower, I could hear the pulsing beat of music and the low hum of people.

"Where are we?" I asked.

I was answered as the stairway opened to a wide space with checkered floors and a long bar curved against one wall. Low banquettes filled one end of the room.

"Happy birthday!" the crowd cried as my feet landed on the bottom step.

The first face I saw was Lulu's, since she stood at the bottom of the steps grinning and hopping on her toes like a little girl. Her shocking pink tank dress might have caught my attention, too. I was happy to see that Andrew was next to her, an arm around her waist. I hugged them hello and walked toward the bar.

Tamara, Maggie, and Candace had shots lined up on the stainless steel bar top, and one waiting for me. I hugged them hello and Candace shoved the shot at me.

"Drink, birthday girl," she said, an evil grin lighting up her green eyes.

Maggie shrugged and smiled, and we all downed our shots, which tasted like punch—with a punch.

I leaned against the bar and looked around the room. Almost every face was familiar, and I was amazed to see how many people I actually knew, having lived in New York for only six months.

Tom, my neighbor, was dancing with a group of guys I didn't recognize. When the song ended, he joined me at the bar.

"Hey gorgeous," he said. "Meet my friends, Dennis, Alton, and Jem."

They said the obligatory "happy birthdays" and then scooted down the bar to get drinks.

"Your gift is at my place," Tom said.

"You didn't have to get me anything," I told him.

"No. I did." He grinned. "It might kind of be a gift for me, actually."

I raised an eyebrow in question.

"A *rug*, Natalie. I got you a big, thick, noise-muffling rug. Now you and Tamara can dance all you want. At respectable hours, of course, and not with those gut-stomping boots of hers."

"Oh my gosh." I was floored. I had priced rugs and was surprised at how expensive they were. That was a very nice gift. Tom must really want some peace and quiet. "I can't believe you got me a rug!"

"Believe it, sister." Tom smiled and gave me a kiss on the cheek before returning to his friends at the other end of the bar.

There were other people from All Night Media there—Damon included, and he was dancing with Justine in a way that made me wonder if they'd gotten a talking to from Lanie yet.

"Is Lanie still on the fraternization warpath?" I asked CJ as he slid an arm around my waist. "Or has she gotten over it now that I'm gone?" I nodded toward Damon and Justine.

"David put the kibosh on her no-fraternization policy," he said. "I thought I told you this. He sent an official email out saying that we had no official policy but that it was not encouraged. And he must have told her to quit threatening people, because they're pretty open at the office." He nodded toward Damon and Justine.

"You think it's serious?"

"How serious can Damon ever be?"

"I don't know," I said, not wanting to go too far down that path. CJ still didn't know that I'd had my own Damon Michaels interlude, and I didn't want him to find out.

CJ sipped his beer and watched me over the glass as Tamara put an arm over my shoulders and began pulling me toward the dance floor with her.

Fat Boy Slim's "Praise You" was thumping through the room, and it acted like a klaxon call, bringing all the girls to the dance floor. Lulu came slinking toward me with her hands over her head and her long, dark hair flowing around her, and Candace and Maggie followed her. Soon we were all dancing together in the middle of the floor, the whole party moving to the beat around us as the lights flashed and flared.

It was a perfect moment. I was surrounded by my friends, CJ and I were together, and all felt right in my world.

The only thing getting in the way of perfection was the woman leaning against the wall at the far end of the bar. She was older than most of my friends—at least thirty-five, I thought. She was wearing a tight red dress and black heels, and she looked like something out of the pages of Vogue—elegant, refined. She wasn't anyone I knew, and as we danced, I wondered why she was at my party. I guessed that the bar must be open, but that most people saw that there was a function going on and went elsewhere. There was something about the way she was watching us all dance that left me feeling unsettled. She didn't act like a lonely stranger looking for a night out. She was staring at CJ with some kind of intent.

As CJ's hands held my hips and we moved together, I leaned my head in and asked him if he knew who she was. He evidently hadn't noticed her there before, because as soon as I pointed her out, his hands tightened on my hips and he stopped moving. I stared into his face. He looked almost scared.

"Who is it?" I asked, following his gaze back to the woman in the tight red dress holding a martini glass.

"It's ... I don't know why she would be here," CJ stuttered. "It's Irene."

My head swiveled around to look at the woman again.

She smiled, seeing us watching her, and raised her glass.

"Irene from Buffalo?" I asked. "Why the hell would she be at my birthday party?" I didn't like the look on CJ's face at all. He was holding his features still, as if he was trying not to show whatever he was really feeling.

"I have no idea," he said.

CJ pulled me off the dance floor, and we approached Irene together. She was even more stunning up close than from across the room. My stomach turned as I took in the wavy dark hair, the perfect lush red lips and the strange way she was gazing at my boyfriend. Like she knew him well. Too well.

"Cassidy," she said, her voice a purr. "Your girlfriend is lovely." She put out a hand to me. "Hello. I'm Irene Halliday."

I shook her hand as CJ said, "What are you doing here, Irene?"

She smiled, and there was a longing in her eyes that worried me. "You know I don't take no for an answer, darling. I came to convince you to come back!"

My heart dropped as CJ stared at the woman before us. What exactly had been going on in Buffalo?

"This is a private party, Irene. You and I can talk tomorrow. On the phone," CJ said.

"Whatever you like," she said, her wistful smile setting off alarms in my head. "But you know I don't give up easily when there is something I want. And I want what is best for you. You belong in Buffalo." She stared at CJ for a minute, then glanced at me before slipping through the center of the dance floor and up the stairs, her elegant lithe body attracting the attention of several men as she went.

"I'm so sorry, Natalie," CJ said, pulling me close.

I looked up into his face trying to read whatever secrets were written there. "Cassidy?" I asked. Why had I never thought to ask what CJ stood for?

He nodded, looking mortified. "Cassidy James. It's awful."

"I like it," I said, still trying to figure out what had just happened. "She was talking about the job, right?

"Of course," CJ said.

Something was going on. Something that I wasn't going to like. But it was my birthday party. And I wasn't going to let anything get in the way of one perfect night with my friends and the man I loved. Or at least that's what I told myself as I dragged CJ back to the dance floor. I closed my eyes as CJ's hands held me close, and pretended that we could live there in that moment forever.

I knew that my life was never quite perfect and that something would always come along to upset the balance. But for that night, I vowed to live in the moment. I was twenty-five—young and in love, and in the middle of the best party of my life. I threw my head back and closed my eyes, and let myself be swept away by the pulse and swell of happiness all around me. But I knew with certainty that before I was ready to face it, tomorrow would come.

PREVIEW OF BOOK 3

An Excerpt From:
COSMOS AND COMMITMENT

BOOK THREE

the GIRLFRIENDS OF GOTHAM

by

DELANCEY STEWART

1. A COUGAR ON THE PROWL

Natalie

"YOU ARE the coolest girl I've ever known." CJ's warm hand slid across my stomach as we lay side by side in his bed, staring up at the ceiling of his bedroom. One jagged crack ran from corner to corner. On my worst days, I imagined it would cave in and we'd be suffocated under the weight of someone else's bed, someone else's life crashing down on us. CJ always laughed when I mentioned this fear.

I turned to look at him. "I've never been cool. I think I've spent most of my life trying to figure out how to blend in and not make a jackass of myself."

That slow sexy grin spread across his full lips as his brown eyes danced. It both honored and irritated me that he found my confession amusing. "You should never try to blend in. You're amazing, Natalie." CJ rolled toward me and kissed me gently on the lips. Not a suggestive kiss, just a sweet reminder that he was mine and I was his. That we were finally together.

"Thanks." I kissed him back, letting myself lean into his warmth for a few seconds, and then rolled out of bed, excusing myself to the bathroom. I took in my reflection with appraising eyes. Blue eyes, maybe too close together, and blond hair, long and straight. Ears that were slightly asymmetrical, and front teeth that I'd always thought were too big. Was I the coolest girl in the world? Definitely not. I was twenty-five, living in New York City, and just trying to figure out how to get from day to day without dropping one of the balls I felt like I was always juggling.

CJ's assessment of me certainly stroked my ego, but even after a year in New York, I didn't have much confidence in myself. I had great luck, as it turned out. I'd stumbled into a position as marketing director at a start-up Internet company, and I'd convinced the greatest guy I'd ever met that I was somehow worthy of him. As I stared in the mirror, all I could feel was that I somehow didn't deserve any of it. I was sick of that feeling. I was sick of being a pushover, sick of waiting on luck and the whims of others to decide my destiny. 1999 was going to be the year of Natalie Pepper. Sure, it was already late September, but a lot could be accomplished in a few months. If these two months went well, I might just declare myself to be destined for greatness in the next millennium too.

I brushed my teeth and hair and splashed some cold water on my face before wandering back into the bedroom, a plan forming. There were ways people worked on themselves, professionals who could help get to a person's true essence, right? I was going to find one of those.

CJ had turned the television on and was intently watching some financial news show. The man could find investment news at any time of day or night. He ate it up like the girls and I devoured *Friends* or *Sex and the City*.

I settled onto the bed next to him and leaned over, blocking his view of the television. "I'm gonna head out. Meeting the girls for brunch."

His dark eyes sparked. "You sure? We could just stay here in bed all day..." His voice was low, and his fingers traced up my arm. My stomach tightened as my skin heated under his touch. CJ was the one thing I couldn't resist in the world. I'd wanted him for so long that sometimes I still couldn't believe he was mine.

I was about to give in when his phone rang, breaking the moment. "You get that," I said, standing up. "I'm gonna sneak out."

"I'll call you later." He rolled to pick up the handset out of the base station.

I glanced at the phone as I left the room and wished I hadn't. The caller ID displayed the name Irene Halliday. Not a name I enjoyed hearing or seeing, but one that didn't seem to want to go away. I lingered in the living room, putting my shoes on and gathering my things slowly while CJ talked. I wasn't really eavesdropping. I just hadn't left yet.

"I understand, Irene," he was saying. He sounded exasperated, and that made me feel better. "I just don't think it's the right time. Even if it is in the city."

I took my time latching my watch, which had been abandoned on the breakfast bar.

"Well, I'm not exactly qualified, for one thing," CJ said. "It'd be a pretty big jump for me."

Irene must have been making her point for quite some time, because CJ was silent. It was awkward just standing in the living room, so when CJ said nothing else, I picked up my bag and headed for the door. I pulled it open, and as the door swung shut behind me, I thought I heard CJ say, "Fine. We can meet to discuss it. I'm free tomorrow."

My happy mood dissipated as I rode the elevator to the lobby of CJ's Upper West Side building. By the time I'd reached the sidewalk, any giddy elation I'd been feeling had evaporated in the face of the ever-present Irene. What the hell did she want? She'd tried unsuccessfully to lure CJ back to Buffalo, and now she was here in the city. She was way too old for him. I hoped they both knew that. I poked around at the discomfort that always bloomed inside when Irene's name came up. Did I really think CJ would do anything to jeopardize the relationship we'd fought so hard for? Not really. But Irene's presence made me uncomfortable all the same. The sooner she was back in Buffalo and out of his life, the better.

I got on the southbound subway at 72nd Street and hoped mimosas with the girls would help lighten my mood.

By now, the staff at Cafeteria knew to expect us most Sunday mornings. Not everyone made it each week, and sometimes boyfriends or even straggling remnants of what would become one-night or weekend flings joined us. But as often as we could, we had brunch together, and it was one of my favorite things. Brunch gave us a chance to catch up, to recap what had happened each week. Lately it felt like everyone was getting busier, and those occasional Sundays were the one day we could all take to slow down and spend some time catching up, pulling our little group back together. This week, Candace had come solo, but Lulu and Andrew were both there. I got to the door at the same time as Tamara, and we wandered over arm in arm as Lulu continued her monologue. Tamara and I sat down at the round table.

"I know you had planned to move, Candace, but Brooklyn? Why not just move to New Jersey? Or Queens?" Lulu sounded disgusted at the thought, and while her words were nearly venomous, her intentions were not. Lulu was hard to understand sometimes, but I'd gotten to know her well. She was an exaggerated personality, and she often made off-the-wall proclamations and completely judgmental pronouncements. She wasn't intentionally argumentative, just passionate. "We'll never see you." She pouted, the full lower lip pushing out as she pushed her long dark hair off her shoulders.

Andrew, Lulu's boyfriend, put an arm around her and smiled. "I think we can manage the subway out to Brooklyn, Lu."

"Seriously," Candace huffed. "If you can find me fifteen hundred square feet on two floors and a garden in the city, we'll move back."

"You have a garden?" Lulu sat up straighter. "You're a gardener now?"

Candace rolled her eyes. "I'm not a farmer, Lulu. It's a green space. Somewhere to sit outside."

"I'm just glad you got it." Tamara pulled a roll apart. "I had like six other couples come in the same day you applied." She was in real estate and had found my apartment for me. Now she'd helped Candace and Gregoire find theirs. "You guys had the best credit profile by far, though."

"Of course we did." Candace sipped her mimosa. "Gregoire has the best everything." She winked, but then her gaze fell on Andrew. "I mean, no offense Andrew. I'm sure your... assets are impressive."

Andrew blushed.

"So, hi, by the way," I cut in.

"Sorry, honey," Lulu leaped up, nearly knocking down a passing waiter as she rushed to my chair to hug me. People at nearby tables turned at the commotion, and the waiter looked offended, moving around Lu to another table. "How are you? How's CJ? How's work?" She stopped to hug Tamara on her way back to her chair.

"Everything is good," I answered. "I think."

"You think?" Tamara looked skeptical, and her blue eyes flashed. "That means something is not good. What is it? Wait, is it breakfast-appropriate?"

"Lulu's here, so we've already veered into inappropriate. No worries there." Candace smiled.

"You're the one who wants to know about my boyfriend's penis size!" Lulu pointed across the table.

Andrew pulled Lulu's pointing hand back into her lap. "It's okay, Lu. They're kidding."

Lulu sniffed and took another sip of her drink.

"What's wrong, Pepper?" Candace put on her problem-solving face. She had a way of seeing the world that made it easy for her to blow through obstacles, but she wasn't exactly subtle. She went after what she wanted like a linebacker, which wasn't my style.

"Remember how I told you about Irene? The woman in Buffalo who offered CJ the job last year?"

"The old lady?" Tamara said.

"She's not that old. Maybe forty."

"That's pretty old." Tamara nodded at her own proclamation.

"Well, she's older than us, for sure."

"What's going on? Is the cougar on the prowl again?" Candace leaned in. "Someone should put that old cat down."

I shrugged. "I'm not sure. She called CJ this morning as I was leaving. He said something about meeting her."

Lulu sat up straighter. "Oh, honey. I'm so sorry."

Andrew raised his eyebrows, a puzzled expression pulling one side of his mouth up. "It's a phone call. What are you sorry for? He's not cheating, if that's what you're thinking."

"How do you know?" Lulu asked him.

CJ and Andrew had been hanging out for the last few months, since Lulu and I spent a lot of time together. They'd developed kind of a bromance, and they always seemed to have the other's back when issues came up, like they'd signed some kind of man pact.

"CJ's a good guy." His expression was serious. "Like a *really* good guy. He's not the cheating kind. Plus..." He looked at me. "He's head over heels in love with you, Pepper. He'd never screw it up on purpose."

A blush crept up my neck as my heart warmed just a bit.

Andrew was right. If CJ had told Andrew how he felt about me, then it was certainly true. "Thanks. That makes me feel better." I looked up as my waffles were placed in front of me and thanked the waitress who delivered them. "I still don't like it, though."

Tamara shook her head. "I wouldn't either. *This* is why I don't get involved in relationships. Too much potential for confusion. Too much drama. Too much everything." She was the only one at the table not involved in a serious relationship. She dated. A lot. Like really a lot. But she didn't seem to fall for any of the guys she went out with. I hadn't quite figured her out.

"You just haven't met the right guy," Andrew said. "Let me set you up. There's a guy at the hospital—"

"Wait," Lulu interrupted. "Who is this guy? Why are you saying 'guy'? If he was a doctor, you'd say, 'there's this doctor at the hospital.' Is he a janitor or something? Tam won't date a janitor."

"There is nothing wrong with the custodial arts," I volunteered, feeling protective of the janitors of the world for no discernable reason.

"I'm just saying. If Andrew's setting Tam up, it should be with someone impressive." Lulu sniffed.

"Janitors can be impressive," Andrew said. "Like, what if he's a janitor who goes home and studies opera in his spare time? Or is dabbling in the custodial arts while he's finishing his doctorate in theology? Or what if he's the best damned janitor there is—like if janitoring is his calling?"

"Is he a doctor or not?" Lulu said.

"He's not a doctor," Andrew said. "He's actually a nurse."

Candace spit out her coffee then looked around apologetically. "Sorry," she said, wiping her mouth with a napkin. "I was just picturing a dude in one of those little white hats, with the squeaky shoes and the white skirt."

Andrew squinted and pursed his lips in irritation. "It's 1999, Candace. Men are nurses, too, and we all just wear scrubs." His face cleared, and he turned back to Tamara. "He's a really awesome guy. He plays rugby, is part-owner of a bar in Soho, and he's pretty handsome, according to all the girls at work. You interested?"

"Why is this incredible man-nurse still single?" Lulu asked.

"Why is Tamara still single?" Andrew returned.

"Hmm. You touched me." Lulu leaned back in her chair as everyone at the table began to giggle. She looked around blushing, and demanded, "What?"

"I think you're looking for 'touché,'" I suggested.

Andrew was practically crying, he was laughing so hard.

Lulu stared at him, her eyes squinting slightly like she was trying to decide whether to be angry at him for making fun of her. Finally, she shrugged and turned to Tamara. "Tamara? Why *are* you still single?"

Tamara's wide smile made her blue eyes gleam and then sipped her lemonade, shaking her head slowly. She wasn't talking.

Lulu shrugged again and turned her attention back to her food.

We ate and enjoyed the zinging atmosphere around us as New York City woke up and stretched, recovering from its Saturday night pursuits in the brightening Sunday afternoon. Traffic picked up out on Seventh Avenue, and from our table near the window, we could see people heading out for runs and shopping outings, dressed in shorts and T-shirts as summer's warmth lingered into the last sultry days of September.

2. ALONG CAME A SPIDER

Tamara

CANDACE SEEMED determined to spend the day with me Sunday, despite the fact that I'd planned to head home, get a workout in, and begin work on plans for the week. I had several open houses and a few clients I was pretty sure were ready to pull the trigger on the next good thing I found for them. It was shaping up to be a good month, and I had been expecting to get a jump today and keep it rolling.

"So what are you going to do?" Candace asked as we strode up Seventh Avenue.

"I was going to get some work done..."

"No. About the man-nurse." Candace stopped walking and grabbed my arm, tugging me into a bodega where she continued talking as she pulled water from a refrigerated case and grabbed a pack of gum. "I think men can be nurses. There's nothing wrong with that, of course. And if he's hot, well, that obviously makes up for a lot..." She gave me a mischievous gleaming look and began digging in her purse.

"I don't care if the guy's a friggin' manicurist."

She turned to me and raised an eyebrow.

"Okay, well, that might be a stretch, actually."

She nodded and turned back to pay, her dark bob shining under the fluorescent lights.

"The point is that I'm not looking, Candace. I know you and Lu have found love and Natalie and CJ are finally together, and you all think the world is romance and roses, stinky cheese, and champagne, but there's more to life." I knew that implying career-focused Candace was becoming distracted from her high-powered career by her boyfriend would stir up her ire, and then she'd get busy defending herself and quit harassing me. "I'm twenty-four. I'm not looking to settle down. I could've done that in Indiana."

Candace steered me out of the bodega, and we were walking again, side by side up the busy avenue as horns blared, children wailed, and life of all stripes beat on around us. "First of all," she began. "I'm not exactly laser-focused on my love life to the point that I'm ignoring my career. Or my friends." She raised her eyebrows at me over her large dark glasses. "But when the opportunity presents itself—in any part of your life—you go after it."

"Right."

"Right." She was staring at me. "So?"

"So I don't need to go chasing down men at hospitals trying to create opportunities, either."

"But if someone knows someone who might be a great fit..."

"Andrew was just pulling this nurse guy out of his butt because Lulu was pressuring him. It isn't like he's been at work thinking, 'This guy right here, this scrub-wearing man-nurse, he'd be perfect for Tamara.'"

"Hmm. I guess you have a point."

"I do." I tilted my chin up slightly. People didn't often win in debates with Candace.

"I'm just saying don't ignore opportunities."

"And I'm saying I won't." I was the last person on Earth to miss an opportunity, but Candace had no idea that just my being here—in New York City on my own, healthy and alive—was the perfect illustration of me taking an opportunity by the balls.

She smiled at me, leaned in, and gave me a quick hug. "I'm gonna head back uptown then. I've got boxes to pack, thanks to you."

"Sounds fun!"

"Not really, but we get the keys next weekend, so I guess I'd better be ready." She stepped to the curb and shot a hand out, hailing a cab that stopped suddenly with a grinding of gears. "See you later!"

The cab pulled away, and I continued a strolling pace back to my own apartment. As I fitted the key into the outer door, I thought about what she'd said. I knew I wasn't missing opportunities. I was doing the opposite of that. For a long time, my life seemed like it was going to be devoid of opportunities altogether, filled instead with bleak pronouncements and family who refused to let me do anything for myself. And it wasn't like I hadn't been in relationships. I'd even been in really long, really serious relationships. Now I was ready for other things.

I threw my keys on the side table as I let myself into my apartment. Home. I always breathed a sigh of relief on returning to my own space, my own refuge, a normal reaction to finally having a place to call your own after growing up with four brothers. This apartment, small though it was, was my own. In every way. The exposed brick held a painting that I'd done in junior high school, a scene of Lake Michigan that captured the winter's lonely grays with a reflection of hopeful sunlight off the sand at the water's edge. The mantel held my collection of bright, clear glass boats—something I'd been hanging onto since I was a tiny girl. To me, they had always represented the chance to move on, to get away.

I flopped down on the bed against the far wall, my hands

rubbing against the muted colors spread, my head on the few bright pillows. My closet was open, the clothes inside mimicking my bed's hues. Staples of individuality. A predictable constancy with small deviations. That was me.

I flopped down on the bed and stared out the window for a few minutes. Was there something wrong with me? Why wasn't I excited by the prospect of being set up with some manly rugby-playing nurse Andrew swore was hot? It wasn't as if I never got excited about the prospect of meeting men. I liked men, no doubts about that. I liked them tall, broad and lean. I liked them in my bed, and I liked them to leave in the morning. I always set the agenda where men were concerned. Being in control left little room for misunderstandings, for anyone to believe that something was possible when, really, nothing could happen at all. At this point, I wasn't interested in the back and forth necessary for a long-term relationship. Not yet, maybe not ever again. I definitely wasn't interested enough to distract me from all the other things that demanded focus. Work, friends, family, and just looking after myself kept me plenty occupied.

A light flashed at me, so I pushed the button on my answering machine. Two messages.

"Hey, sissy. It's Hal." My brother. Hal was two years older than me, and we'd been more like twins than siblings. He was having a rough time, which meant I was having a rough time. "Just calling to, uh... check in, I guess. Things are... well, they're okay. Clarissa left today." His wife. "And before she went, she told me some stuff. I guess I'm going to be a daddy..." Hal coughed, and I couldn't hear the rest of the message because it sounded like he moved his mouth away from the phone. My head spun as I replayed it. She was leaving? And she was pregnant? Oh, God, poor Hal.

The second message was even less expected. "Hey, Tam. It's Spider. Hal told me how to reach you. Hope you don't mind me calling. Hey, I'm gonna be in the city. I'll look you up."

My blood froze in my veins. Spider. In the city. Looking me up. I pushed down the agitation that began as a swirl of excitement in my gut and then spread out through my limbs in the form of a thrumming pulse of anticipation I had always felt when Gaige Spydell was anywhere nearby.

I squeezed my eyes shut and wished I'd never heard either message. I sat down and flipped open my laptop. I could at least pretend I hadn't heard them. I could pretend for a few hours. Maybe a day or two.

Work and coffee became my best friends for the next eight hours.

Thanks for reading this excerpt of COSMOS AND COMMITMENT! Keep reading! Get it here!

ALSO BY DELANCEY STEWART

Want more? Get early releases, sneak peeks and freebies! Join my mailing list here or scan the QR code and get a free story!

The Kasper Ridge Series:

Only a Summer

Only a Fling

Only a Crush

Only a Secret

Only a Touch

The Singletree Series:

Happily Ever His

Happily Ever Hers

Shaking the Sleigh

Second Chance Spring

Falling Into Forever

Singletree Box Set 1

Singletree Box Set 2

The Digital Dating Series (with Marika Ray):

Texting with the Enemy

While You Were Texting

Save the Last Text

How to Lose a Girl in 10 Texts

The Text Before Christmas

The MR. MATCH Series:

Prequel: Scoring a Soulmate

Book One: Scoring the Keeper's Sister

Book Two: Scoring a Fake Fiancée

Book Three: Scoring a Prince

Book Four: Scoring with the Boss

Book Five: Scoring a Holiday Match

Mr. Match: The Boxed Set

The KINGS GROVE Series:

When We Let Go

Open Your Eyes

When We Fall

Open Your Heart

Christmas in Kings Grove

The STARR RANCH WINERY Series:

Chasing a Starr

THE GIRLFRIENDS OF GOTHAM Series:

Men and Martinis

Highballs in the Hamptons

Cosmos and Commitment

The Girlfriends of Gotham Box Set

STANDALONES:

Let it Snow

Without Words

Without Promises

Mr. Big

Adagio

The PROHIBITED! Duet:

Prohibited!

The Glittering Life of Evie Mckenzie